LOVE. BETRAYAL. DEATH.

THE
UNFORGIVING
SHORE

GIL HOGG

Matador
9 Priory Business Park
Kibworth Beauchamp
Leicestershire LE8 0RX, UK
Tel: (+44) 116 279 2299
Fax: (+44) 116 279 2277
Email: books@troubador.co.uk
Web: www.troubador.co.uk/matador

ISBN 978 1784622 596

British Library Cataloguing in Publication Data.
A catalogue record for this book is available from the British Library.

Printed and bound in the UK by TJ International, Padstow, Cornwall
Typeset in 12pt Bembo by Troubador Publishing Ltd, Leicester, UK

Matador is an imprint of Troubador Publishing Ltd

For Maureen

CONTENTS

PART 1

THE LETTER

1

Ellen thought that she would rather live on Mirabilly for the rest of her life than go back to England.

John continued to speculate vaguely about where they might travel when they left Mirabilly and this went on for several months. The disconcerting factor for Ellen was John's unsettled attitude. He seemed to have lost some of his enthusiasm for new places and, plainly, he felt confined at Mirabilly, vast as it was. Life on the station appeared to be a phase which was over for him.

Ellen was as cooperative as she could be and gently guided him with an itinerary which was going to take them to Broome, Perth, Adelaide and Sydney and then New Zealand. On the way back, they would visit Melbourne and Brisbane and after that, America. This journey would take endless time. After that? God knows.

They would have to slow down on their travels at times to allow the trickle of money from John's trust fund to form a puddle and then they could go on. Ellen packed their schedule with new places to ensure that England was as far away as possible. John tacitly agreed on these destinations without considering them closely.

She also realised that there was an element of absurdity in her behaviour in planning, or at least thinking of a journey without end. She was trying to avoid what the end might be. She was frightened by what the end might be; she didn't want to think about it, much less discuss it with John.

Their departure date had not been finally decided in June when the DC3 supply plane from Darwin brought a letter for John; Ellen couldn't help noticing it amongst the leaflets and newspapers placed on the sideboard in the dining room by the maid; it was the kind of letter which John didn't receive. The envelope was stiff bluish paper with an embossed sender's address on the back: Leyton's, Solicitors, Leadenhall Street, London.

When John came in to breakfast after his morning ride he kissed her cheek absently and scooped up the mail from the sideboard; he placed it beside him at the table as he always did. She watched his face when he noticed the letter; he picked it up, felt it and turned it over curiously. He ignored his coffee and toast, opened the envelope and began to read.

He was completely silent for a while, frowning. "Bloody hell! This can't be right," he muttered. He flipped over the pages, going back to the beginning to read the letter again.

"What is it, John?" Ellen tried to sound casual. This was the world beyond Mirabilly reaching out to John, intruding. She felt that the unknown, in relation to him, could not be good news for her. She had already done what she could to construct a flimsy potential existence for them beyond Mirabilly. In a perverse way she didn't want to leave. Mirabilly was crude and while it had at first been unattractive in comparison with the excitements of Sydney, here they at least had each other. John was more completely hers on this remote station than perhaps he could be anywhere else. But after their long stay he was restless.

"Something very odd has happened, Elly." John's voice was unsteady. He looked radiant. "It seems I've inherited a major interest in all the Marchmont booty! *By accident!* Can you believe it?"

He dropped the letter on the table and buried his face in his hands, his long pale hair falling forward. He made a weird wailing noise. "Can you bloody believe it, Elly?"

She forced a smile and pushed her plate away. She should have felt elated. She actually felt ill at the uncertainty of what it meant. "That's really great, John," she said in a very low voice.

He was too enthralled to notice her grudging reaction. He began rereading the letter. "It's all completely against the odds. Not what anybody planned. Old Geoffrey wouldn't have left me a cent."

He explained, waving the letter. "You remember old Geoffrey at the Grange, Elly? He was the elder statesman of the family. He was also a crafty old fox who had either inherited or acquired the bulk of the Marchmont interests. According to the solicitors, he was talking to them about a new will, but he died suddenly at nearly eighty. Only then was it found that he had *already* destroyed his existing will! He was a bachelor, as you know and the old boy's next of kin was his older sister, Bernice. Dear old Bernice. She inherited everything from him. Then *she* died, only a few months after Geoffrey. Nearly ninety she was. In a nursing home, in Hove. And guess who, out of the whole Marchmont clan, was her favourite?"

Bernice had a valid will made many years before and although her estate was small, it would have been a welcome inheritance for the young man she idolised, John Charles de Vries Marchmont; but as the solicitors explained, with dire warnings about the effect of taxes, Bernice lived long enough to inherit from her brother.

"Oh, Bernice! Lovely old duck. She was one of my holiday minders when I was younger. Took me to Paris when I was fourteen. I hated every moment. All that walking and bloody art galleries. Ungrateful sod, I was!"

"I've never heard you mention Bernice, John."

"No, well, I'd more or less forgotten about her to be truthful. I've only seen her once, I guess, in the last ten years and that was only for a quick slurp of tea at her doll's house in Chelsea. I never did get around to visiting her in Hove. Always meant to. I'd have written every week if I'd known!"

She didn't know if John was joking or being naively honest. "How much are you worth, then?"

"I don't know," he said, looking up at the ceiling. "The solicitors don't say. The estate hasn't been valued yet."

"Does it include Mirabilly, and even the Grange?"

"It looks like it."

It was hardly worth speaking. John was in a reverie. "When you put the money in the bank…" she began. She wanted to know what he, a person who was careless with money and appeared to despise it, was going to do.

"In the bank? What do you mean, Elly? It's taken about seventy-five years for the family to run out of steam. I'll be picking up the pieces and trying to put them together."

She shook her head in confusion. "We've often talked about what you were going to do and you always said you could have gone into the family business at any time, but you weren't interested."

John looked at her curiously as though she hadn't understood the obvious. "That's right, Ellen. I never wanted to be a piece of dead wood pushed in place because of my family name. But I'm not going to be a family place-man. I'm going to be the boss, the fucking boss! Well, according to the letter, I'll be far and away the major owner. I've just inherited a piece of British history, a tradition, a part of the old Empire. And that brings with it duties…"

She left John to his euphoria. She spent the day distractedly walking in the shaded paths on the Hill, or sitting under the trees and looking out over the golden territory which rolled toward the horizon; and she worried about what was to happen to them. In the evening when they were having a sherry together before dinner, she tried to be as vivacious as she could, but John hardly seemed to notice. When they sat down at the table and the girl had served the food, he spoke seriously and without preliminaries.

"I need to get back to the old country, Elly."

"Surely it can all be fixed from here?"

"The solicitors say there are papers to sign," he began importantly and then changed to his more casual self. "I'd like to have a look at the goodies. You know, the odd cargo ship and tea plantation."

She played with her fork in the salad. "What about us, John?"

"Yes, of course, Elly. I've been thinking about you…"

His voice tailed away. She looked down the glassy surface of the oak table, with its candles in silver candlesticks giving a rich mellow light, at the face of the man with whom she had spent so much time alone. She was surprised by the firmness, immediacy and calculation behind the smooth geniality. The blue eyes, usually so clear, were now almost glacial.

"Would you rather stay here, Elly? I know you love the place. I do, too."

She bowed her head. He was thinking of her comfort, not their relationship. She remained silent.

He got up and came around the table and took her hand. "Ellen, you can come back with me, if you want…"

"The grand tour is off?" she asked, trying to keep back tears, and knowing the answer.

"Yes." He spoke decisively, almost coldly.

She could see clearly the end she dreaded. Back to King's Lynn. Ellen Colbert returns, dumped by her lover!

"I had a feeling you might not want to leave Mirabilly for a while, since we can't go on with our plans."

"I don't want to leave, John. I'm happy here, but I love you more. I'd go anywhere with you."

"I'll be busy when I get to London, Elly. You can't pick up the threads of an old colonial empire with interests all over the world in a few days, or even months."

She could see herself working in a shop or factory or waiting at tables in a Barton Village café. 'Don't you know who that is?' people would say. 'That's Ellen Colbert. Deserted her sick husband for John Marchmont. A fat lot of good it's done her! Not so high and mighty as she was, not by any chalk!' She could already hear Aunt Hilda's stinging condemnation.

"I don't feel I have any home, not now," she said.

Standing beside her, he ran his hand through her hair as she was slumped at the table. "We've had great times together..."

It was all past tense. "Can't we go on?" she asked looking up at him, her voice dry, a croak.

"Things change, Elly."

"People change, John!"

"They do... I think the best thing you can do in the meantime is to stay here as long as you want. Look after the Big House. You'll be in charge..."

"You mean housekeeper?"

"Housekeeper, guest, manager, what you want." He was vague. "I'll leave plane tickets and money for you and you can come to London when you're ready and... we can meet."

After all they had done together, they could *meet;* that

was all. She looked beyond him through the wide windows, across the lawns to the dying flare of red clouds and the prickle of early stars. The sun had set while they were talking. The room beyond the glow of the candles was shadowed. She remembered Doris at the Grange. Doris had called John a young toff and said he would drop her like a hot coal when he was ready. And wasn't it true? Wasn't that what was happening right now?

And there was something else Doris had said, when she understood how determined Ellen was to go with John. 'Everything with John will be all right if it doesn't spoil things for you.' Ellen had pondered what Doris meant by 'spoiling things' at the time. Now, she thought she knew. You can't go back to working at a café in Barton Village, Norfolk after living in the Big House, dining in this room with nobody between you and the hills a hundred miles away and nobody even beyond that for thousands of miles. You can't go back to being a skivvy after you've been a queen. If you have to go back, your life is spoiled.

Doris had been right in seeing that her life could be spoiled. She wasn't a waitress having a fling with one of the gentry any more. That was the way it had started, but as time passed she had come to think of John as *hers,* as she was his. The pain of losing him would be unimaginable. She couldn't believe she would ever recover.

She clung to John that night in bed and sobbed herself to sleep, but it made no difference to him. He had, unusually, drunk himself into near insensibility after dinner. In the few hours since he had received the letter he had become a different man.

A week later she was stoically at the airstrip seeing John off on the supply plane bound for Darwin. Half a dozen other senior staff were there too. She was the only person who knew of John's fortune; his telephone calls to the solicitors in London had been very guarded and the news had not leaked so far.

John took her in his arms in front of the Farrells and the others, as the pilot was gunning the engines of the Dakota. His lips touched hers perhaps for the last time and she pulled away from him in a cloud of red dust.

"We'll meet soon," he said, releasing her.

She seemed to recall something in *Casablanca* like this, but there was nothing romantic about the parting here; it was a cold moment of rejection. She held her head up and smiled. As soon as he turned to the aircraft, she walked quickly away. By the time the plane had cleared the trees, her driver was churning the Jeep in low gear up the drive to the Big House.

She went into the cool, quiet interior. Other than two schoolgirl daughters of jackeroos who were doing odd jobs and two Aboriginal maids, there was nobody in the 'owner's wing' where she and John had lived. Jim Farrell, the general manager of the station and Maureen, his wife, maintained scrupulous privacy in their wing. Ellen gave the girls a week's pay and told them it wasn't necessary to come back. She could rely on the maids to deal with her requests and not to bother her.

In the solitude of the bedroom she started to cry and she may have cried for a day and a night. When she awoke her eyes and lips were swollen and her chest was sore.

It was over.

After a week, Ellen went out of the Big House and walked or rode alone in the early morning or evening. She walked past the Village down to the Juduba River, now shrunk to a muddly trickle, like her relationship with John.

She couldn't be bothered to supervise the maids and she let them get on with the housework and cooking. She rebuffed all callers and ate alone at her place at the long table in the dining room, with the crystal glistening in the candlelight. She took little notice of food except to swallow it. She had no confidant and kept Maureen Farrell and the other wives on the Hill at a distance. Maureen had brothers, sisters and children of her own and knew a troubled heart when she saw one; it wasn't a secret Ellen could keep from anybody on the Hill or in the Village. All she could do was hide in the shadows of the Big House.

She wanted to write to John and she sat for hours at the antique Dutch bureau in the lounge trying to make notes of what to say. She had followed an assiduous course of self-education since she met him, reading books and newspapers, always with a dictionary beside her, but she couldn't find the words for the purpose of this letter. When she did find a phrase, her handwriting looked like a child's.

There was nobody to ask for help as a writer. Maureen Farrell and the wives on the Hill, if they knew all, would probably contend cynically that they had foreseen her plight. And the sluttish wives in the Village were as illiterate as she was. She couldn't reveal her ignorance, or share her shame with any of them. She might have found a neutral scribe in Darwin, a parson perhaps. But she couldn't ask a stranger to write a sensitive letter about two people he didn't know, a letter she couldn't clearly articulate herself. It was the same when she thought of the telephone. What could she say to John that she hadn't already said? And what would she want to say with the Mirabilly operator listening in?

Every night in the early days however, she waited in the hope of receiving a telephone call. Once, her contemplation in the dining room was interrupted by Jim Farrell. He came unannounced, swaying in the doorway, a bulging gut, with purple hands like joints of meat.

"Anything I can do, my dear…" he said, moving across the room and putting a hand on her shoulder.

She could smell the beery breath. For a moment she thought she might confide in him. As general manager he was the most powerful person on the station, but she knew almost as quickly what it would have to lead to.

"Don't come into this part of the house again Jim, unless I invite you."

"I was only trying to help." He raised his voice.

"What would your wife say?"

He backed away and left the room.

Later she studied herself in the bedroom mirror. There could be another and different life for her in one of the bright new Australian cities, in Perth or Brisbane or Adelaide. One thing she vowed: she wasn't going back to England, to the rain and wind and mean stares and the shame.

She felt she had lived more than one lifetime. The imperfections in the old pier glass mirror rendered a mysterious reflection. She was twenty-two, five feet four inches tall. Her legs could have been those of a dancer; her delicate ankles gave her a graceful look. The body wasn't quite that of a dancer, too full in the breasts and hips, but it was sensual. Her complexion was pallid and drawn from the recent troubles, but nothing could diminish the lustre of her eyes and hair. It was a face made for fun and love and perhaps lust. There was a whole new lifetime ahead of her if she could put the ache of losing John behind her.

2

John Marchmont returned to Mirabilly after four years. Ellen saw his plane, a white, twin-engined Beechcraft, circle low over the Hill before it landed. Jim Farrell had made up a small delegation from the Hill to meet the plane which Ellen did not join.

In the past few weeks a certain tension had developed amongst the staff in anticipation of the visit. Although John was known personally by some on the Hill, he wasn't known in the character of the owner. A seismic change in the perspective of the station people had occurred when the news filtered back to them that the light-hearted Englishman who had departed on an unspecified errand, leaving his girlfriend behind, was now the most senior person in all the Marchmont enterprises. The gossips were left to consider the girl he had left behind.

Ellen had followed John's life at a distance. The newspapers from England were delivered once a month and Maureen Farrell passed them to her; they were often many weeks old but that didn't matter. She read the thin diet of news about him with sickly interest. John had rallied the company and dropped 'Colonial' from its name; it was Marchmont Commercial Mining or MCM now; but she was more interested in the fleeting mention of John in the gossip columns. He was apparently a fashionable figure in London and in New York which was now the headquarters of MCM. He was usually squiring a new beauty.

On the day that John arrived, Ted Travis, Ellen's husband, came home at lunchtime. "Marchmont wants to meet all the top fellers and their wives up at the house tonight, Ellen."

"I can't go, Ted."

Ted was easy with her about most issues. He had a quizzical look. "Think a bit. If you don't go, it looks as though somethin's eatin' you."

He was right, but later, when the time came to dress, she said she had a migraine. Ted shrugged his hefty shoulders and said nothing. He put on his pale blue twill trousers with razor creases and a white cotton shirt crisply ironed by Ellen. He refused a necktie. This wasn't the way she'd have preferred him to dress, with his sleeves rolled to the biceps; but he earned a second look as a masculine creature with his burned, sunlined face, dry sandy hair and slender muscular physique. He was the head stockman; a hard drinker, a man who settled disputes with his fists. Ted lacked words; he could hardly write and could only read with difficulty. His skill lay in his leadership of tough men and his experience with cattle. He had seldom been beyond cattle stations and small towns. He was ten years older than Ellen.

Ted's life was limited, but curiously full. Before he was married, he would stay in the bush for days on end with a gang of men, working the cattle or repairing roads and stockyards. Work was followed by wild drinking, gambling and whoring in one of the towns. Men like him tended to marry by accident or not at all. But there was a soft side to Ted. He had a gentleness and a feel for the wilderness that was touching. Ellen had never heard a man talk so sensitively of nature, of birds, snakes and grasses and clouds; to him they were important signs of how the land was faring.

Ellen had made a home with Ted. Jim Farrell had assigned them one of the spacious wooden houses on the Hill, with a verandah and an acre of trees and garden. This was Ted's right, to live in the same style as the engineers, master butchers, cattle dealers and pilots. They were very comfortable.

Ellen lay on the bed in her pants and bra, playing with the baby. She had a jumble of fears and uncertainties turning in her mind. As soon as she heard the screen door bang on Ted's departure, she put the boy to bed. She had already showered and she slipped on a frock with apprehension about what might happen if she had the nerve to go to the party. Actually, nothing would *happen* except in her head and other people's heads. If she really wanted to go, she could still get the daughter of the woman next door to baby-sit.

The house was silent. At times, she could hear a shout or laugh as people walked up the drive to the Big House. She sat before the dresser mirror and turned on the lamp. She seemed to be more of a woman than a girl now; an interesting woman, she hoped. Every minute that went by made her possible entry to the party more awkward. As Ted said, people knew something might be eating her.

She sat in a chair in the lounge and switched off the air-conditioning. The heat began to swell in the room. She tried to imagine what John was like now. She had changed; he must have changed. She tried to visualise the party, the overdressed wives, plastered with powder and lipstick, looking like parrots and the men skulking at the bar telling dirty jokes. Time seemed to pass quickly, maliciously reducing her opportunity to make an entrance.

The child stirred in the next room. She went in and soothed him. Footfalls crunched the gravel on the front path. She could hear steps crossing the verandah to the screen door. It wasn't Ted. He didn't move like that. She went back into the front room, not frightened because Mirabilly was a place where people left their doors open and went to each other's homes without formality. Her gut told her it would be *him*. He was in shadow in the doorway, dressed in a bright shirt and white slacks, his fair hair longer, serious-faced.

"Ellen, you're more beautiful than I remember." The room filled with his soft, precise voice. And then he said flippantly, "Were you expecting me?"

Her nerves exploded in a kind of laugh. "That's quite a question!"

He stepped close to her and reached out. She could smell cologne and the sweetness of gin and lime on his breath.

"John, you're in my home," she said, stepping back.

"Don't you feel…?"

"How can you ask that?"

"Excuse me," a quiet voice said from the doorway. "I came back to see how you were, Ellen."

John turned. "Please forgive me." He walked out without looking at Ted.

Ellen cried and Ted carried her to bed and made violent love to her; it was painful because she half-imagined it was John.

In the next few days, John made a number of attempts to see her. He telephoned the house and called when he apparently knew Ted was away. She hung up the telephone on him and locked the door. Two days later he intercepted her outside the Village store. She had Paul with her. He was a big boy, over three years old, with brown eyes and a coppery glint in his hair like hers. She smiled and encouraged the child to greet him, but under her breath she said, "Leave me alone! People know about us and if they see us talking…"

John distractedly tried to chat to the child. "How like you he is, Ellen."

"Go away."

He whispered, "I don't want to make a scene, but can't you give me a few moments?"

She walked with John, towing Paul, down toward the deep course of the Juduba River which threaded through the Village and was nearly dry. A solitary grey heron sat on a rock. The fat barramundi had fled with the waters.

She looked from under the wide brim of her straw hat, over her shoulder, back towards the company store. "I don't want any more to do with you, John. It'll do me no good when the old bags in the Village hear that you and I have been seen walking together."

"I've missed you, Ellen."

"Good, I'm glad you appreciate that, only you haven't done much about it, have you?"

He looked abject. "I can't understand how you can say that, my dear. You married within a few months of my departure… *Married*…"

"You wouldn't even have known. You never wrote. You never called. Years could have gone by."

He wiped his face with his hand as though to remove the look of incomprehension as well as the sweat. "Ellen, of course I knew you married. I was shocked when Farrell told me on the telephone. And the next time I spoke to Farrell he told me you were pregnant. I was distraught…"

They were on the bank of the river in fierce heat. There was no rational reason for two people to stand there talking. John gestured to a row of gums for shade but Ellen turned away to retrace her steps.

"*You* were distraught? Think how hurt I was when you left me. What did you expect me to do? Sit around for four years and wait?"

"There's been a complete misunderstanding here, Ellen."

She swung back toward him, sweat trickling down her cheeks. "If you think I'm going to have a dirty little affair with you every time you come to Mirabilly, like a sort of resident whore, you're mistaken!"

He put his hand on her arm. "I care for you deeply. I always have. Look at what we've done together…"

She looked toward the store to see if they were being watched. Two women were standing under the awning looking toward them. She moved out of John's reach.

"Yes, we've shared a lot, but in the end I'm not good enough for you, am I? I'm great for drinks, dinner tête-à-tête and bed, but when it comes to your family and friends, you don't know me! And marriage, you never ever got around to thinking about that!"

"It's not true." He spoke feebly, raising his panama hat and running his hand across his damp hair.

"All right, John. Tell me what you're proposing now, apart from occasional sex and a few presents? What? Tell me, what?"

The heat on her neck and shoulders was making her head ache. The light was blinding. Flies were beginning to crawl on her shoulders, prickling as though their legs contained electric charges. John didn't speak, didn't seem to have thought it through. The stifling air was a barrier between them. The Juduba reeked of decay. Paul began to moan. She lifted and balanced him on her hip, brushing away the flies.

"You can't answer the question, can you, John? You know what I am to you? I'm an ignorant servant woman from your family kitchen. I may have been a lot of other things too, but I never ceased to be an inferior. You're imprisoned by your snobbery."

"Ellen, my dearest, you've got it all wrong…"

She set the boy down and hurried up the slope, jerking him along. It had hurt her to speak so to the man she once loved and in the right circumstances could probably love again, but the weight of his rejection of her was crushing; it wasn't inconstancy or carelessness on his part; she felt it was a rejection of everything that she was. She climbed to the level of Piccadilly, as the main street was called. She turned round before she went into the shade of the store.

John was standing forlornly where she had left him, hands in pockets, shoulders bent, hat askew, yellow hair plastered across his pink forehead. A sliver of still water in the Juduba, directly behind him, caught the sun and glowed like molten metal. She had to look away.

3

The outback seemed unchanged for long periods, months on end, glaring sky and hard, golden landscape; it was as though time wasn't passing; and then in the spring or early summer, in October or November, a fury would be unleashed.

Paul Travis heard the rain on the roof all day; it fell in determined squalls and then faded, seeming to be exhausted, only to redouble its pounding. He was eighteen and if the day had been clear he would have been flying a stock-check for the station either as an observer or a pilot with his new licence; instead, he was at home, worrying about his mother worrying.

Ellen Travis was standing in the gray light of the lounge window. At times she went into the kitchen to listen to the short-wave radio. She bent her head, narrowing her eyes at what she heard, anticipating trouble. The station had mustered two hundred head of steers in the afternoon and the beasts were now trapped on a flat in a bend of the Juduba River, with the water rising from a cloudburst.

The Mirabilly station's general manager, Dick Mather and the men at the Juduba crossing on the west range, fifty miles away, were talking on the radio. The Juduba River was like a sick artery of the body of Mirabilly, niggardly in its nourishment of the pastures at one time and at another, flooding destructively. Paul could hear his father on the radio speaking to Dick Mather; clipped, unemotional work-talk about the condition of the herd and their progress.

'We'll lose the beasts unless we move 'em across the river to higher ground,' Ted said to Dick Mather.

Paul couldn't identify all the voices crackling over the air, but Ted was unmistakable, as were the tones of Dick Mather who was only a few hundred yards away in the radio shack adjoining the Big House; they discussed options. The weather was wild but the voices were dry, calm, hesitant as they explored the possibilities. Eventually, it came to abandoning the cattle, or trying to drive them across the river. In the reluctant way the stockmen and the general manager exchanged views Paul knew and his mother knew too, that there were risks they were thinking about but not mentioning.

'The horses are in good shape and I can do it with three men,' Ted said.

'It's up to you, Ted,' Mather replied cautiously, sounding worried about his men, but also worried about the possible loss of prime stock.

The voices were silent for a while and Paul stayed with his mother in the kitchen, looking out as the wattles and acacias thrashed in the garden. Daylight was darkened by the thick clouds. The only light in the kitchen was the red pilot bulb of the radio receiver on the table. After quarter of an hour Mather began to call the Juduba team. He called every few minutes but got no answer. Ellen sat quietly, staring ahead. She didn't seem to notice that Paul was there.

Then one of the Juduba hands called the station, tense tones coming through the distortions of the signal. 'We're moving them… It's deeper than we thought…'

'Everybody OK?' Mather asked.

'I guess so,' the Juduba hand said. 'Can't see Billy Kimball or Ted… the herd's moving… twenty or thirty have made it across already.'

The whining note in his voice suggested to Paul that he was thinking that they shouldn't have started this. Mather called back every few minutes asking if Billy or Ted had been sighted. For a while there was no answer.

Then another call from a stockman. 'I see Billy on the other side. Lofty Mandarik's pulled back here. We're on the ledge above the flat... the current's too strong. We got maybe a hundred head across, the rest, hell, they've gone... we lost 'em!'

In the gloom of the kitchen, Ellen's eyes were on the red point of light on the receiver. The radio hissed again and Paul picked out the words; it was the station operator this time. He said, 'Dick's on his way. Still too rough for the chopper. Two and a half hours if he can get the Land Rover through.'

Mather's decision to go himself confirmed the seriousness of the trouble to Paul.

"I can't listen any more. Your father hates the water," Ellen said, switching off the power.

It wasn't so much hate, Paul thought, as the fact that water was an alien element to Ted Travis; vital to the land, yet rare and on the occasions when it was plentiful, cruel. He put an arm around his mother's shoulders as she was shaken by a sob, but she shook herself free and went to the bedroom. Paul never believed any harm would come to Ted Travis because he knew him as the best horseman and one of the toughest and fittest men on Mirabilly.

The inquest had returned a verdict of accidental drowning on Ted Travis. The funeral was to be held at Tennant's Creek. Dick Mather piloted the Cessna 235 from Mirabilly, with his wife, Gus Lorio the station engineer, Ellen Travis and Paul as passengers. The plane landed at the Creek before lunch, in time for the men to go to the pub and for Ellen and Paul to see Arthur Lucas. Lucas was a solicitor who kept a room in the ANZ Bank building on Barlinnie Street. He visited there from his other offices at Mt Isa and Katherine, a day a week. He had telephoned Ellen, saying that he was the executor of Ted's will and he asked her to see him.

Paul had been at home when his mother received the call from Lucas. Afterwards, she had said to him, "Lucas was one of Ted's boozing mates. Why does a lawyer mix with jackaroos?" She always classed Ted as that, although he was a boss. "Buffalo Lodge Number 42, that shed down by the stockyards at the Creek, that's where they go. What do they do there, except drink? 'Men together talkin', Elly'," she mimicked Ted, but not in a humorous way.

Ellen and Paul climbed the stairs to Lucas's dusty office, scattered with files and piles of paper curling in the heat. Lucas himself was fat, seventeen stone, with thin, damp hair and an eroded face hanging in wads of red flesh. He had wet, bloodshot eyes. He was probably in his late forties, but looked sixty.

"Lovely to see you, Ellen," he said, the gravity he had assumed for the funeral sliding into a leer as he waved them to seats.

"You're starting early," Ellen said, seeing the beer can on the corner of the desk.

"Have one," Lucas said, pulling a can of Fosters out of a small refrigerator on the floor behind his desk and offering it to Paul.

"Don't encourage the boy!"

"He's eighteen," Lucas said, taking a long pull at a can.

It surprised Paul that this stranger knew how old he was.

"What do I have to do?" Ellen asked impatiently.

"Well, now, Ted's will is short and simple. He's left

23

everything to you, Ellen." He handed a document over. "Problem is…" he halted for another drink.

"What's the problem?" Ellen asked sharply.

"Ted left a few debts. Some are gambling debts and needn't be paid, but where Ted has borrowed and given security, those debts have to be paid or the security given up."

Paul knew that his mother wouldn't be surprised at the mention of gambling. Virtually all the men on Mirabilly drank and gambled.

"You didn't know it was serious, Ellen?"

"How serious *is* it?" she asked in a chilly voice.

"The car, the holiday house in Cairns and all Ted's insurance policies are in hock. When it's all added up there'll barely be enough to bury him. The insurance payable by the Mirabilly owners comes to you directly."

Ellen sat silently considering this. A fly buzzed. Lucas reached for a cigarette, lit it quickly and sucked the smoke into rheumy lungs.

"This is what happened on binges in Katherine and here?" Ellen said, outrage quivering in her voice.

"Yeah, I guess."

"You ought to do more than guess. You were there! I can't understand how Ted let this build up without telling me."

"I reckon Ted believed he could recover."

Paul thought that was probably right. His father wouldn't have meant to do anything to hurt his mother; they were a close pair, but she had a definite attitude: drinking and gambling weren't fun, they were despicable and there must be something wrong with anybody who persisted with them.

"I expect you can remain in the Mirabilly house for a while, but you'll have to give it up, Ellen."

"What about Paul's education? He's got a place at Sydney University. Will we be able to afford that?"

"Look, Mum..."

She silenced him with a gesture.

"Yeah, I'm glad you mentioned it. I'd like to speak to Paul," Lucas said, crumpling the empty beer can in his fist. "In your presence of course."

"You *what*?"

"Ted asked me to," Lucas said, scuffling behind his chair for another can.

"Stirring up trouble where none was before! It's bad enough Ted's dead, bad enough he was in debt, and now you want to finish off his memory by belittling him to his own son!" Ellen's voice was raised, fury in her face.

"It's not like that Ellen. I have a signed statement by Ted. And I promised him. I have to talk to Paul."

"What's the big deal in talking to the man, Mum?" Paul was confused by the conversation. Surely they could *talk* about anything?

Ellen stood up.

"Please stay and hear this, Ellen," Lucas wheedled.

"Never," Ellen said. "You'll spoil my life and Paul's for a lot of drunken pub-talk and promises! Are you coming, Paul?"

Paul sat without moving. He didn't understand the reason for his mother's outburst. He knew that there was something she could have explained to him. He was well used to her dictatorial stance and inclined to frustrate it if he could. As an only child, who had been brought up in the solitary world of correspondence school lessons, there were many things about the so-called adult world that he didn't know because nobody had explained them to him; he had an underlying resentment about this. He decided to stay.

Ellen moved away. Lucas stumbled after her and stopped her by the door. "I want to help you, Ellen." His puffed fingers like sausages reached out for her breasts.

"Get away, you sot!" Ellen went out slamming the door.

Lucas came back to his desk sweating and irritable at his rebuff. "You better listen, son. We have to talk." He sank back into his reclining chair, his hairy navel protruding from a gap between the buttons on his shirt. His breath rasped. He stared at Paul over an extinct volcano of scorched paper and cigarette ash.

"Ted Travis was a mate of mine, Paul. Ten years ago he asked for my advice on something that was worrying him. He told me that he had promised your mother, before they married, never to reveal that he wasn't your father." Lucas reached for the beer can without taking his eyes off Paul, knocking the can off the edge of the desk.

"Not my father?" The ugly words stuck in Paul's throat.

Lucas swore, recovered the can and belched. "S'right. Ted wasn't sure he should keep the promise. He was a decent man. You were growing up and you and your real father were entitled to know. It worried Ted. I told him *he* had to sort it out with you and your mother. Ted said he would think about it but if anything happened to him, he wanted me to tell you. I took notes at the time." He held up a few yellow handwritten pages and copies of a marriage certificate and Paul's birth certificate. "Ted's signed each page. And take a look at the dates on the certificates."

Paul heard this as though it was a story about somebody else. Ted had always treated him affectionately as a son. He loved and respected his father and had been distraught at losing him. "I don't get it," he said, taking the notes from the lawyer's outstretched hand, but after a minute he couldn't focus on the pages and dropped them on the table.

"Who's supposed to be my father, then?" he asked in a shaky voice.

"Surely you've heard the stories?" Lucas smirked.

"I haven't heard any stories!" Paul shouted.

He was speaking the truth. Nobody had ever said anything directly to him. What he *had* heard were obscure (obscure to him) remarks relating to his mother, about her being 'the duchess' and him being 'the young prince'. These rare comments were usually accompanied by laughter ridiculing him and his mother as though they were very funny. Paul thought that they arose from his mother's superior attitudes and her pampering of him. There were all sorts of people on Mirabilly and a lot of them were rough and rude but not in an aggressive way; that was simply the way they were; nevertheless they were good people. Paul had therefore taken very little notice of these jibes. He had accepted that there was some difference in gentility between him and his mother on one side and the Mirabilly hands on the other.

"All right! OK! Everybody else on Mirabilly has," Lucas said cynically.

"Not me!" Paul shouted, standing up.

"Sit down, son, calm down." Lucas's eyelids slid up over his inflamed eyes. "Your father is Marchmont. The mighty Marchmont. The lord high panjandurum. Surely you know your mother came out from Pommie-land with him when she was a kid?"

"No. Not *with* him!"

"You've been cosseted! He went back to Pommie-land and left her on the station with a bun in the oven. Namely, you."

Paul's head was aching. His father wasn't his father? Why? How did this happen?

27

"What's the proof that my father is Marchmont? Why not somebody else?" Paul snapped.

"You're a smart kid to make that point. There isn't any actual evidence. Ted doesn't say who the father is. He didn't want to write anything about that. But he told me. And the chain of evidence is clear. Lord and Lady Muck arrive at Mirabilly. He goes home, leaving her. She is pregnant. She extracts a promise from Ted, marries him and has a baby three months later."

"Somebody else could be the father." Paul's voice was feeble.

"No way." Lucas wiped the beer foam from his lips with the back of his hand. "Now you see where your education comes in. Your old man could send you to Oxford or Yale tomorrow, never mind Sydney. Now, I'm going to set you up for life…"

Paul walked out of the room before the lawyer had finished, impelled by the cocktail of emotions in him which had ignited.

Lucas caught him up on the landing, grabbed his arm. "Listen kid, I meant that about setting you up for life…"

"Let me go!"

Lucas had lost his patronising manner. Paul jerked away and stalked out of the door. He couldn't have sat down again with Lucas, watching his navel squirm.

As he was going down the stairs, Lucas leaned over the railing. "You're a stupid young bugger!" he called hoarsely. "You're walking away from a fortune!"

The funeral service that day didn't stir anything in Paul except a faint and distant warmth for a man whom he had liked and admired; a man who had apparently engaged in a deception against him and deprived his mother of future support. The coffin rested in front of the altar. He had a clear picture of the body inside, although he had not seen it as a corpse, cleaned of river mud, laid out with orifices stuffed with cotton wool, hair combed, cheeks rouged, dressed in Ted's best blue suit: the body that was supposed to have sired him.

While the parson droned through a commendation of his father and tried to coax a hymn from the tardy congregation, Paul thought of Marchmont. His father? No, his sire, perhaps. He could remember the man from occasional meetings over the years: when he was about ten helping Dinka Djawida in the kitchens at the Big House and two years ago when he was a waiter at a Mirabilly banquet. Marchmont was plump and pink and friendly with lank yellow hair; a man of authority, while Ted Travis had been inarticulate, lean and bleached from a lifetime in the dust of the outback, like a piece of bone, part of the vast dry land.

When the mourners moved away from the graveside after the coffin had been lowered, they sought the shade of the gums along the fence-line of the cemetery. People were hugging Ellen and shaking Paul's hand – which he suffered coldly. He walked with the crowd as some turned off at Trail Street, in the direction of the bar of the Commercial Hotel and a smaller number walked back to Maude Geary's house on a new subdivision two blocks away.

The house was on one level, low and spacious with a tiled gable roof; it was set square on a quarter acre plot, in a street of new upmarket houses all set square on quarter acre plots. Every house was trying to be different, with slightly different panels on the facade and slightly different muted colours, but really they were all the same. Guests gathered in the Gearys' lounge behind almost closed venetian blinds, able to breathe in cool air.

Paul watched, sickened, as Maude Geary, with Ellen's help, brought out plates of food; cold roast ham, fried sausages, a leg of lamb on a carving board, bowls of salad, roast potatoes, sweet yams, breadfruit and fresh baked bread. Beside the table was a cool box filled with canned lager and on the sideboard, backed by a regiment of glasses, two bottles of Johnny Walker Red and a bucket of ice.

Paul couldn't eat and went to the room Maude had given him for their overnight stay. He lay on the bed turning his past over and over. He had to wait until six o'clock in the evening for the guests to depart before he could corner his mother alone in her bedroom. She was sitting in a chair by the window, awake and motionless.

"I want to talk to you about what Arthur Lucas said," Paul began.

"This isn't the place to discuss such things, Paul. The walls are paper thin."

"No place is the right place for you. Why haven't you told me?"

"Don't raise your voice. You don't want to listen to Lucas. He's a drunk. Him and those Buffaloes!"

"Why have things happened this way?" His voice and hands shook. "Why this secret?" He couldn't stop his voice trailing away, thin and incredulous.

"What nonsense!" she scoffed.

"It's not nonsense. Lucas knows. Dad talked to him. *You* know. You knew what Lucas was going to say before he said it. You told Lucas he was stirring it up. You knew!"

"Get yourself something to eat from the kitchen. There's plenty left."

"Don't put me off. Lucas made notes at the time and Dad signed them. There's no mistake. Years ago. Why would he do that if it wasn't true?"

"Because he was a stupid, weak man who had doubts about his paternity. He did what his drunken friends persuaded him to do."

"Lucas said my father was Marchmont."

"Do you want to believe an alcoholic in preference to me?" She turned to him fiercely.

"Lucas had a marriage certificate with the papers. Dated three months before I was born."

"So you were conceived before Ted and I married, but we were married when you were born and he signed the birth certificate, isn't that enough? Don't you think I know where my body has lain?" Ellen said calmly.

"No! I want to see you, you're not going to hide in the shadows!" Paul snatched at the blind cords, filling the room with light. He saw an imperious woman with carefully waved short, dark brown hair, smooth olive skin, scarlet lips and even today in her mourning, sensual. Her brown eyes were unflinching.

"For God's sake tell me about myself!" His heart was like somebody inside him kicking his chest.

"Keep your voice down. You don't want to share our business with the Gearys."

"I have a right to know!"

She sniffed. "You're my child. There's no doubt of that." She was still in the sunlight like a waxwork.

One part of him was attached to her by the unseverable umbilical cord of maternity; another, at this moment, hated her with a violence which made his fists clench.

4

In 1967, when Paul Travis was twelve years old, he had the first encounter that he could remember with John Marchmont, on one of Marchmont's fleeting visits.

In the afternoon when school lessons on the radio were finished and his set work had been marked by Ellen, he was free. The marking was a formality and seldom delayed him. He knew his mother didn't understand his lessons properly because she couldn't read and write as easily as he could. He stopped for a hurried scone and a glass of orange juice in the kitchen. His schedule for the rest of the day was crammed with business.

To avoid enemy patrols, he had to keep to the grove of wattles and acacias around their house. He moved carefully to high ground where he could get a clear view of the Hill. He scanned the orange tile roofs of the houses scattered through the trees below him. He checked the weather and compared it with the records in his notebook, inserting the temperature figure he had taken from the thermometer in the garden: 84 degrees fahrenheit. He wrote, 'Clear sky, stirring of an afternoon breeze. Usual for July.' He could see clearly downhill, to the Village, where there were shops and stores and small houses. There was no sign of enemy activity.

Then he headed for the Big House. He slipped through a fringe of newly planted pines, then through the gums which ringed the Big House. He broke cover briefly as he crossed the lawns, pausing to cool himself in the spray of the sprinklers. His cotton shirt sodden, he dashed for the safety of the wall of the house, flattening himself against it.

This was an alien place, headquarters of the enemy with secret rooms and passages. He'd never been inside, except the kitchen and the storehouse. Ellen had told him about the 'owner's cabin' in one of her rare reminiscences. This was the name of the most secret place; even Dick Mather the general manager wasn't allowed in there. The word 'cabin' was misleading; it gave the impression of a small room when in truth, Ellen had said, it was vast, like a palace. Paul had read that the owners of cargo ships on the Australia run, like the Marchmonts, often had a special cabin set aside for themselves and this was the origin of the deceptive name for their palace.

Paul edged round the shrubbery and looked in the laundry doorway. Dinka, the boss of the maids, was bending over a tub. He crept inside, drew the Colt 45 he carried in his belt and let her have a couple of rounds right up her big backside: *Pow! Pow!*

She leaped up with a scream. "Jeezgod Paul Travis, you damn scared me!"

"You're dead, Dinka," Paul said, replacing the Colt. "You need a decent security system around here."

"Don't need security 'gainst anybody but you, boy." Dinka led him outside, heaving with fright. "Goffy says you clip the hedge." She pointed to the low macrocarpa surrounding the kitchen garden.

Paul went to the tool shed, selected a pair of hedge clippers and surveyed the task; it would take an hour to give it a neat shape and clean up afterwards if he didn't cut too close. And the money would be welcome for his secret Swiss bank account. He calculated that he would still have time to check on enemy action at the airfield and log the makes and registration numbers of any new aircraft for his intelligence report.

He began to work his way along one side of the u-shaped hedgerow. He finished this side two minutes ahead of schedule according to the old pocket watch his mother had given him. He braced himself to begin the next side, realising that he was going to suffer exposure to nuclear radiation slanting in with the sunlight. He also became aware of a man on the lawn, watching him. The man was about as old as his mother, with a plump boiled-looking face, stringy poet's hair and blue x-ray eyes. He was a stranger, possibly a mutant from another planet. Paul took no obvious notice, but classified the man temporarily as Class A: dangerous.

The stranger, grinning, ambled over the lawn in his loose shirt and dirty white trousers, one hand in his pocket, the other shading his eyes. "Hullo," he said, "who are you?"

The stranger had the same poncy voice that Paul had heard on English radio programmes. He knew his schedule would slip if he paused. He didn't reply, but lifted his head and gave the man his gamma-stare which usually had a withering effect.

"My name's John Marchmont," the stranger said, unaffected, coming so close that Paul could smell his aftershave, which was probably lethal. "What's yours?"

Paul had recognised the name immediately. In the sloppy shirt and trousers the man could be an imposter. He expected that the merchant prince who owned Mirabilly would be dressed in a white suit with a collar and tie, so he went on the offensive. "Edward Silveras," he said, giving Marchmont one of his aliases. He went on clipping while Marchmont followed, exuding his flowery poison.

"Where do you live?"

"With a family in the Village."

"Not your family?"

Paul went on clipping but gave the stranger a cover story. "My mother died last year from radiation sickness and left me with the family. My father was a scientist and he died earlier from the same radiation. They were in the Monte Bello Islands."

Marchmont pondered and then said, "I'm very sorry to hear that. Would you like to have a look at the radio shack?"

This was the one offer that could deflect Paul from his plans, an opportunity to penetrate the enemy command centre. If he could get inside he could microfilm and memorise priceless data for his intelligence report. He put the clippers down and followed Marchmont across the lawn. As they went past the back door, Marchmont said to Dinka, "I'm taking Master Edward Silveras to see the radio room, Dinka. He can finish his work later."

Dinka squealed, "That aint no Silveras you got there! That's Paul Travis, more tricky than a box of brown snakes!"

Paul signalled to Dinka behind Marchmont's back with this hands and facial expression: the fate in store for her was death by strangulation.

Marchmont didn't seem to mind. He chuckled, "I thought you might be pulling my leg. So you're Ellen Travis's son, are you?"

Paul felt uncomfortable but it had to be endured for the opportunity. When they moved into a room like an office, Marchmont's eyes were consuming Paul. "You certainly are your mother's son," Marchmont said, nodding as though Paul would understand this idiotic point. Paul knew he had the classification right: dangerous.

In the radio room there was a young operator whom Paul knew as Terry. Terry addressed him as if they were old friends. Paul returned a blast of gamma and concentrated on absorbing all the secret information he could. There was a bank of radios along one wall faced by chairs and headsets. The dials and switches were complicated and there were masses of wires. You could switch on a speaker and hear pilots talking. Marchmont attempted to explain, but he didn't really understand and Terry took over. Paul learned that you could not only talk to aircraft flying around the Northern Territory and Queensland but reach out to houses anywhere in the world. The enemy was certainly formidable.

Terry seemed to think that Paul would find it interesting to know how his school lessons were transmitted. At this point, Paul said he had to go. He was glad to get out because Marchmont kept staring at him but didn't say much.

Paul finished the hedge and decided he had gathered enough intelligence and there was no need to check the airport. When he got home Ellen subjected him to the usual interrogation but despite her experienced probing he did not yield. However, he thought that since Ellen had actually been mentioned, he might be able to turn the tables on her and obtain some of her secrets. He explained that he had been arrested by a suspicious stranger that afternoon who had taken him to HQ at the Big House, but he had managed to escape. The stranger's name was Marchmont.

His mother's reaction was odd. She didn't cross-examine him at all. Not one question. She stopped talking and went off into space. It confirmed what he thought. The man was dangerous. His mother told him to go and wash for dinner. Nothing much happened that evening except that Ellen was quiet. When his father asked her why, she said she wasn't quiet. When Paul went to his room later to go to bed, she came in.

"Paul, I've decided I don't want you working at the Big

House any more." She spoke in a low 'I–mean–what–I–say' voice. "If you want a job, get something on the Hill or in the Village. Don't go to the Big House again. I'll speak to Goffy Jones in the morning."

Paul said, "I need to know the reason for this embargo. My gold reserves are going to suffer."

She smiled weakly and said he would have to do as he was told. Ellen, like many Category A people, threw an immediate security screen round all her proposals. That was why she was dangerous. All her operations had to be questioned and ultimately penetrated and understood. Not a clever way to work. On the contrary, his father was one of the few people who didn't need to be classified.

Paul retired to the security shelter under his bed sheets with a flashlight, special ink mixed from ochres found on the eroded banks of the Juduba, and a pen and paper; he compiled his report. He checked with his commander on his high frequency transmitter and it was confirmed that he should disregard Parental Order 6/3902 as necessary.

5

It wasn't until 1971 when Paul was sixteen that Marchmont came into his life again.

A party was to be held under a marquee on the lawn of the Big House to celebrate the arrival from New York of Mr and Mrs Marchmont. Mrs Marchmont was a new acquisition. She had two children of her own who were not much younger than Paul and they were to be at the party too.

Ellen seemed to have had a change of heart and the long-standing prohibition on Paul's presence at the Big House was in abeyance.

The marquee for the party had been sent from Brisbane. Paul helped his father and the gang set it up. It was like a fairy castle with a pale blue and white lining. Cold air was pumped into the space between the canvas and the lining. When the system worked properly, the interior was chilly and uncomfortable; when it didn't work the air was stiflingly hot. The portable air-conditioning plant made an unpleasant vibration even parked as far away as the length of the hoses carrying the air would allow. "Ours is not to reason why," Ted said to Paul. His father had a way of accepting wacky things like that.

At this time Paul was working and saving to fulfill Ellen's ambition that he should go to Sydney University. She had had her mind set on this ever since Paul could remember; it had become an accepted fact of life. He would finish his secondary schooling mostly at Mirabilly by correspondence from Darwin, supplemented by radio lessons and short courses in Darwin; and some classes with the Hill and Village kids. Ellen said he was lucky to be having a private education, like those posh Bloomsbury kids in the early twentieth century who were even smarter than their professors.

Paul was over six feet tall, strongly built and looked more like nineteen or twenty. To earn money he was helping build a road on Mirabilly, working with a gang forty miles from the Hill, where a cliff a hundred feet high in places marked off the highlands from the lowlands. The high ground, part of the Barkly Tableland, was the best cattle-raising country on the station. The lowland to the south teetered out into desert. Paul had to crinkle up his eyes if he wanted to look toward the shimmering boundaries of their land, millions of acres away.

On Mirabilly there were jobs where you could earn twice as much for half the effort of building roads. A worker in the fellmongery scrubbed cattle carcasses with a water brush as they came past him on the line. The man next to him trimmed the fat. They worked in the cool, scrubbing and slicing and talking all day. Ted knew Paul needed the money and he could have muscled Paul into a job on the killing line, but Ted didn't operate that way.

In the week before the Marchmonts were due to arrive, Paul was part of a gang of six men and earning almost as much as they were. He disliked the work. The men were alien to him, harsh, monosyllabic. He was doing it because Ted said that if he wanted to work on Mirabilly he had to start at the bottom. No privileges. He intended to qualify as a pilot as soon as he could. He had already mastered the technical manuals for the station's light aircraft and flown sometimes as a stock observer.

At eight o'clock in the morning on the day when John Marchmont was going to inspect progress on the road, Paul and the gang were breaking boulders with pickaxes and spreading the fragments on the road near the top of the cliff.

Their task wasn't a simple matter of excavating a track. They had to safeguard their work against rains in the summer which could destroy it in a few days. The road had to be compacted, paved with stone and drained. They didn't have an engineer or any drawings for this work; they did it according to common sense and their knowledge of the climate. Two weeks before, Ted had described what he wanted, pointing to a possible line up the rock face and then driven off leaving them with the grader, bulldozer and dynamite. He noted progress each day when he came in the truck to pick them up after their shift, usually with the serious joke that it seemed to be taking a hell of a long time.

The gang had bulldozed, dynamited and hewn out a road to enable cattle driven from the lowland plain to take a twenty mile shortcut to high ground and the slaughterhouse. Ted said you could work out the value of the road by calculating the weight a cattle-beast would lose on a twenty mile drive in the high eighties. Now it was June and they were starting to get those temperatures. They worked an early morning shift of four hours and a late afternoon shift of four hours. At noon, only lizards could move against the face of the rock.

Paul could just about keep up on the labour side. He had been doing heavy manual tasks on and off for months. He hated cracking rocks and hanging on the end of a shovel because it seemed mindless. After each day's work he fell on his bed with hardly the energy to eat, let alone think.

The experience gave him a different perspective on the gang; they were all in their thirties or older; it was as though their bodies were made of wood and steel; they didn't bleed or hurt; their heads were lumps on their shoulders which registered what to do next: lift, shove, punch, drink. For them, life was hard yacker and drinking and eating.

He couldn't imagine the sexual lives of the gang. All except one were unmarried; they were the dregs of Mirabilly in the sense that they weren't reliable or skilled enough for any task, except the hardest and least rewarding labour. Paul feared to be like them because what rock-breaking had done was to turn them into bullocks with jellied brains.

The gang took a ten minute break after every hour and on the nine o'clock spell, Paul found a shady place in a crack in the cliff and sat down. He was too tired to go up the road to recover a bottle of orange drink he had stowed under a bush. He'd have a quick gulp after he'd rested and before he started work again. He lay back against the stone with the usual feeling of light-headedness. His heart was thumping at first and the effort had driven away thoughts. He began to feel drowsy. He was in the cool of a cave where there were Aboriginal paintings. His imaginings were interrupted by what he thought at first, absurdly, was rain. A fine spray fell from above, breaking on the outcrops of rock as it fell. He put his face up into the spray and caught its pungent smell.

He moved out from the rock face to get a clearer view upward. About twenty feet above, Shorty Molins was standing with the toes of his boots over the edge, drinking orange juice from a bottle. At the same time, he had opened his flies and was urinating.

"How y' doin' down there, mate?" Molins yelled when he saw Paul. "Coolin' off?"

Paul heard the laughter of men he couldn't see. A black

temper exploded in his head. He sprinted to the top of the escarpment, stumbling painfully on the rocks. Molins had cast aside the bottle and Paul could see it was the one he had left under a bush. Molins's pug face was creased with amusement.

"Bastard!" Paul shouted and launched a fist at the small-eyed head.

Molins, a foot shorter than Paul and twice the thickness, had remarkable speed. He squared to Paul, knocking his arm aside and crashed his fist into the side of Paul's head. Paul fell in the dust.

"Pissing on you from a great height, Professor!" Molins said, dancing from foot to foot.

Paul was foolishly down only for a few seconds. He thrust himself at Molins again, his fists uncoordinated. Molins caught him quickly with two blows. One scrunched his nose and cheek, the other hit his chin.

Paul was on the ground again, his mouth gulping the dirt. He couldn't get up. He could hear laughter. And then another voice cutting through the hilarity: "What the hell are you doing with the boy?"

Blue Murphy, the boss of the gang, put a hand under Paul's arm and dragged him to his feet. He said quietly, "There you go, mate. I'd keep y' paws to y'self if I were you."

"Yeah," Shorty Molins snorted, jigging and shadow-boxing at the audience. "Y' might get hurt!"

"Are you OK, son? What happened?" Marchmont demanded, his face glowing under a digger's hat.

Paul's cheek ached. His nose felt as big as a balloon. His left eye was closing. He wanted to say that Molins was a bloody animal who stole his drink and pissed on him. Instead he choked the words back. "I'm all right. It was just a bit of fun."

The men were suddenly silent. Paul scooped up his hat, turned his back on Marchmont and hurried back to his place down the hill.

At the end of their day, Ted Travis arrived in the truck to inspect the work and drive them back to the station. His eyes didn't dwell on Paul's face for more than a second. He never asked a question or made a remark.

When the gang climbed into the back of the truck, Molins was next to Paul and elbowed him in the ribs. "Why don't you tell Pappy, Professor?" he snorted.

Paul didn't answer. Ted stopped at the Village and the men got out. Ted said to Paul, "You better come into the club and wash up. Your Ma'll go mad if she sees you like that." Ted didn't ask what happened.

Paul went into the shed which served as a club; it was a bar for workers on the station, a billiard room with one-armed bandits and a refreshment counter with chilled sandwiches and ham rolls. He went to the washroom and cleaned his hands and face with a paper towel. He examined his head in the mirror; it wasn't as bad as it felt. One eye was puffy. His lip was split. His nose was red and looked bigger.

When he came out of the washroom and passed through to the bar, Ted was talking to a circle of his mates and he nodded to Paul to join them. One of the men saw the marks and asked what happened. Paul said a camel backed into him and they all laughed and forgot it.

Ted led him out of the bar after an hour; he was light-headed with the beer. "Your Ma ain't goin' to like this," Ted said. He drove to the house and halted outside the gate. They made their way unsteadily up the path to the door. Ellen came out on to the verandah. She had been waiting and watching, trim and severe. This was the critical time when

Ted could arrive somewhat tipsy. When she saw Paul's face her manner changed.

"Oh, my God, you've had an accident!"

"It's nothing, Mum."

"The boy's OK," Ted said calmly.

Ted could hold a lot of booze, but the effect showed quickly. He smiled more easily. He relaxed. His hands weaved around ineffectually. Ellen knew the signs.

"So you've got the boy into your ways at last, have you?" she hissed, "I've told you often enough that I'm not one of those Village tarts that you can come home to like this!"

Ted met Ellen's onslaught with smiling silence, as he usually did. He didn't really understand her standards of refinement. As Ellen was fond of telling him, Ted didn't know anything before they were married except a bar room and the back of a horse. It was said that Ted could half kill a man like Shorty Molins with his fists, but he would never even contradict Ellen.

Ellen took Paul inside, bathed his face, put iodine and plasters on the cuts and anxiously satisfied herself that nothing was broken. He didn't mention that his nose was painful and floppy. He told her he'd fallen off a horse and she said riding was dangerous and he should stay off horses. Ellen herself rode occasionally. If she knew what had really happened she'd have stopped him working with the gang and probably banned him from the Marchmont celebration.

The Marchmont party had arrived by plane from Darwin a few days before Paul's fight. They were seen about the Big House and gardens as preparations were being made, interested, but trying to keep out of the way so that they could make a grand entrance as guests of honour later.

John Marchmont acknowledged Paul from a distance, as he cut across the lawn of the Big House on an errand for his mother. "Mr Alvarez!" he shouted with a salute. Paul waved back, but scuttled on. In a way it was flattering to be remembered by this man whom everybody on Mirabilly held in awe, even if he did get the alias wrong. There was a caution in what people on the station said about Marchmont. They felt they lived by his grace and he had access to worlds beyond their comprehension.

Paul soon spotted the wife, Katherine, behind the glassed-in terrace, trying not to look curious as she looked out. She was long and fair, graceful and tanned and she wore transparent flowing clothes. Then there was her son, Alexander, said to have been adopted by Marchmont, about Paul's age, slinking around outside, watching haughtily, pale, with blond hair and light eyes like his mother and, oddly, like his stepfather. And the girl, she was fourteen, but you'd honestly think twenty. She paraded herself around the patio, rolling her eyes and her bum, inviting everybody to get a load of her. She had, Paul thought, the most superb knockers and she knew it and put them about. She had dark red hair and an unfreckled, creamy skin. She noticed Paul and she knew he noticed her. He felt it would only be a short time before they were friends and the thought made him hot.

He figured that to get to Emma (Dinka had given him the lowdown on the names as well as a potted history) he needed to be matey with the weedy Alex. He resolved to speak to Alex as soon as possible.

Paul's girlfriend from the Village wouldn't be at the party. He was free and his girlfriend wasn't for publication anyway. She was the daughter of one of the workers in the hide store. She had five brothers and sisters and no mother. Her mother ran off with another man. Ellen would have killed Paul if she knew about Charlene. To Ellen, Charlene was trash, but Paul liked Charlene a lot.

Ellen had taken a completely different attitude to this party and the Marchmont visit. Usually she didn't want to know anything about the Marchmonts or said she wasn't interested. This time she planned to go to the party herself. Paul saw that she was making a yellow sun-frock which left her arms, shoulders and back mostly bare. Paul watched the dress rehearsal. Bearing in mind that she was around forty her body had shape. Paul couldn't judge her face which he knew too well. To him she was mostly fierce, didn't smile a lot, but was capable of moments of effervescent high spirits, dancing and singing.

Paul didn't know what made Ellen change her attitude about the visit; it was like so many things with her, you never knew. She was a phony in the sense that she tried to create a picture of herself for you, what she thought she was like, but forgot it didn't have any credible context or any background at all. Paul didn't know anything about her family in King's Lynn in England. He wasn't even sure how many brothers and sisters she had. She didn't write to them and they didn't write to her.

Once, in one of the drawers of her dressing table, Paul saw a photograph with 'From Ivy' written on the back. It showed a grave in a churchyard with an elaborate cross engraved 'Peter Burnham' and the dates of his birth and death. Ted told Paul confidentially that at one time, Ellen had letters to her relatives in England returned unopened. Ted didn't appear to know any more than he did, but Ted didn't care. Paul did care. If he pressed Ellen about her family she would say she couldn't remember, or that Paul didn't need to know, or if he pushed harder, 'Mind you own business!' Paul felt like saying it was his business.

Ellen was all dark corners and black holes. She had scrapbooks of information about odd places like London, Aden and Singapore but there was nothing very personal in them. She had taken out all the personal photos. You could see the gaps. When Paul asked her why, particularly, those places, she said because she was interested. If he pressed harder, he got the old 'mind your own business' routine. So her change of heart about the Marchmont visit, like so many things, would remain inexplicable.

In contrast, Paul felt that he knew his father through and through. What you saw was the actual man he was. Ted Travis was completely real. He was a simple man. Paul knew Ted's history and Ted often recounted funny episodes from it. He was one of a large family. His father was an ex-railway guard who plunged his savings into a smallholding in New South Wales and impoverished his family. Ted was raised on 'roo meat and rabbit stew and never had a pair of shoes until he was in his teens. He had been a happy kid who wasn't in the least sorry for himself.

You never sensed there was anything hidden or dark about Ted. If you didn't know something about him it was because it hadn't come up, not because he wanted to conceal it. Sometimes Paul used to ride with Ted and they would lie in the grass when they were tired (after they had beaten it for snakes and spiders). They would talk about the weather, or the state of the herds, or how the new work on the stockyard was progressing. Ted was like the governor of a vast territory philosophising about what he had done and planning what he was going to do, talking of the rain and the fire and the wind, entities that he had parleyed with and would outwit.

Paul's mind was mostly on how to manoeuvre close to Emma and he was up early on the morning of the party, helping to prepare the marquee with Dinka, the maids and Mrs Mather, the general manager's wife, who was in charge of protocol. He set out the round tables and collapsible chairs for the guests as Dinka directed and the trestle tables for food and drink. There were white linen cloths for the guest tables, with pale blue linen table napkins and pale blue tablecloths for the buffet tables. The caterers from Darwin provided 'silver' cutlery and crystal glasses. Every table napkin had a real silver ring engraved 'Mirabilly, John and Katherine Marchmont, 1971' intended as a personal memento for each guest.

The food was being kept, until the party began, in chillers behind the serving table and there were reserve supplies in the refrigerated store room, ready to be moved into the marquee by a small army of waiters. Mrs Mather had hired chefs from Darwin to prepare special dishes on the day and they had been working since three in the morning.

It was going to be a garden party followed by supper and the guests were expected to wander around. Since it would be too hot outside the marquee, Ted had suggested that they join the marquee to the doors of the Big House with an awning. A bright blue and white striped sheet of oiled cotton was flown up from Townsville and strung up fifteen feet high, creating a pleasant shaded area where guests could promenade or talk; and the hall and reception rooms of the Big House were also opened.

Paul helped Dinka put out the specially printed menu cards written up in part in French by the French chef. *Menu for the garden party and supper at Mirabilly Station in honour of the visit of Mr & Mrs J C deV Marchmont etc.* This inscription was set out in a grand scroll on the front of the cards and inside was a menu of food and wine such that Paul had never seen before. He had observed the crates of Dom Perignon champagne. He counted fifteen dozen bottles in the crates in the cool-store; it was going to be served like beer.

Paul couldn't understand the description of the food in French but he had seen the stores in the kitchen. Old Dinka couldn't stop giggling about them. Bluff oysters from New Zealand and Sydney rock oysters by the gallon; lobsters had been flown over live from Maine; there were buckets of whitebait and prawns, all to be washed down with the champagne. Paul had never tasted any of these delicacies. And there was more; smoked salmon, blue fin tuna. Monster fresh sea salmon and rainbow trout from Scotland were cooked to be picked off the bone and eaten cold with salad. Then there were the meats: the fillet of beef killed on Mirabilly and aged to perfection, supported by lamb and venison; the partridge and grouse were imported from England.

"We're goin' to need a whole lot of people to eat all this," Paul said to Dinka.

She leaned over and shielded her mouth with her hand. "They aint goin' to eat it, Paul. They just goin' to pick it around and whoomf it up!" and she cackled with laughter.

With three other kids of his age from the Hill, Paul was supposed to be serving drinks; that meant pouring champagne and wine; and orange juice if anyone wanted it. Mrs Mather had hired a barman from Darwin to serve mixed drinks and cocktails because she said nobody on Mirabilly could be trusted to remain sober enough to remember the ingredients of a gin and tonic. She was wrong about the barman. Paul helped him lay out the bar table in the marquee and then, the first thing he did was to wink at Paul and have a snort of Glenmorangie himself.

Ted had asked Paul that morning, with a grin, to go easy and Paul knew what he meant. Coming from Ted, a liberal drinker, that was quite a statement. Ted was conscious of his duty to be a more or less sober partner at Ellen's side. Paul thought Ellen had probably spelt this out to Ted in so many words.

The party was to start officially at 4 pm to use the cooler part of the afternoon and evening. It was the usual bright sunshine, about eighty degrees and pleasantly dry. By three-thirty everything had been ready for hours, with Mrs Mather wandering round checking, grilling the waiters on their procedures and getting annoyed with Dinka and the maids about little things. She also got annoyed with the barman when she caught him having another quick one.

Paul's instructions were to make sure the guests got a glass of ice cold champagne when they arrived and keep them filled up. The guests were mostly families from the Hill and a sprinkling of nobs flown in from Brisbane, Townsville, Cairns, Darwin and nearer towns. They were all going to be staying the night either on the Hill or at the Big House. The visitors were the buyers and agents for stock, hides, wool and meat; they were freight and aircraft contractors. The bankers were there and the accountants, lawyers, consulting engineers, pilots and surveyors; all the services and skills that had an important role in the business of Mirabilly.

About fifty guests arrived by 4pm and then more seemed to arrive suddenly in crowds. Paul served champagne on the run. All the time he was thinking of Emma and noting that none of the Marchmont clan had made an entrance, except Alexander. Paul saw Alex wandering alone at the fringe of the crowd, trying to look self-possessed. Paul offered him champagne and Alex took it coolly as if it was a glass of water. Paul tried to start a conversation hoping it would lead to Emma. He said he'd like to hear about England and their journey out. He had to rush off to his duties, but as he saw to the needs of the throng, he revisited Alex regularly. He always found him with an empty glass and left him with a full one.

Paul reckoned there must have been a 150 people there, the men in white shirts throttling themselves with neckties; some arrived in linen jackets but soon removed them. The women were dressed in the finest silk and cottons in every colour, with lots of tanned flesh showing and so many bright straw hats that all the brims seemed to touch and form a multi-coloured awning over the crowd. The marquee and the shaded area under Ted's canopy were crowded; some guests were inside the Big House but Paul, like his co-servers, had been told he need not go there, meaning he wasn't allowed there.

As Paul pushed through the guests with his tray he saw his mother and father; they were with Mr and Mrs Marchmont and Emma. He had been too busy to notice the arrival of the guest party. He hesitated, trying to decide whether he should approach, but Ellen stopped him and made a point of introducing him.

"This is my son, making himself useful," she said in a stagey voice Paul had never heard before.

He could see Emma looking at him in a way which suggested that they could now get to know each other. Even in that moment his eyes got stuck on the swelling of her breasts. Marchmont slapped him on the shoulder and said they'd already met. He chuckled and said Paul seemed to have recovered from his fight. Ellen reacted with a needling stare which signalled a forthcoming inquiry, but fortunately the talk passed on quickly to other subjects.

Mrs Marchmont took no notice of him; she was concentrating on his mother. Kate Marchmont had tired eyes. She was troubled by the heat. She had a line of sweat on her brow and her long hair had become damp and stringy; under her eyes were blue marks of exhaustion. "I'm sure you could do it admirably," she said to Ellen.

There was a complete contrast between the two. The tall, fair Englishwoman and Ellen's dark vitality. Ellen looked astounded. She turned toward John Marchmont who was nodding agreeably.

"It's a damn silly idea," she said emphatically; again, in the strangled voice that Paul couldn't recognise.

Ted stood mute, grinning at nothing and swaying as he tossed down the dregs of whatever was in his glass. Paul was startled that his mother had spoken so sharply and slipped away to replenish his tray. When he came back and handed Emma a glass of orange juice he whispered, "What was so silly?"

Emma smiled and drew away from the adults. "My mother thinks it would be a good idea if the Big House had a full-time housekeeper and my stepfather suggested she ask your mother. Your mum doesn't seem to like the idea. She certainly speaks her mind, but then she knows John from... before. Doesn't she?"

Paul wasn't that interested in the answer to his question. He was giddy in Emma's sweet odour and the possibility that some time that afternoon he might touch her. "Why don't you come over near the bar and we can talk?" he said with a boldness buttressed by two glasses of Dom Perignon.

"I might just do that later," she said lightly, with a glance that meant she certainly would.

By about 6.30pm Paul was aware that strange things were happening. When the first guests arrived in the tranquil afternoon heat it was difficult for them to find words, even though most of them knew each other; dressed up and in unfamiliar surroundings, they were tongue-tied. But the golden liquid did its work and the noise in the marquee gradually rose to a deafening level.

The guests were not strangers to champagne but their usual drink, including many of the women, was cold lager beer. Paul began to see that he and his fellow servers were at least partly responsible for the change, because they had poured the champagne like lager. No glass had been allowed to empty.

Paul had reduced Alex, who now lay hidden behind the bar, to a comatose state. Alex's eyes couldn't focus and he babbled nonsense when Paul spoke to him. Paul's plan, when he could sneak away from his duties, was to call Emma over on the pretext of consulting her about her brother's health.

A number of people were not far from Alex's condition, lying on the grass or slumped in chairs. Drunkeness was socially acceptable on the Hill. At a point in the later afternoon, the gathering had decided that it was time to eat instead of merely picking canapés from trays and they had advanced upon the buffet en masse, pushing and shoving, guffawing and shouting, grabbing handfuls of food, piling their plates with lumps of chicken and fish and lamb and salad, all in a mess and to hell with the Frenchie's menu. When the diners retreated with their piled plates to the dining tables some couldn't find clear seats for their party of friends of the moment. Chairs were pushed aside and knocked over, tables were pushed out of line. Plates were jolted off the table-cloths on to the grass.

Paul noticed that people seemed to start eating

indiscriminately with any dish. One man wolfed strawberries and cream, while another had a whole plate of king prawns fried in butter; with sleeves rolled up, he tore them apart with his fingers and stuffed them into his mouth. A woman with a lobster was so frustrated by the armour plate of the creature that she banged her shell-cracker on the table and threw the carapace at her husband, opposite. He threw it back.

Paul continued to ply his trade until Mrs Mather ordered all their team to stop and not serve unless requested. This was his chance to call Emma to her brother's side and when he did so, he was pleased to see that she was indifferent to Alex's fate.

"Why don't we go outside, out of this racket?" she said.

Paul led Emma Rainham Marchmont to the swimming pool with no particular action in mind. It was on the far side of the Big House, screened by trees and with a canvas awning so that bathing, even at noon, would be tolerable. As soon as she saw the sheet of clear blue water, Emma slipped out of her dress and shoes. She touched a button and the dress fell off. She dived into the water without giving Paul much time to see her in bra and pants. Paul had never bathed in the pool before; it was off-limits to him, but he dropped his denim trousers, tore off his t-shirt and dived in after her. The water was dreamily warm and thick like syrup. He swam to Emma and put his arms round her, only to be distracted by a groan from Alex who had appeared at the side of the pool. Alex swayed on the edge, cheese-faced. He then bent over and honked up the contents of his stomach into the pool. A stream of half-digested shrimp, salmon, chicken and fine fillet steak, marinated in champagne, spread in a lumpy slick on the surface of the water.

"Let's get out of here," Emma said to Paul and they

scrambled out of the pool, scooped up their clothes and, ignoring the prostrate Alex, went into the Big House by the back door. Emma led him through the halls to her bedroom. They saw nobody on the way.

"Now we can talk," she giggled, shutting the door and throwing herself on her bed.

She was lying in front of Paul with a tiny pair of black silk pants on, which didn't even cover her red pubic hair and a thin black bra that showed the outline of the big, dark nipples on her breasts.

Paul was unsteady. His head and belly weren't synchronised. He felt suddenly cold in the air conditioning. He had a lump in his stomach from bolting chunks of steak and an aerated feeling in his head. In his groin he had nothing.

"Look at your hands! They're as rough as the roots of an oak," Emma said.

He looked at his hands. Normally, he never thought of them much; bony, calloused, with fingers thickened by manual work.

"It's all right, Paul. I like you better that way. You can touch me."

Paul couldn't move.

"You are a silly boy," she said impatiently, sitting up.

She reached out, putting her fingers in the waist of his underpants and pulling them down. He was exposed, useless. Emma smiled wisely and moved her hand toward him.

He had no time to feel more than a ripple of excitement. The door was thrown open behind him and Katherine Marchmont stood there, choking.

"Get out of here you perverted beast!" she shouted. "The child is fourteen years old!"

Paul pulled his underpants up from his ankles and slipped past Katherine Marchmont, leaving his trousers, t-shirt and loafers behind.

He fled out of the Big House by the back door, a shadow startling the servants in his way, into the trees and home. He sat in his room for five minutes wanting to get under his bed, to hide in darkness. His life was in ruins. And then he heard his mother's voice from the path. She and Ted had come home. He couldn't face her. He was still expected to be helping in the marquee. He pulled on a shirt and slacks over his wet underpants, slid into sandals and went out of the back door, a fugitive.

It was quiet as he approached the marquee. He found a scene of ruin and desolation. A few guests were still present; those who couldn't move, heads down over the tables or prone on the grass; some were groaning as they spewed up the food and liquor they had taken in; their vomit mingled with streams of spilt sauces and liquor which trickled down from the tables and over the chairs. Glasses and empty bottles and half-eaten plates of food were scattered over the grass, tables collapsed and chairs overturned. Here and there was the gleam of a silver napkin ring which a guest had forgotten to claim. The pale blue table napkins were flopped everywhere, like gulls roosting on a rubbish dump.

Now Paul's mind alternated between gritting his teeth and helping to clean up, waiting for the fateful hand on his shoulder, or running to the Village and hiding out at Charlene's cabin until... until when?

Dinka and the other maids had their backs bent restoring order, their task vast. Paul found the barman, Harry, emitting a strong stench, snoring in a flower bed, a florid stain over the front of his white dinner jacket. Dinka muttered instructions to Paul as though he wasn't a fugitive.

He began to help, carrying dishes to the kitchen, scraping off the ravaged food into waste buckets, folding chairs and tablecloths. Emma came up suddenly behind him. She was in a different dress and looked calm. He could not speak. She smiled as though they shared a sweet secret and handed him a paper bag.

"Here's your clothes, Paul. Don't mind Mother. She's a bit old-fashioned." And she skipped away with a snigger.

6

Paul stayed on a few weeks at the Hill with Ellen after Ted's funeral and although they talked occasionally, they were remote from each other. His qualification for a light aircraft licence enabled him to make some money flying one of Mirabilly's planes, doing stock-checks and short errands to nearby towns in the outback. He had no commercial licence but that didn't worry Dick Mather.

Paul also had to decide how to deal with the place he had obtained at Sydney University to study law, a choice of Ellen's, made from almost complete ignorance, which he had passively accepted. It was soon confirmed that Ted's debts would wipe out everything Ted owned except the furniture in the house. Ellen offered her insurance pay-out, but Paul pointed out that it was plainly insufficient for courses lasting years. Neither of them had any clear idea how he could earn during his studies. Ellen agreed that Paul would have to postpone his education for a year or perhaps two years.

In the meantime, he was happy to join one of the small outback airlines and get a commercial licence. He knew the pilots who were flying into the station regularly. He was particularly friendly with Nick Karantis who worked for Dart Airways. Nick persuaded Paul to come to Darwin to meet the proprietor who was looking for another pilot. Nathan Dartmell was only around thirty but he had the clipped, bossy way of a big executive. "So you can fly," he said. "You don't have a commercial ticket. We'll get you one. Join a real outfit, Paul. Have a career!" They shook hands. "Nick's word is good enough for me," Dartmell said on the issue of references.

Paul moved to Townsville first, then Darwin. He had a room in a widow's house near the city; it looked over a field of goats. He bought a third-hand Honda 125 bike to get around. He liked, but didn't love, flying. In the first few months he hardly ever seemed to be on terra firma and then only for a quick meal, or to go back to his room to sleep. He began to hear whispers about Dartmell's private life.

One night, in the bar of the Flying Club, a wooden shed near the Darwin field where the pilots lounged when they were off duty, Nick took Paul aside. "Nat's in trouble." His dark Greek eyes were wide.

"What do you mean?"

"Booze, a woman who ain't his wife and a father-in-law who wants his lolly back. Nat's in pieces. He barks at us as though he was on cloud nine, but it's the gin talking."

"Shit! We're going to be out of a job." Paul had a sudden feeling of helplessness.

Nick and Paul sipped their beer quietly, thinking, and then started to criticise Dart's organisation.

"Are you going to go to Nat with a rescue plan?" Paul asked.

"Nah. He'd never listen. Too far gone."

"So why don't we get in on the act?" Paul said, having no clear idea how they could do this. But the idea that it could be done was simple and logical.

"Yeah," Nick said slapping him on the back. "I been thinking the same! Dart's reputation's going down. The customers are nervous. We know that. Slip–ups with deliveries. And the word about him is on the wire."

Nick and Paul resigned, collected their pay on their last day with Dart and headed for the Flying Club to develop their plans. They sat at a table under the trees by the roadside and ignored the occasional dust that settled on them as the heavy trucks passed. They could see the shimmering airfield through the wire fence; light aircraft were continually landing and taking off, each one drilling urgently at their thoughts.

Nick urged Paul on. His idea was to hire two planes and when they had some business, go to a bank and borrow money to get planes on long-term leases. Easy. Paul wasn't entirely convinced but Nick's enthusiasm was infectious.

"Let's have a go!" Nick said, raising his stubbie in a toast.

"I'm not sure my savings are enough," Paul said, grinning.

"How much have you got?" Nick asked seriously.

"About a thousand dollars."

"Ha! Me too! Hell, we won't need much. My old man will stump up a few thousand bucks for the first few weeks. We just have to get out there and get those deals!"

Both Nick and Paul had contacts with the bosses at the stations they had been servicing. Mirabilly was Paul's baby and he approached Dick Mather. He flew down in a Cessna 235 hired for the day. He had an edge with Mather who was having an affair with Ellen and Mather knew Paul knew. Paul didn't like Mather, who reminded him of the sleek seals he'd seen in the Townsville Aquarium and he felt sorry for Betty Mather.

He sat opposite a confused-looking Mather in the shadowy office at the Big House. "I heard Dart was in trouble. The service has been flagging," Mather said, "and I've been talking to one or two of the boys about what we should do…"

Paul had no scruples about spinning Mather a yarn. "My partner has finance for a small fleet of aircraft and we want to pick up as many of Dart's contracts as we can. We know the business. We've been flying the routes."

Mather wasn't going to refuse Paul readily. He seemed more interested in personal gossip, the fall of Nathan Dartmell, the drinking and infidelity which must have resonated with his own pecadilloes. He scratched his scurfy head, wriggled his neat moustache and looked for catches.

Paul imagined his mother in bed with Mather; it hardened him from a kid asking for a favour, to a deal-maker. "No catches. We pick up the Dart load at the same rates."

Mather was silent for a moment. "Can't see what we have to lose. It'll save me looking round. I'd only be having this conversation with somebody else. Damned if I thought I'd be dealing with you, Paul. How old are you?"

Nick and Paul weren't doing anything extraordinary; they were two of a number of pilots freelancing around northern Australia in beaten-up hired machines, making a small turn on the traffic. It was touch and go whether the new firm of Karantis & Travis would get enough work to keep them flying. The loads had to be small because they didn't have the capacity to haul heavy freight; they had to be medical supplies, perishable foods, mail and payrolls and any small delivery that was urgent, plus the occasional passenger: a dog, a cat or even a human.

7

Paul used to fly in to Mirabilly every week and occasionally take the time to see Ellen, who after almost two years from Ted's death was still living on the Hill. He didn't know whether his visits to Ellen were out of consideration for her, or to lacerate himself. The atmosphere between them had hardly changed since Ted's death; a superficial calm covering dark, forbidden spaces.

On a visit he met Dick Mather coming out of the house as he approached through the neatly clipped and watered lawns; they exchanged uneasy greetings. Mather hustled past in embarrassment. Paul pressed on through the screen door into the house.

"What did Mather want?" he asked, although he knew already, as Ellen came out in her dressing gown, drying her hair with a towel and humming a tune. "I ran in to him as he was leaving."

"Bad news, I'm afraid. I'm going to have to move in a few weeks. Dick's a friend. He's going to get me a house and a job in the Village."

"Yes, a very good friend." Paul was sickened at the thought of Mather pawing his mother.

"I can manage Mather," Ellen replied in a biting tone.

Indeed, she had managed him quite skilfully for almost two years.

"And what's more I believe he's done you a good turn or two," she said.

Paul was grateful for Mather's early support with the Mirabilly work. At the same time he was nauseated, knowing the leverage which earned the favour.

"You'll hate it in the Village, Mum."

"I'm not leaving Mirabilly."

"You ought to get a house near Maude Geary's at the Creek, or in Townsville. I'll look after the rent. You could probably get a job there."

"It's final, Paul."

It would be a wrench for Ellen to leave this place, the head stockman's house with its neat white walls, glassily polished floors, bright rugs and the seclusion of the garden; but she didn't share a word of that with Paul. She, and Ted at her direction, had worked hard to make it a showplace, but hardly a home. Ted had definitely not been allowed to bring his mates home.

Ellen called the homes in the Village doss-houses. She loathed the style of the villagers. In fact, they had money and their cabins were in good repair. They were the people Paul had grown up with and liked on the whole. She would protest, "The women smoke cigarettes and talk in loud voices; they wear trousers and dig the garden. And the men sprawl on the front porches and drink beer. The dogs chew bones under the kitchen table and go to sleep on the children's beds!"

Paul cringed inside at the thought of his mother moving from the Hill to the Village amongst the Mirabilly workers, because of her view of them and because what had happened to her was as plain as if she had shouted it from a rooftop. She was snidely laughed at by many and perhaps pitied by some. She had often been referred to behind her back as Lady Jane and Paul couldn't, when he first heard that kind of expression years ago, understand why. He understood now. Dumped by Marchmont, impoverished by

Ted Travis, in bed with Dick Mather and now set to live and work in a community of jackeroos whom she despised. Paul's flesh crawled as though it was happening to him.

Later, Ellen was allocated one of the better cabins in the Village; but it was still a cabin rather than a house, in a row of similar cabins, surrounded by a few yards of lawn and a chicken wire fence. Mather also got Ellen a job in the commissary and sometimes she worked shifts in the cafeteria. She retained her profound contempt for the families around her. She was always curling her mouth at what she described as the shouty, dirty, sozzled men, their ever-pregnant wives and wild kids.

Ellen never mourned for Ted in any visible way that Paul could detect and never mentioned him affectionately. He was like a distant acquaintance who was no longer around. Ted had eventually become one of Ellen's many taboo subjects and this left Paul unable to reconcile, for himself, the essentially gentle man of the outback whom he knew as a father, with the improvident gambler and deceiver who had emerged after his death.

Two years after Ted's death was the time to which Paul had agreed to postpone his further education. He had seriously meant postponement at the time, because he had been attracted by books and study and was disappointed at having to wait. Ellen was now questioning him month by month about his intentions.

"Isn't it time you got on with your studies?" she would say and he would reply that he was 'working on it.' He hadn't entirely dismissed the idea, but instead of the savings Ellen thought he must have accumulated, he had big personal debts and a commitment to Nick Karantis. If he pulled out of their business Nick's livelihood would collapse or be severely damaged.

"I've decided not to go to university," he told her at last. He wasn't going to say to her that it was impossible because he had no money.

Ellen was quick to condemn. "A plane is more fancy than a car, but you might as well be a cab driver."

But a living had developed around him by his own efforts and imagination, aided by Nick. He had a genuine reluctance to give it up quite apart from the lack of money. The thought of writing papers for academics seemed to belong increasingly to a part of the past that he had missed and to which it was becoming too late to return.

Nick's early, perhaps reckless confidence had boosted them into business, but Paul was surprised how quickly Nick's spirits sank as their borrowed capital was eaten up by unforeseen expenses and their cash flow slowed down. Paul decided that he was not going to give up without pushing further. He argued that they had to get cheaper and better planes. He found, from a classified advertisement in *Flight Monthly,* that a firm named Burrundie Finance of Darwin were offering four repossessed aircraft in good condition for sale or lease. He persuaded Nick to look over the planes which were stabled in a compound near the field. The security guard stood at the wire gate jangling his keys and keeping the dogs quiet. They patted the noses of the planes in a friendly way as though they were horses.

"We'd never be able to afford the Beechies," Nick said, "but that's what we need."

Paul pulled his head out of the cabin of a Piper Apache. "These old buses are OK."

Their next stop, the next morning, was the office of Burrundie Finance. "Huh," Nick said, eyeing the hairdressing salon on the street front and peering upstairs into the gloom. "A back-street outfit. Run by bean-counters creaming it off as money-lenders. Whadda y' think they know about flying?"

Nick and Paul had dressed in their best and only dark suits; in Paul's case formerly Ted's second best. They both wore white shirts and dark ties.

"OK," Paul said, "we play it very calmly this time. Say little. No attempt to deal."

"Right," Nick said, straightening his tie and looking at his partner. "Goddamn it, Paul, you look five years younger'n you already are in that outfit!"

Upstairs, the receptionist was impressed with Mr Karantis and Mr Travis. She lingered huskily over their names and then opened a door behind her to reveal a shiny-bald man in rolled shirtsleeves and braces, wedged behind a desk. He didn't get up.

"Come in and siddown boys," he said, hardly appearing to glance at them. "You wanna take the planes or are you enquiring on account of your daddy?"

Paul was confused. It was their first real business meeting. Getting freight loads from station managers and suppliers had been like talking to friends. This was different. Nick showed for the first time a quality of temperament that was to be important to them. A red coin-sized spot appeared on each of his cheeks and his eyes swelled. "We been flyin' fuckin' aircraft for years, mate!"

The accountant's face wrinkled up and he paid attention with his damp eyes behind his spectacles. "Just kidding, boys, just kidding," he said. "Tell me."

"No, you tell us," Nick said, pushing over the desk a long and quite professional list of questions that they needed to answer to assess the planes. Paul had got a girlfriend of his to type it.

The man held the list between finger and thumb delicately as though it had a bad smell. He studied it for a short time and said, "Yeah, I can get you this stuff but can you guys deal? Premium. Bank guarantees. That crap."

Nick's olive cheeks were suffused now and his eyes focussed hypnotically on the accountant. "Listen, Mr Burrundie…"

"Dooley," the man said.

"You give us the info. Then we consider it. Then we come back to you if we like it with a deal."

"We need bank guarantees, fellers."

"We'll prove our credentials and experience and give you a third party guarantee. Forget the premium. And the bank guarantee. It's a buyer's market, mate. We're looking at other aircraft when we leave here."

"I understand the market, boys. We'll talk about it when we've got the details."

"If the birds are up to scratch," Nick growled, jerking his head at Paul to signal their departure.

Over a beer at the Macquarie Hotel, Paul realised he had learned something. Nick had established an emotional dominance over Dooley and by agreeing to talk later, Dooley appeared to have cast aside the bank guarantee and the premium.

"You did great, but what about this third party guarantee?" Paul asked.

"My old man has three bakery shops. As soon as we're under way I'll repay the old man and get a bank guarantee."

"We already owe your dad a bundle."

"You know what he said to me when I asked for the advance? 'I'm seventy-five years old, son. You have it now – or later'."

Nick and Paul thought they had nothing much to lose.

They weren't worried about bankruptcy because they didn't fear or even understand the stigma, but they had been and probably would be a hair's breadth from it for years. And Nick didn't seem to be worried about the risk to his father. It was an advance on his inheritance.

They leased the planes and soon Paul was working harder than he had ever worked in his life. They never seemed to have any money. At first, they paid a girl in a secretarial agency to act as receptionist and booking clerk and flew every hour they could, serving six stations and small towns spread out over the Northern Territory and Queensland. When they were in Darwin together, they were up until three or four in the morning with bookkeeping and business arrangements. They were enjoying themselves in a masochistic sort of way, but they could see this couldn't go on for very much longer.

Nick and Paul named their company Northern Airlift. In 1975, when Paul was twenty, their office was at the end of Trafalgar Street in Darwin, where the town started to run out and the suburbs began.

The office was in a two-storey building with a fish and chip shop on the ground floor and their office up a flight of stairs over the top. The smell of frying fat came in the windows on most days and it was too hot to close them. Their office, two rooms, was looked after by Melda Turner, a middle-aged married woman whose children were in high school. She lived two doors along the street and could be relied on to be at the office at odd hours or during the weekend. She was an expert typist and telephonist, once a secretary for a mining boss. She had taken to 'the boys' as she called them.

Nick and Paul, in their everyday uniform of t-shirts and jeans stood in the front office with Melda one Saturday morning. Melda always wore a smart dress and had her dark hair back-combed to stand high on her head. Nick threw Melda a coin.

"You do it, luv," he said. "We don't want any mistakes. Heads, I'm grounded; tails it's Paul."

Melda squeezed her bulky figure out from behind the desk, the coin in one of her beringed hands. "I'm not used to this," she said, as she balanced the twenty cent piece on her thumb awkwardly.

Paul watched her movements as if they were in slow motion. "This is the big moment," he said, trying to be flippant.

Nick and Paul had hired two more planes and pilots in a year and now had their own part-time engineer to supervise the servicing. They had a sprawling business, a huge overdraft, lots of bills to pay, and almost no money of their own – but the accountants said they were doing fine. It was simply a matter of flying further and faster and running faster and faster in their office.

The pair weren't always the best at communicating and perhaps that was because they were apart during most of their working hours. But they had both independently arrived at the thought that one of them should be grounded to manage the business, a task that couldn't be passed to anybody they could afford to employ. The only way that came naturally to them to resolve the problem was to toss a coin.

Paul would not have admitted it openly but he was becoming bored with flying. Looking after the business on the ground wasn't attractive, but it would be a change. He hoped almost desperately to for the coin to ground him. He assumed Nick felt the same.

Melda giggled and threw rather than tossed the coin into

the air; it turned over lazily a few times but both men declared it a valid toss. The coin bounced on the linoleum floor and rolled under a desk; they all had to crowd around to see it lying in its resting place. Paul looked past Melda's bundle of hair at the disc with the over-pretty bas-relief of Queen Elizabeth II in profile. The disappointment was like being winded.

Nick straightened up and put his sallow face close to Paul's. "A head. Agreed? Fair enough?" he said, holding out his hand. "I gotta push paper!"

Paul determined not to show his real feelings. "Yeah!" he said, shaking the proffered hand.

Nick chucked the coin idly in his palm and slumped into a chair, frowning. "Well, fuck it, somebody had to get the short straw! Sorry, Melda. Shit!"

Paul was staring stiff-faced out of the open window, the images of passing cars unseen, the smell of frying unsmelt.

"What's the matter with you, misery-guts?" Nick asked him, "You're flying, man. You're fuckin' free!"

Paul started hesitantly. "Hey, Nick. I think we've got a cock-up here. You're not happy. I thought you wanted to be grounded. You got a head and you are grounded."

"Balls," Nick said, "I may as well tell you. I wanted to *fly* and I'm not, but OK. We have to move on."

"But I wanted to be *grounded* and I've got to fly!" Paul protested.

Nick was bemused. "No kidding? You don't want to fly?"

"Flying's OK but I'd like a change. I thought you felt like that too, Nick. I thought we were both bidding for the job as manager of this outfit."

"No way! Hell, I don't want a change! You crazy guy! My wonderful partner," Nick said, leaping up, spinning around and letting out a yell. He jigged to the office fridge and pulled out a six-pack of Fosters, throwing cans to Melda and Paul. "Drinks all round. To our new office manager, accountant, managing director and chief toilet-roll buyer. I give you Paul Travis! A long and successful career to you, mate!"

Paul let a big pull on the beer hit his throat and detonate. He was flooded with relief. "Hell, I got it arse about."

"Jeez, yes," Nick said, putting an arm around Paul's shoulders. "You sit here and smell the fry-ups while I'm out there in the big blue. Yes, please!"

When Paul was installed in the Darwin office he had a chance to do, or try to do, all the things he had thought about in the air. The company was beginning to become well-known; they were young, informal and enthusiastic. The only requirements were to deliver on schedule, safeguard the plane and sweet-talk the customers. Paul could sense after another year that they had achieved a critical mass. The business was starting to grow as though it was alive and at a rate that seemed to be independent of his and Nick's personal efforts.

8

On his visits to Mirabilly since Ted's death, Paul's instinct had been to keep away from the Big House except for necessary business, although the fact that Mather continued to see Ellen brought him in touch with them. He heard from Terry Dunn in the radio shack that Katherine, Marchmont's wife, reputedly an alchoholic, had been killed in a car wreck in New York. Terry also provided him with information about Marchmont's latest girlfriend, Linda Ryland and her daughter. Paul wondered what had happened to Emma. And he felt a cold curiosity about Marchmont.

The new mistress's daughter's name was Sophie; Paul met her in the radio shack with Terry Dunn on a weekend when he had come to see Ellen. She was sixteen, four years younger than him, tall, full-bosomed with thick golden hair, clear, white, babyish skin and candid gray eyes. She wasn't in the least like the wild and wilful Emma. She was calm, mature for a sixteen-year-old and sisterly rather than flirtatious. She talked freely about her life and questioned Paul about his. Her manner was very direct and when she said she'd never flown in a light plane before, Paul offered to take her up some time.

"How about tomorrow morning?" she replied instantly and it was arranged.

What had been no more than a macho gesture toward a pretty girl that would come to nothing, became a date.

Paul slept in the tiny box room at Ellen's cabin. In the morning, he borrowed one of the station's utes and drove to the Big House at eleven. Sophie was outside, in trainers and denims with a thin t-shirt and her hair tied back, looking very young.

As she climbed into the ute, John Marchmont, whom Paul hadn't seen since the garden party four years before, came out of the house. He was frowning. He had thickened a little with the indulgence of affluence, but Paul discerned the same vigorous and calculating character.

He searched for something of himself in Marchmont's appearance, something in the shape of the forehead, the nose, the chin, a mannerism. Possibly it was there... no. The colourings were all wrong. Marchmont was fine-featured and smoothly contoured, while Paul was inches taller, bony and swarthy.

"Where are you going, Sophie?" Marchmont asked.

"I already told you last night, flying with Mr Travis," she said with a sweet smile.

Marchmont didn't respond. He strolled up to the ute and bent down at the passenger window, addressing Paul. "Travis, I hear you're working for us now. How's business?" He extended his hand through the window.

"Tough," Paul said, taking the clean, manicured, white hand.

"I'd like Sophie to take a flip with her mother and me this afternoon."

The pale eyes searched Paul and his blood quickened at the silky voice that was effectively giving him an order.

"Hey, wait a minute, boss-man," Sophie said. "The arrangements are mine. I met Mr Travis yesterday with Terry Dunn. *I* asked *him*. I've gotta go." She was coolly emphatic, with the simplicity of a child.

Marchmont ignored her and stared straight at Paul. "Well, Travis?"

Paul hit the starter and eased the ute forward. Sophie turned her head towards Paul and opened her eyes wide; it was an 'I don't care' gesture.

"You look a bit white around the gills, Paul," she said as they moved down the slope, "Are you scared or something?"

"Are you kidding? I'm mad!"

The engine noise from the Cessna 350 filled the cabin as they lifted off the dusty field. Paul talked to Mirabilly flight control, Terry Dunn, as they climbed, explaining their route.

"I'm going up to seven or eight thousand feet," he said to Sophie through the headset, "and you can see how big Mirabilly is, well over two million acres."

The perfectly blue and cloudless sky was only touched by the occasional wisps of smoke from small bushfires below. The land was covered with a haze of dust. To the north was the green smudge of the Gulf of Carpentaria. Paul took the aircraft down in a dive. He flew low, down valleys, over dry river beds, along miles of low cliffs and ridges; it was a huge wild floor of brown and green. At times they were so low the cattle-beasts were startled and started to run. "This is how we check stock around here. Flying cowboys!" he laughed.

Paul had intended to give Sophie twenty minutes in the air and then return, but the row with Marchmont made him want to hang on to her a bit longer and he decided to land the plane. He throttled off over a cluster of deserted tin sheds and a stockyard. "Believe it or not, this is a landing strip," he said, as the plane settled over the level stretch in front of them, bumping and bouncing to a stop.

Paul turned the plane and taxied it to the sheds, telling

control their position and saying they were going to take a look around. It was three o'clock and still blisteringly hot. He fished out two broad-brimmed felt hats and nets from behind the seats and passed one to Sophie.

"Hope it fits," he said.

"Is there anything here to see?" she asked, sounding slightly suspicious, adjusting the hat over her plentiful hair.

"I'll take you up to the east ridge." He slipped a flashlight into his pocket.

"What's that for?" she asked. "I've never been to such a well-lit place."

"It's a secret."

Although she kept questioning, he good-naturedly fended her off. He didn't know why he had decided to share something with a person he hardly knew and little more than a child at that, unless it was an intimacy that excluded Marchmont. Despite Sophie's willingness to resist Marchmont, he understood that she respected him.

The heat didn't seem to bother her and they walked through arid scrub and climbed to the edge of a cliff. In the distance they could see Brahman cattle grazing. Paul pointed to the dry river course a hundred feet below. "This becomes a roaring torrent in the rains. Over there, on the other side, is the Aborigine Reserve."

"Where's the boundary?" Sophie asked.

"It's supposed to be the water-course but it's shifted over the years. The Aborigines say this is their land. It's a sacred burial ground."

"Are they claiming it or something?"

"Not at the moment. They're in no hurry," Paul said, beginning to move down the face of the cliff. "You get like that when you've been around for tens of thousands of years."

"Can we go across there, to the caves?"

"I guess so."

"You don't seem sure."

"I'd prefer permission from the tribe."

"They don't have an enquiry office here?" she smiled.

"Sure, there's a little green kiosk down the hill with a man in it, selling tickets."

"Maybe there isn't another person for a hundred miles, maybe..." she said, uncertainly.

"Right. More than a hundred miles."

They made their way down a trail in the steep face and crossed the water-course. The light was so bright that they had to keep their hat brims well pulled down and the occasional fly created mayhem by getting under their nets.

"Is it bad luck to be here?"

"It's not bad luck," Paul said, trying for the right words to express ideas he'd never talked about with any white person except Ted Travis. "This is where they believe the spirits are."

"But you don't believe that, do you?"

"My father once asked me that. It's like going into somebody else's church or graveyard or temple."

"Sure. Respect," Sophie said.

He helped Sophie over boulders and they climbed up a cleft in the escarpment for about fifty feet, stopping frequently to get their breath. Patches of wet showed on their shirts. They came to a cave and he beckoned Sophie inside. After a few moments their sight adjusted. As they went down deeper the cave became more spacious. At last they reached an amphitheatre and their sweaty shirts felt chilly. The space was quite cool and lit by a shaft of sunlight coming through a fissure in the roof. At their feet was a noisy stream.

Paul took the flashlight and moved the beam around the walls which were covered by brilliantly coloured paintings in blue, red, yellow and brown. "I don't know how far this goes back historically. But thousands, maybe tens of thousands of years. Tribes have worshipped here and sheltered."

"It's very moving," Sophie whispered.

Paul searched the walls with his torch until he came to a place where a piece of rock about six feet high and a yard wide had been removed. "I've never been in the Big House, but isn't there a stone in the lounge?"

"Oh, my God, yes!" Sophie said. "A lovely panel with figures. So somebody broke it off from here? Stole it, I guess."

"Yeah. I've known this place since I was a child and I've never come here without feeling I was trespassing. These are ancestral paintings. The Aboriginals believe they can assume the character of these figures. They sometimes paint the outlines on themselves."

"Do you believe that?"

"Believe isn't the right word. It suggests that there is something practical and provable. The spirits are part of the mythic history of this place. The sacred stones that tell the history of the tribes are said to be buried near here."

"Can we go there?"

"You get a lot of marks for enthusiasm and nerve, but no. We better go back to the east ridge now."

"Why nerve?"

"Crocs."

He led her back across the water-course and as they were climbing, they came to another cave. He beckoned her inside. "There's a whole cave system under the ridge, leeched out by the river torrents over years."

This time there were no paintings, only natural shapes and colours of yellowish rock. "Look at this." He pointed to a white vein feeding through the yellow mass.

"What is it?" Sophie asked.

"Gold. A reef of gold."

"You're kidding."

"No, I'm serious, but of course it's been examined and found to be so trivial that it isn't worth mining."

"Does John know?"

"He must have been hearing about gold finds on Mirabilly all his life. This place is known to the odd prospector, a few kids on Mirabilly and the indigenous people."

They drank water from the underground stream but had no food. They were hungry. When they came out of the cave the sun was low. Sophie's natural buoyancy had given way to quiet thoughtfulness. They walked slowly back to the Cessna and as they strapped themselves into the seats, Sophie said, "I'm sorry it's over."

Paul checked the switches and turned the motor over, but it showed no sign of firing. He checked the gauges. The battery was weak. He gunned the motor again and again and again, until the battery lost the power to turn the propeller.

At Paul's suggestion, Sophie climbed out of her seat and sat in the shade of the hut. Paul tried to turn the propeller by hand but the motor refused to fire. He was steaming, annoyed and feeling a fool. He climbed into the cockpit and tried the starter once more and then put his head out of the cabin window and said, "I can't get her to start, Sophie. I'm going to call Mirabilly and let them know."

When he contacted Mirabilly the approaching night had filled the clefts and water-courses with gentle grey-green shadows, like a rising tide of water and the high points of the ridges were tinted red. He talked to Terry Dunn; they agreed that even if there was a spare pilot, it would be too late to attempt a landing unless it was an emergency. Paul told him they were OK and Terry said he would get a plane to them in the morning.

Paul had the depressing feeling that it would be awkward telling Sophie and Marchmont would be furious.

"We're going to be stranded here for the night, Sophie," he said, carrying a pair of blankets and a tin box from the plane. "We should have something to eat and drink in the huts here. Emergency supplies."

Sophie looked amused before she was annoyed and critical, but those thoughts soon came. "How do we get back, walk?"

"You'll be home for breakfast, I promise."

After a while Sophie sensed his embarrassment: the flying ace who couldn't start his machine! Her attitude softened. They walked around the musterer's huts.

"There should be emergency bedding and supplies in one of these." He searched until he found a large, but not locked cupboard in one of the bunkrooms. Inside were bottles of chlorinated water and a sealed tin of dry biscuits. "Nothing keeps very long out here," he said. In the Cessna box there was more variety; tinned corned beef and more biscuits. In the medical kit he found a flask of brandy.

Paul pulled a small table and two hard-backed chairs into the doorway of a hut. They ate lumps of corned beef on biscuits, washed down with brandy and water; it was an oddly tasty meal. While they ate, the sky became a diamond-studded vault and the chill began to bite.

They talked about their lives. Sophie was natural and uninhibited. Her mother had walked out on her father, a

TV electrician who was a violent drinker, taking Sophie who was six. They had a bad time in a leaky, rat-infested apartment in New York while her mother worked in a small clothing factory. Linda Ryland sometimes acted as an escort at business dinners. There was always an executive from out of town who needed a partner. At a showbiz function she met a television actor and eventually became his girlfriend.

"John was a stroke of luck for mom and me. She met him at one of the dinners her boyfriend used to take her to, a TV award ceremony, I think. John sat next to Mom and they all had quite a lot to drink and he got her telephone number. He called her up, they began to meet and when she was sure enough of him she changed horses. I hope John will marry mom, but she's got the next best thing. He's looking after us."

Paul told her about growing up on Mirabilly and what he'd learned when his father died about being broke. How it changed his life. How he and Nick Karantis were lucky to survive with their business. He didn't mention that his mother had come out from England with Marchmont and married Ted Travis later. He couldn't confide to a sixteen-year-old girl he hardly knew, the issue about his own parentage and the fact that Ellen had once been Marchmont's mistress. But Sophie surprised him by knowing some of the story.

"Your mom was John's woman like my mom. Hey, that's quite a connection between us. That's right isn't it?"

"I guess so, as far as I know. My mother doesn't talk of such things."

Sophie was amused and then she saw the darker side. "Your mom was jilted. Maybe mine will be."

"I don't know anything much about my mother and John Marchmont. She's never confided in me. I guess the busybodies on Mirabilly think *they* know it all."

The last thing Paul remembered was Sophie whispering that they were related and they dozed off, swathed in blankets, slumped together on the chairs.

In the early hours, Paul awakened. The room was bright with moonlight. The insects chorused like a brass band. Sophie stirred too. Paul pointed to the bunk beds and lay down on the nearest. He felt Sophie climb on to the same bed behind him, pressing against his back. His pulse raced until he realised she was sobbing, clinging to him and he could feel her tears on the back of his neck.

In the morning when they stirred the sun was up; they began unwrapping themselves from the tangle of blankets, gluey with sleep, dry-mouthed and stiff. Paul put his arms around Sophie and gave her a hug and she responded by pressing her lips against his cheek. Paul thought that they had achieved a peaceful understanding.

It was like an aircraft fighter attack; they hardly heard it coming. The plane approached very low and fast and the roar hit the hut without warning; shook it and rattled the panes of glass. By the time Paul and Sophie had thrown the mess of food wrappers into a garbage sack, scooped up the blankets, returned them to the cupboard and opened the door, the Piper was on the runway wheeling toward them.

Jim Lomas, the station's second engineer, was at the controls. He looked suspiciously at their sleep-creased and slightly dazed expressions from the window of the plane. Then he got out and without speaking, climbed into the Cessna. After checking for a few moments he found the battery had recovered sufficiently to turn the engine over and it fired into life immediately. He left the engine running and climbed down.

"Nothing wrong with it," he shouted. "You flooded it last night."

Paul's embarrassment was screened by the noise. He saw from his watch that it was 6.30am. At Mirabilly the day was well advanced.

"I guess we sat around the campfire too long," Sophie laughed.

Jim Lomas was unamused. "You wanta come back with me?" he said to her, "They're getting excited about this back at the station."

"Of course not!" Sophie said. "There's nothing to be excited about. I'll go with Paul."

Paul and Sophie hardly spoke as they flew back to Mirabilly. Paul felt that they didn't need to. Sophie had said that she would like to meet Ellen and he agreed without thinking; it seemed to complete the 'relationship' circle which intrigued her. Sophie appeared to be confident that she could handle Marchmont and her mother if they complained about her being out all night. "They'll be irritated but not desperate about my absence."

Just before Paul let Sophie out of the ute in front of the Big House, she said, "Thanks for being so nice. That plane really did break down, didn't it?" Before he could reply, she was out of the cab and running for the front steps of the house.

In the afternoon, Paul met Sophie as arranged at the gate of the Big House under the shade of a grove of eucalyptus trees.

"I'll show you where we used to live before my father's death," Paul said.

He walked her along a path to the head stockman's house. It was on short piles so the air could circulate, the windows shaded by a deep verandah. They could only stand near the gate under the wattle tree and look across the lawns, bright with bougainvillea bushes and rhododendrons. The house gleamed, neat and white.

"Not exactly the Big House style," Paul said, "but a show-place and a temple to my mother."

"She sounds ferocious."

"In a way she is."

Paul didn't mention that he hadn't told Ellen that he was bringing Sophie to visit. He knew that Ellen would refuse. If he wanted to introduce a girl, as he never had, he thought she was bound to say, 'Are you going to marry her?' and if he said no, or 'Don't be absurd. I'm only twenty,' she'd say, 'Then why bring her here?' She was like that.

Paul and Sophie walked down the Hill to the Village and along the modest row to Ellen's cabin. It was as neat and well-painted as the house on the Hill, but the strip of lawn, small bushes of flowers, wire fence and shed-like shape were a contrast. Paul showed Sophie inside to a spotless sitting room, crowded with an upright piano, standard lamp and the chintz covered lounge suite from the Hill.

They sat for a while talking and then Ellen, whom Paul suspected had been listening behind the slightly open door of the bedroom, entered. She was dressed smartly as always on a Sunday, although Ellen never attended the all-faith chapel on the Hill. She wore a dark blue dress with high-heeled court shoes, her neck and arms smooth and golden. Her figure swelled into attractive curves in the simple dress and the skirt was short enough to emphasise her slender calves and ankles. Her fingernails were painted red like her lips. Her hair was wavy dark-brown, worn short. She was a voluptuous woman but for the cold set of her cheeks and the firmness around her mouth which promised, in time, to flare into lines.

As Ellen stepped into the room she looked over their

heads and out the window. "Well, to what do we owe this visit?"

Surprisingly, Sophie spoke first. "Paul asked me to come and meet you, Mrs Travis," which wasn't strictly true.

"Mum, this is Sophie Ryland from America..."

"I know who she is!" Ellen said, addressing him as though Sophie wasn't there.

Sophie stood up, half a head taller than Ellen, red with confusion. "Perhaps I'll see you later, Paul. I better go."

"No, don't go," Paul implored.

"You've satisfied your curiosity, Miss. You better go," Ellen snapped.

"For God's sake, Mum!" Paul said angrily.

"What did you bring *her* here for? The daughter of Marchmont's tart!" Ellen snarled.

"What were you?" Paul replied. The words just came out.

Ellen's assurance cracked. He could see the turmoil of her uncertainty. She rushed into the bedroom, slamming the door.

"I don't need this," Sophie said, going out the front door.

Paul saw her running fast along the street toward the rise. He sank down on the couch. He listened, thinking he might hear Ellen crying, but he had never known her to cry. He fancied that she too was listening behind the door.

The clumsiness of what he had done, bringing the three of them together, began to come to him. All he meant to do was to reveal something of his life to Sophie. Not out of friendship; they had just met. And it wasn't so much precisely *her*, as her connection with Marchmont. He was in touch with Marchmont through her. He was saying this is me, this is how I live.

But for Ellen, the mere sight of Sophie was too much;

light playing round the edges of her golden hair, exuding youthful sexuality. He thought Ellen had probably imagined Marchmont caressing the breasts of a new mistress and *now*, in Ellen's home, the new mistress's daughter was casting her eyes toward *her* son…

9

Paul could not easily forget Sophie or Emma because they were so unlike any girls he had ever met, but they passed out of his immediate concerns from the time of Sophie's visit to Mirabilly in 1975. He was busy with Northern Airlift and it was an era of rapid growth and change. His visits to Mirabilly ceased to be so frequent and he had to take care to arrange them in advance with Ellen, to avoid unfortunate meetings with her callers. Sophie's disastrous visit was never mentioned between them. Paul realised that if he rebuked Ellen for her wrong-headed rudeness, he would only provoke a tirade of abuse about Linda Ryland and Sophie.

Early in 1980, he became increasingly concerned about Ellen's health. He had no firm evidence, just that she seemed to be fading. Some of her old zest was gone. She was always tired. She refused medical attention, saying she could heal herself. She kept a Bible annotated by Mary Baker Eddy by her bed. It was at this time that Paul heard from Terry Dunn that Marchmont was visiting again with Linda Ryland, whom he had not married and Sophie, now twenty-one.

Paul rang Sophie at the Big House and asked her to go riding. He was prompted by the same impulse which made him agree to introduce Sophie to his mother, a kind of subterranean contact with Marchmont. He could tell that she was pleased by the call. She joked that they better not take a plane ride. They made a date.

He met Sophie at the stables in the Village at six in the

morning. She was friendly and cool. She offered her hand. Her face was a little thinner, her hair crammed under a white stetson.

Paul's stomach wrenched when he heard Marchmont's unmistakable commanding tone of greeting behind him. He thought, *Oh, hell, is this man going to try to stop the ride or get in on it himself?* He swung around. Marchmont hadn't changed much. There were a few lines on his face and the thin, longish blond hair suited him. They shook hands.

"I've been hearing things about you, Travis." Marchmont used a schoolmasterly tone which suggested that something was wrong. "Read something in the *Sydney Argus* and Terry Dunn told me. You're selling out to Ansett." He nodded a qualified approval. "You've done very well."

Marchmont was slightly shorter than Paul and uninhibited by it. He stood with his riding booted legs apart, appraising Paul with harsh blue eyes which seemed to be trying to work out how Ellen Travis's kid could have done this.

"I'm selling my half. My partner's staying in."

"What are you going to do next?"

Paul wondered whether Marchmont was being curious or polite. "Take my yacht out to the Barrier, cruise a little…"

"The papers say you've got mining interests."

"Mining? Oh, yeah, sure. What else is there in Oz?"

Marchmont clapped him on the arm warmly. "Good luck. Look after Sophie." He walked into one of the stalls and came back almost immediately. "How's your mother?"

"She's not too well at the moment."

He frowned and it seemed that he was going to take the enquiry further, but after a pause he turned away.

When Sophie and Paul were on a trail beyond the Village, one which Paul thought Marchmont would be unlikely to use, she asked him whether he thought Marchmont was his father.

The question pierced him like a knife-blade as it always did. "Why do you ask that?"

"It's the gossip at Mirabilly."

"Let it be. It's twenty-five year old gossip. Stale."

"The conversation I've just heard is crazy. How could you two talk like that without saying *something*?"

"Shit! I don't know!" Paul said. "I've buried it. What can I do? I mean… it's all a bit late, isn't it? What can he do? Invite me to the Big House for dinner? I don't need a loan. It's too late to pay for my education. At twenty-six I don't exactly need a daddy."

"But you might be father and son."

"I don't think he believes that or he'd have done something about it a long time ago."

"John has talked about what you've done. He thinks you're a hotshot, but he doesn't like to admit it. He started with millions. He's an old colonialist. You're a different breed. You started from scratch and there's something threatening about you, to him."

"Whatever a hotshot is I'm not one of those. I've worked my ass off for the last eight years." It had taken those years of hard, almost obsessional work to get to the present point. He had no regrets. What had materialised as a slightly boring but welcome change the day Melda tossed a coin and he was grounded, had become a demon he fought to conquer. Work was pretty well all he wanted to do apart from sailing his thirty foot yacht from Townsville. He often thought of the studies he might have done and all the books he might have read, but they were like an island he had sailed past in the night.

Nick Karantis was a different kind of man. Nick had

been the driver, the blowhard who persuaded Burrundie Finance that their Pipers would rust on the tarmac unless they did a deal; he was the one who really got them into the air. If it hadn't been for Nick and his easy-going father, Paul knew he might still be bumming around the NT in light aircraft, or possibly finishing university and thinking of becoming a fledgling lawyer. But as the business grew Nick's contribution had diminished. He was a man who only wanted to do what he enjoyed – flying. Then he married and this changed him. He was a first generation Australian, with warm feelings about family from his Greek parents. He wanted to be home with his wife in the evenings and weekends; and when they had kids, his desire for a settled family life increased.

Paul, in contrast, had been pleased to work nights and weekends. He had no attachments and really no family other than his distant relationship with his mother. He had a lot of casual girlfriends but he never let anybody move in with him. After Ellen, he was sure he didn't understand the sex. He had managed to keep the management of Northern Airlift an inch or two ahead of the natural expansion of the business. He had done the prosaic things that could be expected of a novice who studied elementary business administration and accountancy at Darwin Tech, while he directed Northern Airlift. He installed the systems which made the company solid, like personnel selection, computers, cash management, pilot and staff training. He even innovated by introducing female pilots and managers. Nick used to say that this was Paul's harem and a way of saving time chasing women.

Paul learned that men and women find a person who has authority attractive for that reason alone and he began to appreciate that on a much greater scale this applied to

Marchmont. Marchmont had a palpable field of influence around him; people's lives were bent in the direction in which he wanted to go.

After Nick and Paul had mopped up the market formerly supplied by Dart and a few of their smaller competitors, their accountants suggested that the easiest way to expand was to take over other small companies. They added planes, pilots and territory to their business at much less cost than it would have taken them to compete. Paul liked stalking and then the dealing that led to buying other companies. Eventually, they bought a shell company quoted on the Sydney stock exchange and let it take over all their interests. By this time they had extended their activities thinly across the whole continent. Ansett showed an interest in buying a slice of Northern Airlift and Paul, tired of the air transport business, agreed with Nick to sell his share. All Nick's dreams had come true, so there was no difficulty in parting. "Go in peace and make many more millions," Nick said.

Paul visited his mother every few weeks, rarely staying overnight. She continued to work in the commissary and the cafeteria. Dick Mather retired as general manager and with his long-suffering wife, moved to a retirement village in Surfer's Paradise. Ellen had callers and her activities were discreet but probably well-known.

She and Paul found it difficult to talk, except about domestic details and local and national politics (she continued to be an avid newspaper reader) but they never revealed their thoughts and feelings about their lives. "Think about the future," Ellen would say when any touchy subject arose.

Paul offered her a home and a pension in any town or

city in Australia, but her response was always the same. "Mirabilly is my home and I intend to stay here." He tried to persuade her to return to England for a visit at his expense. Her answer was a rapid and peremptory 'no'. She used the money Paul gave her for annual visits to Sydney. She went alone. She had no female friends, but she seemed not to be able to do without the company of men.

She continued to give Paul the impression that she thought she was a young woman whom all the men were chasing. It astounded him that in her mid-forties she could confuse her own undoubted attractions with continued youth. She had retained her figure, her graceful legs and her sensual manner, but even her immaculate dressing and make-up could not hide a weary hardness.

10

The Flying Doctor's nurse rang Paul Travis in March 1981 in Darwin. "I'm sorry Mr Travis, but your mother's ill and Dr Rogers says she's refusing treatment."

"What's the matter?" He wasn't surprised and his worries about her health came to the surface.

"Well… you'll have to speak to Dr Rogers. She needs tests and possibly urgent surgery."

Dr Rogers told him that Ellen had lumps in both breasts, which might be malignant. Paul flew to Mirabilly immediately. Ellen was in bed at home. She was being nursed by the despised woman next door, who had never been in the house while Ellen had been active. Ellen now praised her as an angel. When he told Ellen what the Flying Doctor Service had said, she clutched a hot water bottle over her breasts defiantly.

"If you think I'm going to let those butchers in Darwin cut me about you're mistaken. I'm all right. If I'm not, my time's come."

With anybody else, it might have been possible to give them drugs and take over the management of the case, but Ellen wouldn't take drugs or surrender. She lay on the bed, grimacing occasionally at the pain, with hotter and hotter hot water bottles on her breasts. Paul was unsure when he should step in and order that she be flown to hospital, or whether he was entitled to do this.

He stayed overnight and the next morning she called

him to her. She took his hand and placed it on her nightgown over her breast. He could feel a horrible lump although he scarcely dared move his fingers.

"I'm going to die soon, son."

"Not if you go to Darwin for treatment, Mum."

She looked at him, as though she hadn't heard, only the faintest glint in her eyes now. "Paul, that toper, Lucas, was telling the truth when he told you John Marchmont was your father."

The image of Lucas's hairy navel came to Paul, as it always did when he thought of the meeting with the lawyer and Ellen's contemptuous rejection of him.

"Why didn't you tell me?" The words rattled in his dry throat.

His mother's absolute denial at the time of Ted's funeral had cast him into limbo. Arthur Lucas had been repulsive and unconvincing. Hindsight told him that he had rejected what Lucas said too hastily. He had virtually ignored the notes which Ted Travis was supposed to have approved; he was so upset that he hadn't read them with any attention. He was shocked by Lucas's revelation. He was like a man concussed. He wasn't in any condition to measure anything Lucas had said. He ignored and immediately destroyed subsequent letters from Lucas, exhorting him to make a paternity claim against Marchmont. He pulled a blind down in his mind, not on what he had been told, but on whether it was true and, if so, what to do about it. All these reactions stopped him taking a step toward Marchmont to resolve the issue. *And* he was stopped by an inner pride which said, *If Marchmont is my father and he doesn't want me, I don't want him*. Now, there was no doubt about the truth of Lucas's allegation.

The limbo had lasted for years. Paul often *thought* about

his paternity, but it was like a secret in a tomb on a distant mountain, beyond an impassable desert.

Paul's everyday life may have been ordinary but it was challenging and absorbing. He had luckily become rich and it was easy to let the conjuring of 'what might have been' fade and concentrate on business and his friends. And of course, as the years passed, Marchmont's status as his father became nominal and practically unimportant.

"Why didn't I tell you?" Ellen said, "Because we didn't need Marchmont. You don't need him. Look at you. Dick Mather told me you were one of the smartest businessmen in the territory."

But Paul felt angry and cheated; not cheated so much of a culture or lifestyle, he was at ease with his own, but cheated of *knowing*. He almost wished the doubts had remained.

"I never needed or wanted any money from Marchmont, Mother. It isn't about money."

"I didn't want him to have you, Paul. He'd have taken you away from me if he'd known. He's clever. He'd have gone on treating me like a servant, keeping me below stairs, not good enough to meet his friends. He'd have taken you away to foreign schools and I'd never have seen you. He would have said I owed it to you..."

He thought for a moment that perhaps she did owe it to him.

She looked at the ceiling, her face distorted with pain. "I married Ted to give you a father and a good father he was while he lived... but he deceived us. I wasn't going to let Marchmont have his son, his only son, not after the way he treated me. None of his whores could produce a son. He didn't deserve you..."

Paul felt her folly and selfishness choking him. She loved

him in her way, but she had treated him like an item of her property and used him to spite Marchmont.

"Why didn't you leave Mirabilly years ago, forget it all, instead of living with this suffering?" Paul asked, his voice hoarse with incredulity.

"Yes," she whispered, "the pain I've suffered makes the pain I have now easy to bear. I didn't leave here, because I belong here."

"No, Mother. You have relatives and surely friends in England."

"A horrible place full of rain-drenched people. I was a queen here, a very long time ago, before you were born. What do I want with a cottage in Townsville or those miseries in King's Lynn?"

He thought her reasoning was deluded but he didn't challenge her.

Paul sat with Ellen during the day. Dr Rogers visited and said there was nothing more he could do. He asked to speak to Paul privately. They crouched in the tiny lounge room of the cabin, trying to avoid being overheard by her.

"She's going to die shortly anyway, son," Dr Rogers said. "She's in a very advanced state. She must have known she had something wrong a year ago and decided to ignore it. Flying her out now for surgery would be a huge trauma and I doubt if it would win a few more months. Let her have her way."

Later that day Ellen began to talk to Paul with frankness about her past, things she had never mentioned before. The talking relieved her and even at times brought a smile of memory to her ravaged face.

"I travelled across the world with John. Oh, what a time we had!" She paused and began to paint disordered pictures with her words, which Paul was able to fit into a story, the

95

story he thought that a mother *might* have sketched for her son, scene by scene, over their years together.

"John was a lovely and loving man, but I wasn't good enough for him. He deserted me and he lost his only son. I made him pay that price…"

PART 2

THE SQUARE MILE

11

Ellen Travis's marriage to Peter Burnham ended for practical purposes at about 10pm on a Friday night in spring 1952, not with death or divorce, but simply a blaze of understanding, then ashes.

She was nineteen and they had been married under two years. She worked as a waitress in the Deluxe Milk Bar in Swaffam Place, King's Lynn. She was easing up after a day on her feet, wiping the tables, rubbing spots of mustard and tomato sauce off the shiny menus and thinking of going home to Aunt Hilda's terraced house in Wharf Street where she and Peter had a room. Then Hilda and a police officer arrived in a police car.

Hilda marched into the Deluxe, her thick heels clacking on the tiles, the policeman swaying behind her. She bellowed at Ellen from a distance and the customers all looked up from their plates; their interest guaranteed by Hilda's plaintive tone. "Your Peter's been hurt! He's been in a smash. He's in the General at Castle Rising!"

"What happened?" Ellen choked, but neither Hilda or the officer knew more.

"Come on, luv, I'll run you over there right now," the officer said.

"You go, Elly," the manager said.

She pushed her damp, red hands into her coat sleeves and squeezed into the back seat of the police car, visions of carnage swirling in the dark of ignorance. Hilda whimpered.

At the hospital enquiry desk she inhaled the smell of disinfectant and floor polish and waited while a clerk, his face immobile like papier-mâché, pecked at a typewriter keyboard. Her husband was dying and the clerk went on with his business. "Please?" she said, but it made no difference. After an age, she learned that Peter was in the intensive care unit. She ran along the shiny rubber corridors, Hilda limping behind, taking wrong turnings, misreading signs, begging surprised nurses and orderlies to give her directions and hardly waiting to hear them. When she found the ward, the iron-faced sister in charge started to question her and Hilda about who they were.

"I'm Peter Burnham's *wife!*" Ellen repeated, unable to restrain tears any longer.

The sister softened. "He's unconscious. You can't see anything." She led them to an alcove where a lone bed was connected to machines by tubes and wires.

Ellen's first thought was that Peter was lying in state in a church, his body enclosed in a white sarcophagus. Only a small part of his face round the closed eyes and nose was visible, the flesh angry, suggesting that everything hidden by the sheet was boiling and bloody. She couldn't even tell that it really was Peter.

She had a surge of empathy for the pain of a vigorous creature. Only that morning as Peter pulled on his work-shirt, she had watched the muscles on his back surging under the skin. She had hoped that they would soon draw close as lovers. Now, his life was measured as a pulse on a chart.

She looked round. Hilda snuffled. Fred Fussell, her uncle on her mother's side, who lived next door, arrived in the frayed yellow cardigan he wore around the house.

"Will he get better?" Ellen asked a doctor who was frowning at the dots on the chart.

"Too early to say."

"Can you tell me please, what happened?"

The doctor lifted a record card from the rack at the foot of the bed. She reached for the card. The doctor drew it away. "Spinal injuries. Car accident. One passenger treated and discharged."

"Who was discharged?"

The doctor looked at her critically. "We have to confine ourselves to the medical side. You can get the information you want from the police. I might unintentionally mislead you."

"Look, I don't know *anything!*" she pleaded; and then she could see from the way that the doctor was holding the card that there was only one other name on it beside Peter's. The doctor saw her looking and turned the card away, but she had seen. The name burned on her retinas. The name was Caroline May Kenny.

Her friend Carol in a car with Peter on a Friday night when he was working overtime at Lacey's garage? It didn't make sense. She clawed for the significance of it only for a fraction of a second. It did make sense.

Peter's mother arrived, a little fat woman with a knitted bonnet like a tea cosy, buttoned into a long brown overcoat. She threw her arms around Ellen and started to wail. Ellen could smell her waxy oldness and see the hairs on her chin close up. Peter's Uncle Cedric came in, stomach bulging out of a stained shirt with a phlegmy pipe-smoker's voice.

"Come on!" the sister said, holding out her arms and herding them toward the door. "You can't carry on like this in here. Mr Burnham can't have visitors."

As Ellen rushed out ahead of the others and without goodbyes, she heard Peter's Uncle Cedric mutter to Fred Fussell, "Young bugger always did drink too much!"

When Ellen descended the front steps of the hospital alone, a cab was waiting on the rank and she got in without hesitation; the first time she had hired a cab for herself in her life.

"Orchard Street, near Barton Village," she said decisively. She knew Carol Kenny's address as well as she knew her own. Blakiston Row where Ellen's family had lived was a block away. Alf Kenny, Carol's father, used to work in the grain store with Ellen's father. She had grown up with Carol; they went to school and to dances together; they were not only close friends but Ellen had confided some of the intimacy of Peter's courtship to her.

It was after 9pm when Ellen unlatched the gate and took the three steps that brought her to the front door of the Kenny house. The downstairs lights were on, the curtains open. Carol's mother opened the door before Ellen could knock, drew her inside and put a comforting arm around her shoulders.

"My girl doesn't want to speak to you, Ellen, but she will. I'll see to that."

Ellen faced Mrs Kenny on the lounge suite in the tiny parlour that was only used on Sundays. The light fell starkly from the lampshade in the centre of the ceiling. Mrs Kenny was grey with concern. She gripped her lumpy hands together in her lap.

"Carol's been messing round with your Peter and it's time she owned up. I'm sick of it!"

Ellen sat stiff-backed. Her mouth was dry. She had nothing to say and no tears; only an ache inside.

"I'll get Carol," Mrs Kenny whispered, going out of the room.

Ellen waited. After a time there was a shuffling and sniffing outside the door; then Carol burst into the room with a moan, a faded woollen housecoat around her. "I've got a dreadful headache…"

Ellen noticed how the slovenly garment accentuated Carol's curves. Ellen was silent. She had no accusations to make.

Carol crumbled in the pause. "We hit it off, that's all." She tossed her permanently waved yellow curls impudently. "He started it, coming to the salon for a chat at lunchtimes. I didn't ask him. I told him to get off, but he kept coming."

"So you decided to go to bed with him." It wasn't a question; only a dismal conclusion. She spoke softly.

"It wasn't like that, Elly. He'd come round in one of Lacey's cars. Ask me to go for a ride. Well, I thought, on a nice day, what's the harm?"

"You know what the harm was." Again, the low voice and a distant feeling.

"We didn't mean nothing, Elly."

"How long?" Ellen asked, surprised at her steady, lifeless voice.

"About… I don't know…" Carol had a friendly expression, sharing a naughty confidence with a friend.

Ellen waited, emotions churning but cold outside.

"All right," Carol said. "A year I suppose, maybe longer."

"A year, maybe longer," Ellen repeated. A year of working at the Deluxe, wiping tables. A year of powdering herself on Saturday nights to smell sweet in bed, and getting only beery breath and farts.

"It was only a bit of fun, Elly. We didn't mean nothing by it, I swear."

Every word hit the marriage like a swinging demolition ball. A year and she knew nothing. A year of deception. A year when she searched for little favours to try to show an irritable man who ignored her that she cared for him.

Carol began to talk now and Ellen hardly listened. "I know he really loves you, Elly, but he used to say it was so awful living with Hilda and you couldn't have any... you know... fun." Carol gave a wicked little smile.

Ellen saw the teasing, knowing flash in Carol's eyes. She remembered how quickly after marriage the closeness with Peter faded, his hairy thighs coming down on her, the bed and floorboards moaning in protest. And Hilda's big white ears, like moulded candle-wax, listening at the foot of the stairs.

"I promise, Elly," Carol said, confirming the elegance of the outline of her hair with her fingertips, "I won't ever see Peter again."

Ellen exploded, a hysterical half-laugh at the absurdity. "It's too late for that now!"

She stalked out of the room, pushed past Mrs Kenny who was hovering just outside and went out of the front door. The harsh night air struck her. She slipped on the uneven paving stones and crumpled into the wet gutter.

Ellen was the last of Arthur Colbert's four children and if she was the family beauty, there was a price to pay which she never anticipated.

She was born in 1933 when the depression was biting into the area around Blakiston Row; it was near the wharves at King's Lynn on the Great Ouse River. The family lived in one of the lines of damp, red brick terraced houses. Her father had been out of regular work for years. The family survived on the dole, or relief work when Arthur dug ditches and shovelled garbage. It was not until 1938 when war was in the air that Arthur was able to go back to his old job in a grain store on the river. But nothing much changed and the family continued to exist during the war on vegetables from their garden, bread, pork dripping and milk powder. Only the free issue tins of the Colonial Sugar Refining Company's golden syrup stopped. Occasional treats, a rabbit, a chicken, a pheasant or a duck were obtained in ways which led the older generation to simper and be silent in front of the children. Hand-me-down clothing was all Ellen could remember in those early years. All the women in the extended family swapped garments and set about cutting and stitching to remake them; they passed them along the line of family wearers as the seasons' needs dictated.

The poverty of Blakiston Row didn't impinge on Ellen at the time. The square mile around the tiny terraced house was full of cousins and uncles and aunts and grannies on both sides of the family. She felt she belonged, buttressed by family; there was always somebody to help, always something to laugh at, always a sense of safety and permanence. The Colberts and the Fussells, her mother's name, had lived there for generations.

Ellen's brothers, Arthur junior and Reg, started to do odd jobs for money when they were old enough to lift a pail of water and left school as soon as they could. Her sister Ivy, the oldest, looked after the house and their mother, until their mother died of tuberculosis. Ellen was the only one who had free time while she was growing up. Her widowed Aunt Hilda taught her to play the piano a little and took an interest in her progress at the Ship Lane Secondary School. Her father always joked about Hilda being grand and said she was turning Ellen into a little lady. Ellen could feel the critical edge.

Shortly before her mother died, when she was fourteen and about to start the new school year, she was trying on an old gym frock of Ivy's and admiring herself in the mirror.

"My, Ellen," her mother said, touching her own breast, "you're too big to be wasting your time chittering in class at school. You should be working my girl, earning a little, and putting it by."

"Why, Mum? I quite like school and I don't need any money."

Her mother's mouth tightened knowingly. "Because you'll be married before you know it."

Ellen left school when the year was out. Everybody was expecting her to leave. The feeling in the family was that school was a place that children attended to keep themselves occupied until they were old enough to go to work. Learning, the kind of learning you do at school, was something for the children of bosses who were going to be bosses themselves; it was just a waste of time and a headache bothering with it. That was the attitude in the Colbert home and throughout the square mile.

Ellen got work in Mr Reywin's grocery shop at the end of Blakiston Row, filling shelves at first and then serving customers when Reywin realised that she could count quickly in her head. She fought off his attempts to put his hand up her skirts when she was on the ladder stacking shelves and kept quiet about it. Her mother died and she had to keep the job.

At sixteen she was allowed to go to the Saturday night dance at the Palais de Dance on Market Square, provided she was home by ten-thirty. By 1949, with World War II which she scarcely understood, over, there was a sense of excitement and anticipation. Despite the ruins of the war the world was going to be different, with new opportunities for everybody. But this was no more than an idea received from the second-hand radio in their parlour.

Ellen became an industrious reader in later life, but at this time she had little understanding of the significance of the events of the time; the Nazi war crimes, the birth of atomic energy, the invention of a jet aircraft which would break the sound barrier, or the Churchill government, returned in 1951 with a tottering majority of fifteen. If she heard them, she did not heed the calls for emigration to a new world in Australia. For her, the boundary of the real world was the square mile enclosing Blakiston Row and Ship Street.

Ellen knew, of course, that there were many exciting events happening 'out there', but to her and all her friends, marriage to a young man who worked hard and was kind, children and the comfort of her family, outweighed curiosity about strange places and things; to live this out in the square mile seemed an eminently satisfying prospect. She could visualise exactly how her parlour room was going to look when she married and they rented their first house; the brass candlesticks on the mantelpiece, the figured brass fireguard and matching coal bucket, the floral moquette covers on the chesterfield suite, the carpet square on gleaming, varnished floorboards. All these possessions would have to be acquired over time. And in her trousseau box, which Aunt Hilda had given her for her sixteenth birthday, with a lace tea cloth, was a collection of knitting patterns for baby clothes.

Ellen met Peter Burnham at the Palais and of all the boys she met there, he was the one for her; thick-set and strong, with a serious expression and a mat of short black hair. She was flattered by the attention of somebody five years older than herself; not simply a boyfriend, but a man. He was an apprentice motor mechanic and when you heard him talk, you could be sure that one day he would have his own garage. Even her father approved of Peter.

The marriage took place a year later when she was seventeen. The service was at St George's on Tide Walk where she had been confirmed when she was fifteen. She wore Aunt Hilda's old white satin gown which had gone creamy with age. Nearly a hundred guests were invited to the reception in the church hall, which might seem extravagant, but the families on both sides provided everything. The couple received enough water jugs, tea towels and fruit bowls for a lifetime. Peter said afterwards, as a matter of pride, that he would bet anyone that the quantity of beer and whisky consumed was a record.

He had drunk more than his share when they left the party at midnight after singing around the piano at Aunt Hilda's house. The couple had a room at the Duke's Head on Market Square and a taxi to take them there.

It was a thrill and a luxury for Ellen to spend the first night of her honeymoon in a proper hotel, not just a bed-and-breakfast house. She had never stayed in any hotel before, let alone one as posh as this. The pleasure was spoiled when Peter collapsed on the pillow as soon as he was in bed and then vomited in his sleep. She spent the night on the edge of the bed, as far as she could get from the snorting body and the stench. She roused Peter early and shamed him into checking them out of the room before the chambermaid came in and discovered the mess.

The rest of the honeymoon was in a bed-and-breakfast in Skegness. Losing her virginity with Peter in the marshes by the Ouse, on a Sunday afternoon six months before they were married, was infinitely more exciting than anything that happened during their struggles in Skegness. Ellen had been sweetly tortured by the idea of sharing a bed of her own with Peter, but it didn't happen as she expected. When he wanted her, she didn't quite want him and vice versa.

And it rained. And rained. They loitered in the chilly streets, looking in windows. Peter was bad tempered, but she was confident that they would get used to each other after a while.

After Skegness, they came back to the creaking upstairs room at Aunt Hilda's.

12

When Peter was conscious in the Castle Rising Hospital, he met Ellen's request for an explanation at first with a look of affront – why should a desperately ill man be so harrassed? And then when he had been chilled by Ellen's quiet, he managed liquid eyes. But Ellen was determined that Carol Kenny would be the first subject of conversation when Peter's head had cleared, however badly he had been injured. She leaned over his bed and waited.

"Haven't I paid for what I did?" he asked, tremulously.

She had to admit that Peter had paid a high price for his secret fun. The vertebrae at the base of his spine were crushed and with them, the nerves which controlled the lower part of his body. He would be paralysed for life. The enormity of the harm, in the context of years of living with it, was beyond Ellen's grasp at that time.

The doctor had told her that Peter would be incapable of sexual intercourse, but that had no importance for her; when she thought about it afterwards, it was a relief. When the doctor started to explain sperm donation she was repulsed and didn't listen. Now, she heard Peter's abject declaration of love for her and his rejection of Carol Kenny as *just a bit of stuff*, without being moved. Carol's vow never to see Peter again enraged her.

"Carol should come to see you. Help you get well," she said tonelessly and she meant it.

Peter bridled as much as a man can when he is tightly

sheeted down and able to move little more than his chin, mouth and eyes. "You can't seriously mean that, Elly. It'd be wrong."

She laughed but it was humourless. "No more wrong than what you've been doing. Everybody knows. Why not go on seeing each other? She could take you to the park. You know, where you used to go with her. In fact, she could look after you."

"Never. You're my wife. You surprise me at times, Ellen." He spoke as though he was a moral rock.

It was not only Carol Kenny and Peter who had decided that Ellen was the one to nurse Peter, but Peter's family and hers too; and all the doctors, nurses and social services officials. The hospital delivered the body (that was how she thought of it) in an ambulance, five months after the accident. The upstairs room at Hilda's was exchanged for the ground floor back room at Mrs Burnham's house in the next street. Ellen let Hilda and Mrs Burnham organise the room themselves.

The two old women were taking a more active interest in their own days at the prospect of having an invalid in the house; doctors' opinions and chemists' prescriptions were a constant subject of discussion. The lore and practice of being a carer was passed from them to Ellen in the form of instructions, although neither Hilda or Mrs Burnham had had any first-hand experience.

After a number of determined hints from Hilda and Mrs Burnham, Ellen gave up her job at the Deluxe Milk Bar and became a full-time nursemaid. Mindlessly, she lifted, sponged, changed dressings, massaged, adjusted tubes, gave pills and cooked for Peter for six months, as well as her usual duties of shopping, cleaning, washing and ironing. At times, when she was boiling the copper to wash a pile of night-shirts and sheets and the wash-house stank of shit and urine, she saw with revulsion the unending sameness of the road ahead. The neurologist, Dr Wand, took pleasure in telling her on Peter's twenty-fifth birthday, that with the kind of care she was giving him, Peter could live until he was seventy. Dr Wand probably thought that her outburst of tears was joyful.

At first, Ellen felt only a flicker of annoyance when the doctors assumed she could be relied upon as a twenty-four hour a day body-servant; she understood that they thought only of the patient. Hilda and Mrs Burnham went further; they assumed, in so many comments made to Ellen, that it was fulfilling to empty dirty bed-pans and that a captive husband was a good husband. Ellen could only regard them both as dried out old carapaces, beyond any pleasure but listening to doctors and nibbling buttered scones at afternoon tea; but this was the natural order which nobody in the square mile would seek to question.

"You're Peter's wife," Mrs Burnham said, as though it was an exceptional insight, certain that it settled everything.

Ellen tried to stifle the heat of her resentment as the days filled with catheters, soiled sheets and Peter's choleric temper dragged on, but she couldn't. One Sunday afternoon she was with Peter and Mrs Burnham in the parlour. She had made fish-paste sandwiches with white bread and Peter, in his wheelchair, was gorging them. There was no talk other than the odd remark in an undertone from Mrs Burnham as she fussed around her son and the slapping sound of Peter chewing the food with his mouth open.

"I've got a job," Ellen said.

At first, they hardly heard her. "What did you say, dear?" Mrs Burnham asked, brushing crumbs off the rug over Peter's knees.

"I've decided I want to go out to work and I've got a job," she repeated in a level voice. Both of them turned on her, incredulous, their mouths slack.

"That's impossible!" Sticky lumps of chewed bread sprayed from Peter's mouth. His bloated cheeks quivered. "How will *I* get on?"

"We can get home care," Ellen said quickly. She had thought it through.

"And where might you be thinking of bestowing your labour?" Peter wiped his mouth with the back of his hand.

"The Grange. I've got on the kitchen staff as a waitress."

"You've *got* on the staff. Meaning you've gone behind our backs and fixed yourself up, like?" Peter's voice rose thinly.

Mrs Burnham sat still, her lips crimped into a thin line, the hairs on her chin and upper lip prickling, her small eyes misted with the meaning of the wrong that was being revealed.

Peter took a long look at Ellen. "The Grange is it? That means you'll be working nights."

"I'll be sleeping in at the Grange except for days off."

Peter's cheeks reddened. He trembled. "You fucking slag!"

"Now, Peter…" Mrs Burnham approached the wheelchair and pressed her floppy belly against Peter's face. "Ellen doesn't need to work. Enough of this silliness, Ellen."

Ellen stood up and moved to the door. "I'm not going to ask the charity shop every time I want a coat or a new pair of shoes for the next thirty years."

Ellen had started looking for jobs in the *Barton Village Courier* a long time before she made a move. It was a relief at first, a fantasy, a pretence. On at least one morning a week, after she had washed Peter, helped him into his chair and given him a meal of sausages in brown sauce, or beef mince on toast, she would walk to Barton Village. She shopped for groceries and then sat in the newspaper room of the Council Library in Church Street looking at the *jobs vacant* columns. At first, it seemed hopeless because she wasn't fitted for much. Her handwriting and spelling were poor. She couldn't compose a proper letter. She was quick with figures from her days with Reywin and the Deluxe. Shop assistant was a possibility, or a maid or waitress.

When she first saw advertisements for staff at the Grange she thought that it would be an interesting place to work, but she didn't seriously think of applying. Everybody knew about the owners, the Marchmont family. Old Sir Geoffrey used to serve as the local Tory member of parliament and he had been Lord Lieutenant of the county. The Marchmont family were like aristocracy in the eyes of the locals. But it was the significance of the words *live in* in the advertisements which started her on a new line of thought; not just work, but freedom from the Burnham's back room and Peter's niggling, except on her days off.

She telephoned the Grange's estate agents in Church Close, introducing herself as Ellen Colbert. On the instant, she decided to undertake this venture as Ellen Colbert rather than Mrs Peter Burnham. She was seen by the chief clerk briefly and referred to the butler Mr Grayson. She made an appointment with him by telephone and caught the bus past Barton Village a few miles, to the valley by the Nar River where the Grange Estate lay at the edge of the fen country, boggy, misty and damp. She had been in the Grange gardens twice in the past for picnics with a school party. She was a little disappointed to find that on this occasion, the tradespersons' entrance was opposite the bus stop and led through gloomy passages directly to the kitchens.

Ellen expected, from the films she had seen at the King's Lynn Odeon, that the butler would be a rather superior person, but Jack Grayson greeted her with a grin and a wink and in a flurry of his tailcoat, drew her into his pantry-sized office. He seemed to take only a moment to sum her up. She was plainly dressed, but his manner made her feel lively and she showed it. She lacked confidence in her charms after the disaster with Peter and used them sparingly, but she was conscious that her naturally wavy hair was lustrous; her skin, pure cream. She had a small, supple body with delicate ankles. Grayson was all hustle and bustle and silly jokes. She couldn't help liking him. He was about ten years older than her, short, with thin ginger hair and freckles.

She tried to explain her limited experience but Grayson didn't give her a chance. He scribbled down the name of the manager of the Deluxe Milk Bar as a reference, laughed with her at his own jokes, answered his own questions and fixed a starting date and a wage. He called Doris, whom he described as the 'head girl', a shrewd looking woman of thirty, to measure her for a uniform from their stock and show her the small room she would occupy with another girl. Afterwards, Grayson breezed through introductions to maids and footmen who were nearby and led her up the back stairs to the dining room.

"Take a look. This is where you'll be working, Ellen."

Ellen raised her hand to her mouth as she took in the grandeur of the room. It seemed as tall as the cathedrals she had seen on postcards and was hung with inverted bells of crystal. The dining table was a vista of mahogany, a lucent brown lake decked with small marble statuary and fountains of flowers. Gods and angels flew in the clouds painted on the ceiling, trailing red and blue robes. The sun pierced a stained glass window and blessed the room like a sword.

"This is where Sir Geoffrey sits." Grayson stepped up to a blue plush chair at the head of the table, higher-backed than the others.

Her fingers caressed the carved shoulders of the chair with its gargoyles and chivalric signs; it was like a throne. She thought of Blakiston Row and Ship Street, and suddenly felt very small.

On Ellen's first evening at the Grange the dinner smelt delicious; it made her digestive juices flow uncomfortably in her stomach. She was wearing a straight black skirt, low heeled black slippers, a white blouse and a starched white hat like a paper boat on her head. Her hands were covered by thin white cotton gloves. She was 'marched in' to the dining room half an hour before the guests were due to arrive, with Doris and two other girls. Grayson, grave-faced, inspected them. He muttered tersely if a skirt was marked, or a lock of hair out of place. When he passed Ellen a little devil gleamed from his eye. He swept a slow glance along the table they had so carefully set. He nodded to Doris. Yes, they were ready. Ellen was dismissed to stand in the corridor outside the kitchen while they waited for Geoffrey Marchmont and his guests to finish their drinks in the library and go in for dinner.

Ellen's confidence grew as the days passed. The breakfast buffet and the occasional lunches were easy, but the dinners were tense. Her main task at first was to carry plates and tureens from the kitchen to the sideboard and occasionally, at Doris's direction, hand them to the table. She was nervous at the sight of ten or twenty elegantly dressed people sitting under the brilliant chandeliers and afraid to do more than give a covert glance in their direction at first. The men were usually in penguin black and white, or the red or green jackets of formal military dress. The women's hair was sculptured and studded with stones. And there was a smell of perfume wafting headily over the rich food.

After a fortnight's experience of dinners, when Ellen was about to place a silver tray of sliced sirloin of beef on the sideboard, Doris alarmed her with an order: "You do the left, Ellen." The heavy tray, supported by her left palm and forearm was already making her shoulder ache. She began to work along the line of diners, picking up slices with spoon and fork (a skill she had practiced) while the slices slid about in the gravy, alive; and the brown juice ran around the rim of the tray in a mini-wave. Her shoulder was numb. At the moment when she placed the last slice on a virgin white plate, a fatty brown trickle went over the edge of the tray, on to the black silk collar of the dinner jacket beneath. For a moment, she thought the guest might not notice. She thought Doris might not notice; but Doris appeared at her elbow and took the tray with accusing eyes. Ellen stumbled out an apology.

The guest's bloodshot eyes, as red-rare as the beef, stared up at her. He dabbed carelessly with his table napkin. "Don't worry, my dear. I was going to get it cleaned anyway," he said.

There was mild approval from the guests for his gallantry, but Doris was not so charitable. She dismissed Ellen from the room with a jerk of her head. In the corridor she dug her bruising fingers into Ellen's upper arm. "You're supposed to be an experienced silver service waitress! You don't know a damn thing, my girl!"

Ellen was banished to the kitchen where she sat in a

corner and nervously stuffed herself with smoked salmon; the austerities of war, still present in the country, seemed to have no application to this household.

After dinner, Grayson, frowning, adjudicated on the charge in his office. He listened to Doris's harsh account.

"Anything you want to say?" he asked Ellen.

"No." She was going to say that she never claimed any experience, but she felt a fool. She was in acute anxiety that she would have to leave the Grange, because it meant going back to the Burnhams.

Grayson paused, puffed up his chest and turned down his mouth. "Well," he said loudly, "you're going to have to do better!"

Ellen heard Doris's sharp exhalation of breath and saw the look of contempt she shot at him.

Ellen quickly learned the skills of waiting at table and began to look about her. She began to recognise the different members of the family. She particularly noticed John Marchmont, Geoffrey's nephew, whom she guessed was about her own age. He was often the only young person present. He was strongly built with straight corn-coloured hair and wide blue eyes. His face was smooth and good humoured. It was a pleasure to look at him, when she could, without being noticed. She thought about him romantically when she was walking in the gardens, or in the room she shared with Laura. She also thought of John sometimes when she was in her bed, beside Peter's, on her nights off. If only she could have a lover who seemed so gentle and was fair. All the boys she had ever known were dark and awkward and never laughed much except when they'd been drinking beer.

None of the Marchmont family, including John, or their

guests, seemed to notice the staff as people. Grayson and Doris received rather cursory or jocular greetings but Ellen often felt she was invisible, or at least a mere machine when she was waiting a table.

She came to realise that Grayson, a bachelor, liked her more than the others. And she liked him. He didn't abuse his position with the girls, although he could have had any of them. There was gossip that he might marry Doris, but Ellen knew that she had only to encourage Grayson a little and they could be serious. He wasn't the sort of person that she felt anything physical for; in fact he looked rather silly with his frizzy hair and the faces he pulled trying to be funny; but he was a safe, capable man and if ever she was to marry again, he might be the kind of man she would choose.

In the meantime, she was glad to escape from Ship Street, wear a silly white hat and serve the politicians, soldiers, diplomats and magnates connected with the Marchmont fortunes. Under the muted light scintillating through the chandeliers she watched powerful and beautiful people gorge food and drink. When she retreated to her room after these events, she often felt dazed rather than tired, much as if she, rather than the guests, had stuffed herself with chocolate truffles and tasted too much vintage port. The excitement of a dinner took time to subside.

When the headiness had passed, her mind would often move along the folorn terraces of houses she had known since childhood; Blakiston Row, Wharf Street, Ship Street, Channel Street, Gunter's Alley. The old families were there and always would be there, living within a few blocks of each other all their lives, generations of them. The world for them stretched from King's Lynn to Barton Village on the west and to Castle Rising on the east. Norwich city was far away; the people there were different. London was another country.

For Ellen, being at the Grange was like standing on a hill and glimpsing an exciting and unexplored land in the distance.

13

One Friday night in summer, when Ellen had been at the Grange for three months, she finished work at 10pm intending to go back to Ship Street for the weekend. She had to catch the last bus, but Stan, Sir Geoffrey's chauffeur who had to pick up a passenger at the railway station, offered her a lift. Although the bus would have taken her nearer to Ship Street, she couldn't resist a ride in the Rolls-Royce Silver Cloud, refurbished like new after being commandeered for government service in the war. She was with Laura, the two of them in the back seat, giggling amid the smell of hide and cigars. At Market Square, Stan smoothed the car into a space between the market traders' deserted stands and offered them a drink from the bar.

"I reckon I've got near enough a clear half hour," he said, taking off his peaked cap and slipping into the back with them. The three sat drinking ten-year-old malt Scotch whisky with ginger ale from the bar; they listened to music on the car radio from the sound-track of Charlie Chaplin's 'Limelight'. Ellen wasn't keen on whisky, but she enjoyed pretending that this was her lifestyle if only for a few minutes.

They gossiped about the Grange and then there was a tap on the window; they all started. Even in the near dark Ellen recognised John Marchmont, the silky light-coloured hair, the grin. He was alone. Stan jerked forward with a groan and stumbled out of the door mumbling an apology.

"Don't worry, Stan," John Marchmont said. "The train was early for once. Glad to see you're being hospitable." He handed his small suitcase to Stan and climbed in the back door beside Ellen and Laura. "Now, introductions please. And don't I recognise these two faces? Helen and Lorna from the house?"

They gently corrected him; Ellen and Laura didn't feel in the least embarrassed at first; they couldn't help laughing, especially when John passed Stan's drink to him through the glass partition and insisted that he finish it, sitting behind the steering wheel with his cap on. John laughed too and even Stan managed a feeble smile. They chatted airily for a few minutes until Ellen put down her drink and opened the door on her side, saying that she would have to go. Laura went with her and they faded into the night with John protesting that he would get Stan to drive them home.

Ellen dreamed about John Marchmont when she was in her hard bed at the Burnhams', with Peter snoring drunkenly in the bed next to hers. Friday night was party night and Peter's carers carried on the tradition by making sure he had a quarter-bottle of whisky. In the morning Ellen banished her dreams and imaginings. John Marchmont was light-years away from her. She would remain as invisible as all the other servants.

She was anxious on Monday, the morning of her return to the Grange, when John appeared on the south terrace where she was helping Laura and Doris prepare a table for a buffet lunch. He stood by the terrace door with his hands in his pockets, watching them work. He wore an old sweater with holes in the elbows; his hair was tousled and he blinked in the sun. His face looked sleepy and unwashed. The servants worked without apparently noticing him, but they did notice, every detail.

"Can I have a word with you, please, Ellen?" he asked casually and moved away from their table.

Ellen blushed. Doris frowned and hesitated, then she said, "I expect you have to see what he wants."

Ellen followed John into the shade of the house, her chest pounding.

"Let's go and have a drink at the Green Man sometime when you're free, OK?"

He spoke as though he had known her for an age and he was addressing a girl of his own class.

Ellen knew she should play dumb and uncommunicative, but she couldn't. "I can't go out with you. I'd probably lose my job."

He put his head on one side, weighing her words. "No, I'll see to that."

"I'll think it over," Ellen said, turning away, anxious to get back to Doris and Laura.

He touched her arm. "Please."

She wanted to say, "Yes, I'll come and have a drink with you, yes, yes, yes!" but she jerked herself free and went back to the glare of the terrace.

"What was all that about?" Doris asked.

She thought Doris could feel her heartbeat and the tingling in her breasts. "Nothing." She resumed polishing the cutlery.

"I hope you refused to go out with him?" Doris jolted one wine glass against another, chipping it.

It was no use pretending that John's approach was something else. "I did," she lied.

On their first date at the Green Man, on a sunny Saturday afternoon, they basked in each other's atmosphere; their actual conversation, blurred by the chatter in the bar, was about the village, the town, the old house, anything. The words flowed without either of them taking much notice of what was actually said. John had ordered a half of lager for her and a pint for himself and draped himself in a chair opposite, still wearing his unravelling sweater, with his unwashed golden hair piled untidily over his forehead.

Ellen had tied her full wavy dark brown hair back in a short ponytail. She wore a thin print dress, sandals and no makeup, confident that in these simple clothes John couldn't help focussing on the woman beneath. She was conscious of her slender body which she thought would stand any competition. She had the pale-skin and dark hair and eyes of her family and many of the villagers around the mouth of the Ouse, but the zest in her features was hers alone. She thought to herself, *I don't care what or who this man is, or what I am, I just want him to make love to me.*

She didn't feel shy with John or bothered that she was a servant and he was a member of a distinguished family. She was drawn to him just as she was repelled by life at Ship Street with Peter Burnham; status and rules didn't come into it at that moment, but she knew that the status and the rules were there.

As they walked back to the Grange from the Green Man, John invited her to dinner on the following Friday night. It was like a *Woman's Home Journal* romance, where lovers were always asked out to dinner. Folks from the square mile didn't do that; they had fish and chips wrapped in newspaper, or a milkshake at the Deluxe. Ellen made up a story for Mrs Burnham about having to stay at the Grange on Friday night and promised to be at Ship Street on Sunday afternoon.

Ellen felt grand being driven to Wisbech by John in one of the estate's new Morris Minor saloons. He took her to the United Services Club on a borrowed membership card; it was crowded and smoky. She was wearing a lilac crepe dress in a fashionable style, which she and Laura had made in their room; it clung to her, outlining every curve in her figure, even to her slight embarrassment, her nipples. She was going to be asked to order from a menu and be waited on for the first time in her life.

Ellen did not behave as wide-eyed as she felt. She had watched the behaviour of the rich at table enough to be able to imitate them. You chewed slowly with your mouth closed and didn't wave your knife or fork in the air. She couldn't hide the slight burr of her Norfolk accent, but the mirror told her that her dress would pass and that the young woman inside it was as attractive as any you might see. Her dark brown hair had been parted in the middle and waved back to mid-neck length in the latest style; Laura's work with a curling iron. She looked round at the other diners, at the officers with their gold braided sleeves and shoulders and the lavishly made-up women. She wondered whether it was true, as they said in the kitchen, that Winston Churchill and all the aristocrat types were finished.

She melted into John on the dance floor to the Glen Miller sound of the big band, picked at the food and sipped sweet white sparkling wine. She wasn't at all used to ballroom dancing. She had taught herself the waltz, foxtrot and quick-step with her girlfriends at home on rainy Saturday afternoons – Carol Kenny had been one of them. She had not had much practice at the Palais, where she met Peter, because the boys regarded dancing as wet. The Palais was a place where the boys went, after half a dozen beers, to pick up a girl after a nominal couple of dances, to walk home. But John knew the dance steps and all she had to do was to follow him instinctively.

It was after midnight when they left the club and she was elated and a little in love. Buried in her mind, but nagging her, was how to tell John that she was a married woman with a disabled husband. She tried to banish the thought. When they got into the Morris Minor, John said, "That was fun, but we couldn't talk, could we? Where to, do you think?"

Ellen had already thought of that. "What about Coronet Park?" she said, where Carol Kenny had told her she used to go with Peter. The huge park had a crumbling brick fence and was not locked at night.

John parked the car in the warm moonlight between rows of pines and talked easily about himself. "My mother died when I was three. There was just me and my old man. He was a rather minor Horse Guards officer who retired before the war. He spent the rest of his life in the members' bar at the Royal Sandwich Golf Club, waiting..."

"What for?"

"The inheritance, my love. The old boy had enough brass to buy pink gins, but if his older brother or one of his uncles had died, he had reasonable hopes of being seriously rich. Never happened, of course. Maybe he died optimistic."

"What are you going to do, then?"

"Damned if I know, Ellen. Enjoy myself!"

"You're not studying?"

"Dropped out of Oxford. Probably would have been pushed. I only got in because of my rugger and family name. It must have been that, because I had an abysmal school record. And Geoffrey knew a key don. Probably a case of 'help this poor orphan'."

To Ellen, how a person earned money to live was a first thought. "How will you manage?"

"Oh, well, like my old man I have a modest family trust. Not much, but enough."

She had never met a man so careless and irreverent as John Marchmont, or as charming and candid. The young men she knew were inert rather than hesitant and tongue-tied, especially about personal subjects.

"I've spent my life being shuffled around the family when I wasn't at prep school in Salisbury, or at Sherborne, Ellen. I never knew from one summer to the next where I'd be. Usually with one aunt or another and occasionally here with Geoffrey. Something between a guest and a handy-man."

"Were you lonely?"

"Not a bit! Families are poison. Far better to be on the fringes."

Ellen thought about that. A couple of years ago she would have said it was nonsense. She had defined herself as part of Blakiston Row and Ship Street.

"You could say I've shared the Marchmont lifestyle without being able to support it," John chuckled. "There's a sense of pride in the family, particularly among the female members, that waifs and strays who are relations have to be given shelter like ancient grannies and pensioned nannies."

"Where did they get their money?"

"Merchants trading with China and India in the nineteenth century. Silk, opium, tea. They built mansions in London and the counties, like the Grange. They endowed a college at Oxford. As the clippers gave way to steam, the family fortunes followed. By the 1930s we owned a fleet of refrigerated vessels... but it's all gone to pot now."

Ellen noticed the 'we'. Although he put himself on the fringes of the family, John nevertheless saw himself as part of it, in what she suspected was almost a possessive way.

"They brought frozen meat from Australia, Argentina and New Zealand for the European and North American markets. And the family often owned some of the foreign cattle stations and freezing works which supplied the meat for their vessels."

To Ellen, John's family was like a constellation of stars, expanding to infinity, while her own family pressed around her, wanting to control her, cementing her into Ship Street and Wharf Street and Blakiston Row. Her brothers, her sister, her aunts and uncles and their children, all settled to live and die within a few miles of each other, mired forever.

But tonight, at least, she was free of invisible strings. She let John kiss her. They never spoke about what to do next. The night was warm, even for high summer. The air was silky. Coronet Park had provided them with a deserted place. One look at the back seat of the Morris Minor was enough for both of them to reject it and instead they lay on the ground. The earth was warm, prickly pine needles under her bare bottom instead of the soft cushions of the Rolls-Royce. She wondered whether Peter and Carol had been near this place, limbs tangled in the back seat of one of Lacey's cars and the springs squeaking. It made love with John so much sweeter.

Ellen found it easier to be forgiving to Peter after John; she began to think she could go on working and visiting Peter indefinitely. On her days off she took over full nursing duties. She washed Peter, lifted him, gave him his bedpan and pills and changed his clothes. She had to touch him, her palms on his bull neck and withered thighs. After Coronet Park she had some of the sympathy of a nurse. The injustice of her own imprisonment had subsided, but had not been extinguished.

The arrangements for Peter's care with visits from the district nurse, physiotherapist, and the Meals-on-Wheels ladies worked well. Her sister Ivy and Mrs Craigie next door took turns in the house and she paid them. By the time she had given Mrs Burnham something there was very little money left for herself but life for her was infinitely better.

Ellen's determination to go on working rankled with Peter. Peter's mother tried to sooth his periodic explosions of foul temper. Whenever he erupted, she would make him a plate of chocolate nut fudge, or hot buttered pikelets, and feed him until he fell asleep. He achieved the same effect with whisky on Friday and Saturday nights when they could afford it. He wasn't a reader and his old taste for car magazines had gone. Time passed slowly for him, dozing by the radio. For an hour on one or two days every week he punished himself with dumb-bells. He pumped iron until his body was saturated with sweat. He exercised his fingers and forearms on a set of springs which Uncle Fred had given him. Peter's various helpers, including his mother, complained under their breath, but faithfully sponged him down and changed his clothes after these sessions. While his legs wasted, Peter's hands, forearms, biceps and shoulders became powerful. He liked to crush tin cans, twist cutlery and bend pokers. His nature, never equable, had worsened over time. The lads from Lacey's garage had stopped visiting after a few months, tired of his tantrums.

Peter had become wary of Ellen and less outwardly surly, except for occasional outbursts. She had established that she could think and act independently, a characteristic which was almost non-existent amongst the females in their families. His suspicious glances and down-turned mouth, rather than words, expressed his ingratitude for her efforts.

As far as Mrs Burnham and Hilda were concerned, Ellen's efforts fell well short of wifely duty; they showed this in quiet chilliness and their frequent mention of how devoted Ivy was.

Mrs Burnham allowed Ellen no privacy for the few possessions she kept in the closet and dresser in the bedroom she shared with Peter. A week after Coronet Park, Mrs Burnham found something in the course of 'tidying'. It was Friday night. Ellen had just arrived. She was in the kitchen putting cheese on buttered water biscuits as a snack for Peter before he went to bed.

Mrs Burnham came into the kitchen holding out her open hand and squinting at Ellen. "What's this then?"

It took a second for Ellen to realise that the thin gold ring in Mrs Burnham's palm was her own gold wedding ring. "You know what it is! Stay out of my drawer!"

"So we're a single woman now, are we?"

"None of the kitchen and waiting staff at the Grange are allowed to wear rings."

Mrs Burnham's face was pinched in disbelief when Peter banged the door open with the footrest of his wheelchair and propelled himself into the room. "What's going on then?"

On Saturday afternoon Ellen was alone in the house with Peter; they were in the parlour. She was taking away his afternoon tea plate and wiping spots of food off his chest when she noticed grey hairs at his temples; greying at twenty-six. She leaned over and touched the once-glossy black mane. Peter pressed his forehead between her breasts. She felt a surge of compassion for the broken captive.

She moved gently after a moment to disengage herself. Instead, she felt his arm tighten around her waist. "Please, Peter."

His free hand groped for, and found, the neck of her thin

woollen sweater. With a powerful wrench he ripped it open revealing her white brassiere. He snapped the brassiere ribbons. His teeth sought one of her nipples. She screamed with a sound that made the room vibrate. She rained a panic of blows on Peter's skull, but with her small fists it was like beating a marble bust. She howled against a rising tide of pain in her spine as he bent her backwards, forcing his head against her breasts. At the same time, with an arm round the small of her back, he was drawing her toward him. She pushed and threw herself forward, the only movement left to her to relieve her spine. She thrust herself over his head as the chair rolled across the floor, jerked to a stop on the edge of a mat and overbalanced backwards. They both crashed to the floor.

Peter groaned now, feeling his own pain. He had loosened his hold and Ellen rolled out of reach. He was moaning, watching her, but unable to move his body. He reached across the floor and clamped her ankle with his fist.

The lower part of her body was white hot. "No, Peter, no!"

"I'll choke you, you slut!" He dragged her closer.

She grabbed a heavy glass ash-tray which had fallen from an occasional table in the melee. She struck him on the shoulder. He loosened his hold of her ankle, but caught his fingers in the waistband of her skirt. She hit him again and again and again on his shoulder and back, until he let her go. She slid out of reach.

He lay on his stomach now, his face contorted in agony, mouth wide open, breath rasping in his throat, his eyes staring like a fish landed on a dock. She watched him in horror, calculating through her own hurt whether she had the strength to stand.

She stood up slowly and gingerly. She stumbled toward

the door, skirting him. The ash-tray was still in her hand. Peter had won it a week before their marriage on the rifle range at the Barton Village Show. He had presented it to her in a flare of macho pride. She limped into the bedroom, took a rug from the bed and threw it over him on the floor. She dragged herself up the street to the callbox to get an ambulance. Then she returned to the house and sat in the bedroom alone, waiting.

Mrs Burnham returned from her visiting before the ambulance arrived. Ellen heard her go into the parlour. She heard her cries and Peter's moans. Ellen made no move to get off the bed. Her back hurt so much she could hardly walk.

"Where is that woman?" was Mrs Burnham's quavery cry as she burst into the bedroom. "Leave this house forever and never, never come back!"

"That's what I intend to do, Mother. Look at me!" Ellen lifted her sweater to show the bleeding lacerations and purpling bruises on her breasts. "This is the work of your precious son!"

Mrs Burnham's face screwed up like a dried walnut shell. "It's no more than you deserve, you hussy!"

Mrs Burnham went in the ambulance with Peter and when they had gone, Ellen did her best to ignore her pain. She packed the old cardboard suitcase under the bed with the few clothes she wanted to take, resting two dresses and her winter coat over her arm. She had a last look around the sad room which desperately tried to be bright, with white-washed walls and new blue candlewick spreads over the two narrow beds. The wedding presents were still in beer cartons on the floor and on top of the wardrobe. She could leave all the vases, tea towels and water jugs without regret.

She let herself out of the house, limped a block to Dock Street and knocked at the door of a terraced house around the corner from the one she had lived in as a child. Carrie Chatwin, bent, with a fuzz of thin white hair, took her inside protectively when she saw the red eyes and the suitcase; she made a cup of tea and listened to Ellen. Ellen showed Carrie her breasts and they both cried.

When she had calmed a little, Ellen went to the telephone box on the corner. She couldn't reach her brother Arthur at the transport café where he worked, but she did get Reg, a shiftworker on the railways, at his lodgings. He listened to her quietly.

"I don't hold with knocking a woman about, Elly, but the lad's got a tough number and you're his wife…"

"I'm not going to hang around and get murdered," Ellen said, hanging up.

She called her sister Ivy next and Ivy was even less inclined to see her point of view. "If I know you, you started the row anyway…" Ivy said hotly.

Finally, Ellen rang Aunt Hilda who had been a mother to her and was looked upon as the head of the Colbert family. Hilda was brisk, dismissive. "I've already had a call from Rose Burnham about it. It's a storm in a teacup."

"Auntie, I have teeth marks on my breasts; my back's nearly broken!"

"What you and Peter need is a place of your own. I was talking to Jim Cosby at the council. Peter has special priority. It may only take a few months. We need to put in an application…"

"No, Aunt Hilda."

"May I ask why, girl?"

"Because Peter is a murderous bastard who hates me because I'm whole."

133

"That's how you feel today because you're smarting."

"I'm not just smarting. I've been attacked. I'm in pain. I'm not going to live with a man I'm afraid of."

Hilda exhaled disbelief. "Pshaaaaw! Think of tomorrow, Ellen. You're Peter's wife and when you two get a house of your own…"

Ellen put down the receiver, sobbing at the unfairness.

When she said goodbye to Carrie Chatwin that evening and caught the bus back to work, she sat aching as it rocked and rattled through the darkness. She was on her own for the first time in her life, heading into the unknown. The Grange and John were unknown, glittering, beckoning perhaps, but frighteningly unknown. Ship Street and Blakiston Row were part of her; even the Hildas and Mrs Burnhams would always be there if she wanted, if she followed their rules.

14

A few weeks later, Grayson asked to see Ellen in his office, an alarming sign. Her affair with John Marchmont was the talk of the servants at the Grange, not that Laura gossiped; it became obvious when they were occasionally seen together in the grounds, or at the Green Man. Ellen sat opposite Grayson in his tiny room. His usually jovial face was pale and set.

"There's a house rule, Ellen, about staff mixing socially with the family or the guests." His freckles speckled darkly on his cheeks.

"I know."

"A damn silly rule, because you can't mix unless they permit it. But as usual, we get the worst of it."

Her job, the security and comfort of the Grange, the distance it put between her and Peter, the glimpse of a brilliant life, even if it was the brilliant life of others, all these precious things had faded in her mind with her passion for John; their importance came back to her as though she was clearing her head from a fever. "Are you sacking me?"

Grayson came around the table. His hand on her arm was white with golden hairs. "Never, my dear. I'm so fond of you."

She didn't know whether she was reprieved. She smelt his mint mouthwash; a personal servant always attends to his breath. She liked him. She felt tearful.

"I've had my thoughts Ellen, as you probably know. A woman always knows. At least the tender kind of a woman you are. I'd hoped we might get together. I've got a good place here, and with you… you'd become housekeeper in a few years and it would be perfect."

His dreams had gone a lot further than hers. He gave her a vision of a very different life. Mrs Jovey, the present housekeeper, was nearly seventy and would retire soon. A trusted butler with a capable wife could influence the choice of housekeeper. Butler–housekeeper was the kind of pairing which made families feel safe. Mr and Mrs Grayson would be a comfortable couple at the Grange, living in a genteel style they could never have afforded outside. Life would be ordered; they would have an apartment in the mansion; they would have money and eventually retire, probably to a cottage on the estate. Grayson wasn't offering merely sincere affection and marriage, but partnership in a respected and assured style of life.

Despite his penchant for tomfoolery, Jack Grayson was a competent and well regarded figure in the eyes of the Marchmonts; Ellen believed that all he had suggested was likely to happen to whoever became Grayson's wife.

"I like you very much, Jack." She patted his hand, noticing how long and slender her hands were beside his short and puffy fingers. "But I haven't told you. I'm already married. My husband's in a wheelchair. I can't think of settling down with anybody else at the moment."

Grayson showed no surprise. "I had heard about it, Ellen. You know how they talk. What you say doesn't need to matter. We have plenty of time. Will you think of what I've said and give it some time? I'm sorry it's come out this way. I'm a bit mixed up. I'm supposed to be warning you and I'm proposing. The day I first saw you at the kitchen door you might as well have hit me over the head with a poker. I saw stars. It's true."

Ellen couldn't imagine making love to Jack Grayson, much as she liked him. She could see herself as housekeeper, controlling the servants, treating guests and family diplomatically; she had the imagination and confidence for that and the lifestyle would be dear to her. But poor Jack didn't arouse the slightest sexual feeling in her. She really had no choice. It was an offer she couldn't accept, even if she had not had John. She said, "I'm twenty-one, Jack. I've got a husband who's no good. I want a bit of fun!"

Grayson retreated behind his desk. He stiffened himself up. "I understand, Ellen. Excuse me for being so personal."

"It's good that we spoke, Jack." She stood up, leaned over the small desk and kissed him on his balding forehead.

He sighed. "I've lost the track of what I have to say. All I can say is that if old Geoffrey finds out what you're up to you could get the boot. But nobody on the staff is going to tell him. We think too much of you." He managed a wink.

Ellen knew she was walking on the edge of a precipice. Her work was all she had apart from John. She imagined what it would be like to be told to go, to get on the bus with her few clothes in a bag, to be rattled into Barton Village, to get out of the bus in a cold easterly with a few pounds in her purse. Would John come to look for her? How attractive would she be to him serving spaghetti at the Deluxe, or lodging in the back room at Carrie Chatwin's?

But she knew she would continue to walk the precipice. She wasn't going to give John up. She didn't think it was love, not romantic love, handsome as John was. She was conscious of the abyss between them in background and upbringing but they were capable of being very close. She acknowledged to herself that her feelings were selfish. John filled her days with a radiance from a different life and with sexual pleasure. He had opened the door a crack on a world she had only seen in the movies, or over the shoulders of guests in the Marchmont dining room.

Ellen told John her story, all of it, honestly, one night in Coronet Park; it had become too burdensome for her to conceal it any longer. They sat together after making love, with their backs propped against the trunk of a pine tree, wrapped in a car rug.

John accepted it all without comment and with a slightly reflective smile; he thought for a while. "What do you want to do?"

"Get away from Peter Burnham, his mother, Aunt Hilda, Reg and Arthur and Ivy, all of them."

"Funny that. I don't have anybody to get away from. I've always been rather irrelevant to my family, fitting in here and there when it suits them, or bumming an invitation to keep a roof over my head for a few months when they've forgotten I exist. The complete reverse."

Most of the time John wasn't serious about anything but now there was a tinge of bitterness in his voice.

As summer decayed into autumn, John continued to behave without any mention of the future and Ellen tried to shut her mind to the inevitable; she was on the edge of a dark void.

One day they were sitting in one of their favourite places, a remote part of the estate on the high side of a sunny field overlooking a stretch of the Nar River. The branches of the trees were beginning to point angrily at the sky. The air was chill.

"I've nearly worn out the welcome mat with Geoffrey,"

John said, "and I'm going to have to move on. And he knows about you."

She had a pang of anxiety. "What did he say?"

John imitated his uncle's mincing voice. "'Leave the girl alone. Don't be such a damned cad. I hear she's very well-liked and good at her job!'"

Ellen wasn't amused. "What's he going to do? And what are you going to do? Go somewhere miles away where I'll never see you?"

He paused and looked at her with his pale blue eyes innocently wide. It was as though she was about to fall into a pool which might embrace her with its warmth, or shock her with its iciness. She couldn't tell. Her reflection was there too, a tiny speck poised above the pool.

"It's not what Geoffrey's going to do, Ellen. Or what I'm going to do. It's what *we're* going to do."

We! Ellen couldn't have heard a more important word.

John stretched out on his back, sucking a straw, in no hurry to explain. "I think we've earned a holiday!" he said, sitting up and kissing her.

As long as there was something! A holiday didn't mean much to her. She had never had one, unless you could call an annual outing to Hunstanton Beach with the Barton Village Working Men's Club a holiday. She had never travelled more than fifty miles from King's Lynn. The people she knew didn't have holidays. If they had time off work, they dug the garden, or papered the parlour, or went more often to the pub.

"Why don't we take a voyage on a big ship? See the world? I'd like to go to Australia," John asked dreamily.

"Are you serious, John?"

"Sure!"

"You must have had this in mind all along."

"Damn right I have!" he yelled, throwing himself on her and burying his face in her neck. "One long party, I promise!"

As she unwrapped herself from his arms, the idea of a voyage was marvellous to her, but the thought of Australia wasn't so attractive. Why couldn't it be Paris or Rome? Of course, she knew virtually nothing about Australia. She remembered Grayson sitting in the kitchen at the Grange reading aloud from a copy of *The Times* which he had retrieved from the breakfast room. The girls were cleaning the silver and he was telling them that the British were testing atomic bombs on the Monte Bello Islands near Australia. He said Australia was a desert where the British could do things they wouldn't do in their own back yard.

Ellen asked Grayson if she could talk to him in his office. He must have known it was a bad omen. He shouldered her inside. He looked quite modest taking his seat beneath a framed cartoon of the Admirable Crighton on the wall, with a pile of new menu cards beside him on one side and a wire basket of kitchen accounts on the other.

"I'm leaving, Jack. I'm very sorry to be going. I've been happy here."

"I hope you won't regret this, my dear." He massaged his ginger quiff uncertainly.

"I'll tell you, I'm going to Australia with John."

"John? Er... John Marchmont? Thank you for telling me... I'm a bit at a loss, but I thought..." He stood up, bowed slightly and eased himself out of the door. "I'll get Doris."

After a few minutes, Doris came in. Grayson didn't return. "You've upset him. Only you could do that," she said.

Doris had long, dry fair hair and a firm jaw. Work and

anxiety had carved vertical lines on her face which overlaid a map of smaller and more intricate lines. "I won't say I'm sorry to see you go, Ellen. But woman to woman, I think you're barmy. That young toff will drop you like a hot coal when he's ready, mark my words."

Ellen hardly weighed her words. "Doris, there are hundreds of jobs for servants in hundreds of mansions like this, but there's only one young toff offering to take me to Australia in my life and I'm going!"

Doris had had ten years more experience than Ellen, two marriages and two children, but she thought about what Ellen had said and eventually assented with kindly understanding. "That's the spirit girl, if it doesn't spoil things for you!"

"Why should it spoil things for me?"

Doris didn't answer.

Ellen couldn't face Hilda's unswerving contempt. She had only telephoned Hilda a few times since their conversation on the day she left Ship Street, but she felt obliged to try to find out how Peter was; this seemed to be more urgent now that her life was about to change. In their last talk, when Ellen repeated that she was afraid of Peter Burnham, Hilda had been scornful. "Rubbish! Get and do your chores my girl!"

Now, Ellen summoned her will; she took some small coins to the callbox on the main road near the service entrance of the Grange. She couldn't go away for months without letting Hilda know; John had said it could be months.

"Hello, Aunt Hilda."

"Oh, it's you. You've taken your time." Hilda gave a theatrical sigh.

"How's Peter?"

"Poorly, but it's not my place to be telling you about your own husband."

"What's the trouble?" She knew Hilda could not resist medical details.

"Blood pressure. Heart irregularity. The doctor says he's too heavy."

"Yes, well, we've talked about his diet…"

"You should be here supervising it."

"What say did I ever have in what he ate with you and Rose and Ivy faffing about?"

"Ivy has been like a wife to Peter."

"I'm not coming back home, Auntie."

"Peter's back at his mother's. Ivy's living in there now. She's a brick, your sister. She's nursing him. Not that you'd care."

"I'm leaving the Grange. I'm going to be away for a while."

"Where are you going, Ellen, if I might ask?"

"To Australia."

A pause and Hilda's grating breath quickened. "Australia? What are you talking about, girl? You don't have the bus fare to Norwich unless some man is paying!"

Ellen bit back her reply. "I'll get in touch when I get back."

"Oh, will you, madam. And may I enquire about the rent?"

Ellen was expecting this; it was awkward, but it had to be faced. She had been putting an envelope through Rose Burnham's door every fortnight, with a sum of money that was only slightly reduced to enable her to pay her rent to Carrie Chatwin.

"You're saying Peter is living with his mother," Ellen said, thinking it eased the problem.

"Indeed, but what about Ivy, or does your sister have to sacrifice herself for nothing?"

"Ivy can share Peter's benefit. She might be entitled to one herself."

"Peter is entitled to the care of his wife, or had you forgotten?"

"Peter is an adulterer who tried to murder me, Auntie. He intended to kill me and threatened he would."

"Tsssshaw! What rubbish to cover up the fact that you're not prepared to support your husband!"

Ellen was livid, but controlled. "No, I'm not going to support him any more." There was a pause on the line while she heard Hilda wheezing with anger. "It's no use going on about this. We're getting nowhere," she added softly.

"And how will I know where to find you, just in case you might want to know what's happening in your own family?" Hilda said bitterly.

Ellen thought quickly. "You can get a message to me through Jack Grayson, the butler at the Grange."

"You're so far above yourself, milady! I suppose you think you'll become queen of the manor and never see the likes of Carrie Chatwin's house again? Well, listen to me…"

Ellen knew all about being above herself. Staying at school would put her above herself; reading books and playing the piano were all above her. Anything which didn't involve cooking, cleaning house, having babies and waiting on a man was above her. "Goodbye, Hilda," she said.

"And might I know who's taking you on this jaunt?" Hilda asked, maliciously curious.

Ellen was silent.

"You're a wicked, neglectful girl and you'll rue this day!"

Ellen replaced the receiver not with anger which had

come and gone, but with reluctance and discomfort. Her family would never understand.

It was awkward leaving the Grange because the staff thought Ellen was making a mistake; Jack Grayson tended to avoid her to protect his own feelings, Ellen thought. Only Laura admitted that if she was in Ellen's place, she would do what Ellen planned. The goodbyes were hurried and hushed at a time when Ellen kept telling herself that she was setting out on the greatest adventure of her life.

She stayed with Carrie Chatwin in Blakiston Row while John said he had to make arrangements and see people in other parts of the country. He gave her money which she could not refuse; she had no savings. The fear of being deserted by John lurked in her mind; it was a remote but fearful possibility. Carrie Chatwin and her husband treated her with the same calm affection they had always shown. Carrie's eyes clouded with incomprehension when Ellen had told her about Australia. "I hope you'll be all right love," was all Carrie could say, pressing her veiny hand to her bosom desperately.

On Sunday afternoons, Carrie's son, Malcolm, usually came to the house. Carrie said he always came for an hour now that he was married. Ellen knew Malcolm from schooldays. He was a fitter in the railway workshops at Downham; his big hands had black grease ingrained around the fingernails. He was uneasy with her. In his mind, Ellen thought, women were pale and pregnant home-bodies; and he would know the local gossip. She was hardly notorious, but certainly talked about. Carrie left them alone in the parlour while she made tea.

"You always were a strange one, Elly, like some kind of foreign woman." He wasn't unkindly.

Malcolm Chatwin couldn't have known how well he described her alienation from this cold and rainy place which had hardly changed in her lifetime except to decay a little; and her alienation from the sameness that seemed so important to her family; their square mile of poky houses, with mats on bare floors, an open fire in the parlour fireplace and glassware from the circus fairs on the shelves; all she had ever wanted for herself at one time. And her alienation from the sameness of the events of their lives, the procession of babies, the endless cooking and cleaning, the absurdly optimistic weddings, the drunkenness and the furtive adultery always eventually overlooked, but never forgiven or forgotten by the women.

As Malcolm talked about June, his wife, whom Ellen also knew at school and their baby, she couldn't help thinking of the way life revolved around the men and *their* appetites, *their* work, *their* Saturday afternoons at football, *their* evenings at the working-men's club; and the wife at home with the gas stove and the babies and the grandparents.

For nearly three weeks Ellen had to keep a calm face at Carrie's while she waited to hear from John. She made herself busy shopping and cleaning for Carrie who seemed very weak. Her money had run out. Carrie was watching her sympathetically and sadly. Ellen waited for the postman and listened every day to hear a letter come clicking through the mail slot in the front door. At last it happened. She was beside Carrie in the hall before Carrie picked the letter up; it was addressed to Ellen in a leisured, round hand that could only be John's. She tore it open and absorbed the whole page in one glance. John would come for her in a week!

Ellen read the letter carefully when she took it to her back bedroom. John wrote warmly but as if they had parted yesterday; there was no sense of lost time, or concern that she might be worried. He was a nice but thoughtless man.

John came to Dock Street on the day they were to leave. He embraced her and then sat in the parlour with Carrie while Ellen finished packing; only one small suitcase on John's instructions. Ellen could see that Carrie was surprised that this respectful young man in a thick sweater and corduroy trousers with an untidy crown of hair was John Marchmont. He lounged on the sofa, chatting easily; he wasn't the apparition in tweeds with a loud voice and a moustache which Carrie had probably expected. When they left, Carrie squeezed her tight with happy tears.

"Have a lovely, lovely time, dear."

15

Before the voyage, when Ellen and John walked from Liverpool Street Station into the City of London, the footpaths were crowded with business people in dark clothes. John said that this was where the Marchmont millions were made. He said it in a way which made her think he was disconnected from the family emotionally, that they were people who did arcane and boring business which was of no interest to him.

John took her by cab to Southampton Row and they walked to Russell Square. He pointed to the ornate pink brick façade of a hotel like a fairy castle. "That's where we're staying."

They had a double room at the front of the Russell Hotel, overlooking the square. Ellen looked out of tall windows at trees and lawns; almost like the country if it hadn't been for the deafening noise of the traffic which she found went on all night. The bed would have slept three or four people; the bath in the ensuite bathroom, standing on four short, podgy legs, was made for a giant. This wasn't her first sight of what was called luxury but it was her first taste. The extravagance of swishing around in enough scented water to fill the wash tub at Ship Street three or four times over, was exquisite. She shivered when she remembered her other night in a hotel, the Duke's Head in Market Square and the whiff of Peter Burnham's vomit.

John brought her a whole new wardrobe in Oxford

Street, clothes she never dreamed of having: cocktail frocks, evening gowns, a mink evening wrap, skirts of every kind of weave, silk blouses of all colours and cashmere sweaters; and a vast selection of pink and white silk and satin underwear and nightdresses. He accompanied her at all times, joking with the salesgirls. She realised that he knew what she should wear and was guiding her. For himself, he went to Savile Row and the fashionable Jermyn Street shirt-makers. The results of this spree were packed in their three large metal cabin trunks and consigned to Southampton.

They had time to see the crown jewels in the Tower of London, Westminster Abbey and the Houses of Parliament. They went to a tea dance at the Ritz, saw *Guys and Dolls* in Shaftesbury Avenue and *From Here to Eternity* in one of the new Leicester Square cinemas. They dined at the Savoy Grill. All these things were fresh and fine to Ellen and to John, who spent his money with exuberance and a sense of occasion.

When they boarded the *Rangitoto* at Southampton, Ellen found that they had a first class cabin with a small, self-contained patio. She could open the glass doors and lie on a deck chair in perfect privacy, although it was hard to imagine doing that in rainy Southampton. The ship seemed huge to Ellen; it may not have been the biggest of liners, but there were a confusing number of decks, pools, terraces, casinos, bars and ballrooms.

They could go anywhere they chose on the vessel, but that did not apply to everybody. Ellen went down more than once during the voyage, alone, to the tourist class areas. The people down there were not too different from those she had left in Blakiston Row and Ship Street; many were emigrating and hadn't bought clothes for the journey. Some of the men wore singlets or work-shirts, boots and braces.

The women dressed in the shapeless, washed-out print dresses that they must have worn to scrub the floors at home; and the kids wore ill-fitting older brother's or sister's clothes. The faces of these passengers, even the kids, looked pinched and startled. Ellen knew why they were emigrating.

John was endlessly sociable on the liner, but he rarely detached himself from Ellen. She soon learned to start a conversation with people she didn't know. It was a rare night if they were in bed before two or three in the morning. They had long dinners, danced, watched cabaret, played deck games and swam, although Ellen couldn't actually swim. John gambled a little in his imperturbable way. And they had uninterrupted hours to make love.

The ship sailed through the Suez Canal and they visited the pyramids and the Cairo Museum and went ashore in Aden, Colombo and Singapore. The voyage was an endless party for them both, as John had said.

Ellen leaned over the rail day by day in anticipation as they sailed through the tropics. She watched the sea shade from midnight dark into blue translucence. The weather became milder by the hour as they passed through waters studded with coral atolls. They saw the Great Barrier Reef. With a sighting of the Australian continent, new colours emerged, the bronze line of hills and the pale blue of the mountains beyond.

At last, Sydney in a world repainted in clear, bright colours; the flaking greys and hazes of the Wash were gone. The *Rangitoto* cruised up the fiord-like harbour to Port Jackson. Ellen loved the place immediately; pure skies, yachts on dazzling water, long beaches and low hills with trees shielding the houses.

Ellen and John moved into the Grand Hotel in the Rocks

area and spent a few days with friends from the voyage who didn't want to part; and they met new Sydney people to whom John had introductions. This society was mostly young people like themselves from New Zealand, South Africa, Canada and the USA. Ellen was enjoying lunches, picnics, dinners at noisy restaurants and somewhat drunken parties.

After a few weeks, she began to understand from oblique remarks of John's, that they were running out of money. He didn't seem concerned, but Ellen suggested that they rent an apartment and she even found one in the *Morning Post* at Pott's Point.

"Sounds great and very practical, Elly, but I've been thinking of Mirabilly."

"Mirabilly?" It was a name John had mentioned but not in a way to mark it on her memory. "Where's that again?"

"So much of the Marchmont empire. We have a cattle station on the Barkly Downs in the Northern Territory. We could go there as guests, stay as long as we like and let the old trust fund repair itself. A few months should do it."

She noticed the possessory *we have a cattle station,* which was unusual. "But we can't invite ourselves, can we?"

"There's an open invitation to family members to visit, even poverty stricken ones like me. Nobody there except the manager. I mean there are hundreds of people there, but nobody from the Marchmont clan."

Ellen tried not to show disappointment; they had come thousands of miles to this beautiful city and John was proposing that they stay on a farm *for a few months.* "I can't imagine what you'll do cooped up on a farm, John." But she did think at the same time that his restlessness would ensure that they didn't stay too long.

"By the way, darling, Mirabilly isn't a farm. It's a vast kingdom. We'll be the king and queen."

"You don't really know. You've never been there." She did her best to sound agreeable.

"Oh, come on, Elly. I was going to suggest dropping in at some time during our travels anyway. I want to see the place. It's part of Australia's history. Might as well do it now."

Ellen had to laugh but not with enthusiasm. It was his way. He hadn't told her anything of this part of his plan. She put as good a face on it as she could and prepared to repack all her finery in the cabin trunks which had replaced the two small suitcases they had when they left Carrie Chatwin's in King's Lynn. It seemed that two small suitcases would be all that they would need now.

The idea of being alone with John without friends or acquaintances didn't worry her. Their time at the Grange and a lot of their time travelling together had been spent without friends. She had been a good companion to John socially; but the demands of travelling companions were slight. It would be more difficult for her to entertain his personal friends, not to mention his family if she had to.

John had never given her any sign that he thought she was in any way wanting socially. On the ship there had been a few business and professional passengers who sounded as though their mouths were full of marbles; they talked easily about history, politics and literature. Her method with them was to be quiet and agreeable and move the talk to their family, especially their children, if they had any. She found that most of the people she met on the voyage were so self-absorbed that they seldom asked her questions about her origins. They seemed incurious and more than happy to talk about themselves. If by chance they asked her about her life, she had a ready story which was not actually untrue. She certainly didn't reveal that she had been a servant at the Grange. Her other activity to outfit herself socially was to read as much as she could in her own time (mostly newspapers). She realised her attempts to improve herself were pathetic but she continued with determination. Learning, for her, was like a marathon cross–country run where you just gritted your teeth and slogged on and on.

Ellen remembered that as she and John had walked down Dock Street to the bus stop with their suitcases, she had hoped it would be the last time she ever saw King's Lynn. She had willed herself to be hundreds, thousands of miles away, and here she was in Sydney! But the prospect of leaving for Mirabilly was a disappointment she could hardly contain after the brilliance of the voyage and the promise of Sydney.

16

The thought of visiting Mirabilly made Ellen uneasy because it wasn't just a remote farm; it was apparently a vast, lonely and desolate place. 'Dropping in', the phrase John had used to describe their proposed arrival there, was more than an understatement. She purchased a map of Australia and couldn't reconcile it with John's explanation that they had to 'Go north for a bit and then cut into the interior.' When she made him place his finger on the precise place on the map where Mirabilly was, he touched a point that was hundreds of miles from any road or town, in a part of the continent that hardly had any roads or towns.

John telephoned Mirabilly and they offered to arrange transport from Townsville. Ellen didn't comment and tried to appear to take it lightly. Their trunks were delivered to the train in Sydney and they had tickets for Townsville. This part of the journey seemed to take weeks but it was only days; hot nights and hot days with only desert and scrub to see between stations.

Townsville had a colourful, built-yesterday look and Ellen would have liked to stay a few days but John had insisted that they keep moving. A van and driver were waiting for them at the railway station, with a message of welcome from the general manager. They were driven to an aero-club airport nearby and were soon flying in a small plane across the Great Dividing Range, which shuts off the interior from the coast; over Mt Isa, with the Gulf of

Carpentaria shining to the north. Although this, Ellen's first flight, was thrilling, she soon fell asleep from exhaustion. She awoke as they were landing. The plane was passing over faded, peeling houses and sheds, toasting in the sun. She had little memory afterwards of the hasty introductions, as they were greeted by the general manager and his wife. Ellen's bones felt sore and the dust and the smell of cattle made her yearn to escape into sleep.

Her first real feel for the place was when she awoke in their bedroom, kicking her legs under silken sheets. She heard the hushing of the air-conditioning. John had gone from the room. She looked into a cool void, furnished as elegantly as any room at the Grange. As she found later, the dresser was intricately inlaid and there was an eighteenth century cheval mirror and cream satin drapes. The floor was polished wood, spread with what John later told her were Ushak rugs. She put on a wrap and padded through the self-contained suite, which also had a spacious lounge, smaller reception rooms, a study and dining room as well as spare bedrooms. The oil paintings on the walls were landscapes, like windows, letting in the special blue-gold light of Australia which she had come to recognise on the long journey from Sydney.

The dining room curtains were closed; she parted them and looked out across a shaded veranda with deck-chairs, to a well-watered green lawn and, a hundred yards away, a barrier of blue gums. She could see beyond the line of trees. The land fell away slightly and then stretched across bare acres to a horizon in a bronze infinity.

She went back to the lounge; there was a rich smell of scented wood and the sparkle of small ornaments on tables. Her eye was drawn to a piece of stone several feet high and wide, which dominated the room with its line drawings of fishes and lizards in yellow, blue and red. At first sight, she thought that the stone was a strange and arresting decoration; she knew that there was much art that was incomprehensible to her. She would learn later that the two dancing figures on the stone were said to be linked to the morning star which was guiding them to the land of the dead, where their souls would rest.

Whatever it might be like in the oven outside, she felt that she could enjoy living here. She drifted around that morning like a child, not thinking, picking up beautiful things carved in wood and stone, trinket boxes, crystals, polished shells, fragments of coral. Everything was unaccountably different from the world she knew.

In the bathroom, she bathed in a sunken tub with gold taps. In her trunk, which had been delivered to the suite, she found a cotton dress which hadn't creased too much and put it on.

When she ventured out of the suite, she saw that it was a separate wing of the house. There was an entrance lobby with a pink granite floor, a tropical fish pool and climbing plants and a passage which led to the other wing where she assumed the general manager lived.

She let herself out of the front door into a wall of humid air. She was breathless for a moment and felt the sweat start under her dress. She stood in the shade of the veranda trying to take in the house; it was on a rise, surrounded by green, watered lawns and eucalyptus trees which stirred in the breeze. After a moment she could see dashes of blue and red in the trees, to be named for her later as lorikeets and princess parrots. She had not got over her disappointment that they had come to Mirabilly while all the excitements of Sydney beckoned, but she felt attracted by what she had seen of the place.

A few weeks later Ellen and John had a flight in one of the station's de Havilland Rapides, with Dave Bundy, a Mirabilly pilot, at the controls. The plane hammered down the runway sending up clouds of orange dust. The noisy cabin with its hard seats wasn't welcoming, but Dave was. He was a big, smiling, sunburned man in shorts and a floral shirt. He looked like a holiday-maker from the beach at Manly. "This is the way to go!" he shouted, as they bucked over the potholes in the runway before takeoff. Ellen wasn't afraid, but they *were* racing toward a row of pines and it was a relief when Dave pulled the plane into the air, a sudden upward surge and a lightness.

When John asked Dave to go higher so that he could see more of the country, Dave said, "Strewth! There's damn all between here and the ocean except goannas and a coupla manky towns!"

But it wasn't true. Below was the enormous carpet of Mirabilly, hard, brown-green rolling country with scattered low trees, wooded gorges and curious rock formations in red stone. At this time, the end of the wet summer season in February, occasional thin waterfalls spilled over cliffs. Dave pointed to an escarpment a hundred feet high in places, splitting the land in a more or less straight line as far as Ellen could see. "That's the eastern boundary. It beats fencing."

Jim Farrell, the general manager, had already proudly given Ellen a summary of the history of the station; it was first acquired in 1850 by a Captain Heron, an eccentric ex-officer whose commission in the New South Wales Corps had expired. Heron received a land grant before Queensland was founded. A childless widower, he enticed a wife from a Townsville bar, started a family and successfully multiplied his holding on the cattle-friendly Barkly Tableland. After two generations the Heron family fell out over their rich inheritance. A shipowner from England named Charles Marchmont bought all the leases and freeholds and added more to make over two million acres. He saw the advantage of supplying his own refrigerated vessels in the meat trade with Europe and North America. An abbatoir and freezing works were built near the Village, as the station settlement was called and Mirabilly Station, with dozens of workers became like a town or a country in its own right.

Jim Farrell told her that 'Mirabilly' was the corruption of an Aborigine phrase which Captain Heron had understood to mean 'Where the good spirit brings water and winds'.

Ellen had a small and docile chestnut she sometimes rode. She didn't feel at home on horseback but the little animal was kind to her. Often she went with John, but occasionally with Pete Djawida, the head Aborigine maid's seventeen-year-old brother. John had made her promise not to ride alone. It wasn't that there was any specific danger in the vast spaces, except poisonous snakes and spiders, but rather the possibility of getting lost. Ellen didn't quite understand how you could get lost when you could see in every direction over the stunted vegetation, but she complied.

Pete was thin, with black polished skin, knobbly knees, a spread nose and gleaming black eyes. He worked on the station. Ellen liked him because she sensed he was everything that he wanted to be. He smiled a lot and said very little.

She found the silence and shimmering colour of the outback haunting and mysterious. Little Elly Colbert, who had scarcely been beyond Barton Village in her life, now possessed a vast cathedral of space and calm.

On one particular day, she rode many miles toward the eastern boundary with Pete. He said he was going to show her the burial ground of his ancestors. They plodded slowly across a dusty, featureless plain, through stands of mulga and spinifex. She began to think they had gone too far but she was keen to see what Pete promised. They refreshed themselves and the horses at streams and water holes. The heat beat on Ellen's broad-brimmed digger's hat. The horizon was a fluid line of fire. The sun pricked her skin through her shirt. The flies buzzed continually around the net over her face, occasionally startling her by crawling underneath. Her horse became tired and unsteady. Pete didn't seem to be troubled but she was on the point of saying they should go back, when he reined in his horse at the top of a rise. "There it is," he said proudly, pushing back his hat and wiping his brow with a forearm.

She looked where Pete was pointing. Before them was a long dry rift in the earth, red rock in contrast to the yellow dust of the desert, with a thin covering of saltbush; beyond it the land undulated in irregular ways.

She had expected a more spectacular view. "That's the burial ground?" She hadn't enquired from Pete, but she had been expecting old monuments or at least what she could recognise as a graveyard.

"Sure. Big fishes. Crocodiles. Giant snakes guarding the road."

"What road?"

"The road to the edge of the earth."

Pete spoke matter-of-factly. He wasn't interested in school learning. He said that he and his ancestors were literally part of this land. He felt the blood in his veins was from the earth and would soak back into the earth one day. It was a revelation so strange to Ellen that she thought it merely fanciful.

"Also sleeping warriors, fathers of many tribes."

To Ellen, Mirabilly was sand and sparse grass, windy cliffs and clumps of brush; to Pete, it was alive with spirits.

"Let's get over there, Pete," Ellen said. "We need to water the horses and rest in the shade."

"No, we can't go there."

"Why? It's what we came for."

"You have to look from here." He clicked his tongue and his horse began to pick a path down the steep bank. "I show you."

She had no choice but to follow. Pete dismounted at the bottom of the rift and led his horse to a clump of low palms where there was shade to tether. He secured Ellen's mount and lifted the saddles off the horses' wet flanks, dropping them on the grass. Pete led her into a subterranean cave where she could hear water. She gulped lung-fulls of cool air. They picked their way forward into a natural amphitheatre. There was enough light from a crack in the roof to see a wall of colourful paintings, fifteen or so feet high and thirty feet in length.

"It broken," Pete said.

A section of the painted rock-face had been broken away.

"What happened?"

"In the Big House."

"It's the piece in the lounge room?"

"Yeah. Dinka told me. I never been there."

"You want the stone back?" she asked, because he seemed rueful.

Pete shrugged. "It will come back."

"How do you mean?"

Pete gave her a distant look as though he could see things she couldn't see and never replied.

They drank from the stream and Pete filled two canvas

bags for the horses which they carried back. Ellen lay on her back in the shade near the horses, with her hat over her face, while Pete watered them.

The images on the rock shimmered in her mind. She didn't believe in spirits, but Pete's certainty that the stone would be returned to the ancestors made her uncomfortable. There wasn't the slightest sense of a demand or requirement in his manner; only a certainty that somehow the stone would be returned. Ellen was sure that there wasn't any idea at the Big House that having the stone there disturbed the order of things and that it would have to be returned; it was just an unusual adornment.

Ellen settled into the coolness and quiet of the Big House over the months. She never imagined that she would live in such luxury. She was content wandering through their rooms, having coffee on the verandah and listening to the birds. And of course reading as part of her active course of self-improvement. The house was entirely serviced by Aborigine maids and gardeners managed by Maureen Farrell, the general manager's wife. Maureen was devoted to her husband, her children and her duties. She was friendly, but not Ellen's confidant. However, Ellen was never lonely.

After her ride with Pete, Ellen kept a wary eye on the stone in the drawing room. If she could have returned it she would. She couldn't quite have explained why. She told John about her ride. He laughed and said she was in danger of going walkabout. He said she could expect to hear a lot of superstitions from Pete and his family. Ellen thought that as far as the stone was concerned Pete's remarks were more than superstitions. She suggested to John that taking the stone and then displaying it like a piece of work bought from a dealer, was an act of desecration. He disagreed goodnaturedly.

"It's our land and the paintings will never be seen by anybody, buried in a cave. And besides, it's been here since God knows when."

At first, John found plenty to amuse himself. He went out shooting camels and wild pigs, or riding herd with the stockmen. Occasionally, he and Ellen flew together to Tennant's Creek or Mt Isa or Darwin and shopped in the bright, hot towns. She went with John to parties on the Hill where the senior staff at the station lived, given by people like the station engineer, or one of the pilots. They were rough events and reminded her of the square mile around Blakiston Row, except that they were held in spacious, comfortable and plentifully stocked homes. The men gathered in the kitchen with the keg to drink beer and tell yarns and the women stayed in the front room talking about children, bargains in the mail-order catalogues and vacations. The sexes met at supper. Each hostess as a matter of personal pride tried to outdo the others, producing a variety of cooked meats, salads and sweets – which were actually very tasty.

Ellen was surprised at how easily John fitted in to these gatherings, which must have been so different from the sedate house parties he was used to. The Aussies were no respecters of rank; they must have imagined that John had rank and John had to accept the crudities and the jokes against himself.

The wives were curious about Ellen. She continued to conceal that she had been a servant at the Grange when she met John. In answer to the direct question, 'Where did you meet?' 'At dinners in King's Lynn' was enough. In answer to the other direct question, 'What did you used to do?' she delighted in saying, 'I worked as a carer.' She felt very much a lady amongst these brash, big-thighed women. The wives had no moral feelings about John and Ellen not being married, but were always saying that they should marry, or looking for a reason why they weren't. There were more than echoes of the square mile in the macho family life.

As the months passed, John became more restive. "The pot is full enough for us to move, Elly," he said. "I didn't really intend that we should stay as long as we have, but it's been a marvellous experience." Ellen echoed this and would have felt at home if John had been at ease. Sydney was a faded dream. Without being entirely conscious of it, she had passed from a holiday state of mind, a good time that would inevitably end, to one of seeing her future with John, or rather not being able to see a future without him.

It was more to try to keep up with John than for her own pleasure that she sometimes went riding with him and Jim Farrell in the mornings. They usually left at six or seven, the men with their Winchester Repeaters. She trotted sedately on her chestnut behind the thick, rank-smelling haunches of their two big roans. The horizon was yellow and light green. While it was early, the air was powdery; parrots shrieked in the bush and at times shot past them. By nine the sun was in unrelenting control of a cloudless blue-white sky.

One morning they took a new trail. After two hours they were about to turn for home. They stood the horses for a few moments on a rise, listening to them blowing. Ellen's shirt was soaked with sweat. The endless landscape was spinifex, scrub and stunted acacia. Farrell saw three or four camels in the distance. The men galloped after them and followed them into a dry gulch. She heard a fusillade of shots.

When she rode down to the bottom of the gulch, John and Farrell had dismounted and were pouring rounds into the bodies of four beasts writhing on the ground, groaning and wimpering like human beings.

"Bloody murderers!" Ellen shouted.

When the shooting stopped there was the smell of gunsmoke and the stink of blood and shit. The horses quivered nervously. She turned her mount and rode out of the gulch to the sound of laughter from John and Farrell.

The New Year barn dance was to be held in one of the sheds at the edge of the Village where hides were usually stored. The shed had been cleared and the wooden floor scoured with disinfectant, but there was still a smell of dead meat and fat with a rancid edge. Ellen stood in the centre of the shed and said to Jim Farrell, "Can you smell it?"

"Smell what?" He sniffed loudly, his blue-veined nose raised in the air, thumbs in his braces, easing the tightness around his girth.

"The hides, or whatever you keep in here."

He considered her. He was keen to be polite. "It's not bad. This crowd won't notice. We'll have the food at one end and the bar at the other."

"What about all this?" She waved her arms to embrace the rest of the stifling, inhospitable space.

"We'll put a few chairs round the walls. Build a stage for the band."

"How many guests to do you expect?"

"200. Maybe 250. The Mirabilly New Year bash is the best. Folks come from Tennants Creek, even Darwin."

"And stay with friends here?"

"Hell, they sleep where they fall. Most of the buggers are legless."

She looked up at the timbered roof and tried to picture 250 drunks in this smelly void.

"We hang a few lights up there."

She walked out of the shed. From the door she noticed a party of men digging a trench in a field thirty yards away.

"That's the kazi. Big, wide and deep," Farrell said.

She walked slowly back to the Big House. This was where any likeness to New Year in a pub in the square mile, or a church hall, or the Barton Working Men's Club, vanished. It was a human cattle-pen for a debauch.

John arranged a party at the Big House before they went to the barn dance. Ellen got the impression that Jim Farrell would rather have left his wife to help with the supper, and gone to the club in the Village to drink with his cronies, but he didn't like to thwart John. John had no authority at all and never claimed any, but he was a Marchmont and all the senior staff were slightly wary of him. So the Mirabilly bosses were constrained to be on parade at the Big House, the general manager, the chief pilot and other aircrew, the chief engineer, the office manager-radio operator, the head stockman, the representatives of stock and hide agents, trucking firms and meat buyers all with wives or girlfriends.

John wore a dark blue sports shirt and white slacks which showed off his tan and blondness startlingly. Ellen had a skimpy frock of silver material bought in Sydney which clung to her like a bathing suit. She wore no makeup except lipstick. The sun had added a reddish tinge to the colour of her hair and it reached her shoulders in natural waves; she was able to have it professionally cut on their visits to Darwin.

Ellen felt awkward because the reception was really hers and John's; she had to play hostess to people most of whom she hardly knew. The ship-board experience was some help and she knew that the guests weren't over-fussy provided they had a drink in their hand. Jim Farrell and his wife and Terry Dunn the office manager and his wife, arrived early. There was an awkward silence while they stood in the white lounge feeling conspicuous, but John was relaxed and soon had some talk going. As other guests arrived, Farrell lurched around the room with a whisky bottle filling glasses. Maureen Farrell stood at the fringes, not sure whether she was a hostess or guest and out of place without her children or maids to claim her attention. She tried to smile, but only succeeded in looking as though her bright green dress with puffed shoulders like wings, was pinching her.

The men for the most part were in early middle-age and although wrought from hard work, were over-ripe; their faces were mottled; their bellies pressed against or slopped over their belts. An exception was the head stockman whom Ellen had already met in the Village. He was much the same colouring as John, but leaner and more weathered. The wives were a spectacle, squeezed into garish frocks, faces painted. One younger one was Betty Fallon, wife of a cattle buyer from Tennant's Creek. She was a little bottle blonde with a cheeky face and a black mini-frock which revealed her tanned thighs. Betty seemed to attach herself to John.

Ellen felt like a cattle drover herself as she tried to get the party moving down to the barn dance at around eleven o'clock, or, as she could see, the New Year would come in at the Big House. When the lounge had been emptied, she had walked down to the shed with the company but alone. She lost sight of John in the crowd. She was astonished at the transformation of the shed; there were lights, ribbons and balloons inside and outside. The male members of the band were stripped to the waist except for their bow ties;

they drank as they played. The music brayed out from a piano, a piano-accordion, drums, a clarinet player who doubled on a trumpet and a bass player who doubled on guitar. The group was led by a short, fat girl in a bowler hat who belted out a few verses of the songs, but most of the time rubbed herself rhythmically against the microphone pole. Ellen was momentarily lost in an ocean of people she had never seen before, most of whom were sozzled. The head stockman saw her and pushed in front of her.

"Ted Travis," he said.

"Yes, I remember. I'd like to find John."

"Can't find anybody in this scrum. Come and dance."

She accepted because it would give her an opportunity to look around the shed as they moved across the floor. She could see that there were three main activities: eating from a buffet laid out on three long trestle tables at one end, which was constantly replenished; the wrestling match which passed for dancing in the centre; and at the other end of the shed, the engine which fuelled the show, the bar. Here, the crowd gathered three or so deep. Three barmen only rested to drink themselves, as they hosed lager beer into any available glass. Ted Travis pointed out to her the contests for speed-drinking and forfeits as though this was a delight.

It was a deafening orgy and Ellen had a sense of the drunken instability which was vaguely frightening. She didn't see John. She soon excused herself from Ted Travis and went outside.

Ellen stood on the steps at the entrance. She wanted to observe the decency of staying until twelve, but she felt like putting her hands over her ears and running up to the house. Beyond the bedlam in which she was involved, the night was warm and still and strewn with stars.

She didn't think John was in the shed. She eyed the half-darkness outside, lit by floodlights. A crowd had gathered around a silver Holden sedan; cars were carelessly parked everywhere. She threaded her way curiously toward the gathering. She saw Betty Fallon was sitting in the back seat of the car. Bert Fallon tore open the back door and dragged her out. She fell at his feet.

John stepped out of the crowd and pulled Fallon away. Fallon swiped John across the face with the back of his hand.

"Wrong bloke, Bert," somebody said.

John hit back and Fallon fell down.

"Meddling bloody pom!" Fallon said, propping himself up in the dirt.

"Keep your fists off the woman," John said. He helped Betty Fallon to her feet and then left her. He did not see Ellen and pushed through the spectators in the direction of the Big House.

Ellen was confused and she retreated into the darkness too. Her first instinct was to run after John but she had to move with the herd, in and out of the light, shaking off groping hands, pushing inebriates out of the way, stumbling over insensible bodies. She heard the sounds of whistling and shouting rise to a crescendo in the shed. It was midnight. She could bear this no longer and turned up the slope herself.

When she let herself in, John was already in bed reading, his hair wet from the shower. "Ellen, I couldn't find you. Come to bed, sweetheart!"

He never mentioned the Fallon incident and when Ellen cuddled up beside him, she tried to shut out the Fallons and the alarming turbulence of the crowd.

And so Ellen passed her time, until the day when the letter in the pale blue envelope arrived.

PART 3

THE CLASH

17

After Ellen's revelations to him, Paul Travis knew that he would have to visit his mother's birthplace in Norfolk, England and meet her brothers and sisters if possible, but he was apprehensive; it might arouse uncomfortable memories for them and shock him. He had an inner compulsion to make the visit, despite the fact that it would probably expose him to disparaging views of his mother. Ellen's account of her life before his birth, recounted to him as she lay dying was, he accepted, only her perception of the story. However vehement her views, however impossible she had found it to gain understanding from her family, there was another angle of her life seen from the viewpoint of her family, which lay uneasily in shadow.

Paul retained his intention to visit but put off the event, year by year after Ellen's death, always with the promise to himself that it would be 'soon'. He finally made the journey in 1989, armed with an invitation to stay at the Grange.

Marchmont had given Paul an open invitation in a surprise personal letter some years before. Paul took this to be a genuine gesture toward the son of a woman he had cared for, who had been brought up on Mirabilly; it had nothing to do with biological connection, more with the lord of the manor being liberal with a serf who had turned into a successful businessman. Paul reckoned that despite his mother's relationship with Marchmont, if he had remained a worker on Mirabilly, he would never have been likely to be invited. Sophie Ryland, whom Paul had met briefly a number of times when he was in New York, knew of the invitation and occasionally tried to persuade him to accept it. With her as intermediary, the visit was eventually arranged and Marchmont re-confirmed it with another welcoming note.

Other than to cross and re-cross the Australian continent and visit New York and London on business, Paul had not travelled widely. He felt the compulsion of his business responsibilities and spent only two days in London after his direct flight; then he travelled north to King's Lynn. He took a cab to the Grange from the railway station at King's Lynn. The cabbie offered to drop him at the tradesman's entrance on the main road, but he elected to be let out at the main gate. He hitched up his canvas travel bag and walked through the ornate arch into the walled grounds. Now, he was able to see across the meadows of a shallow valley sprinkled with wild flowers. The Grange itself was on a rise beyond a lake, about half a mile away. The turrets were sharp against the blue sky and the sun shone on tall windows. To him, it was a scene out of Austen or Trollope.

At the house, an old butler showed him inside the iron-studded doors. He stood in the entrance hall blinking in the gloom at the faces of Marchmont ancestors; they stared from the canvases which lined the walls and the stairs. Grayson, as the butler said he was called, pointed to the doors of the library where Mr Marchmont would be waiting to greet him after he had settled in his room.

A girl in a sweaty shirt, jodhpurs and riding boots was also waiting for him. He expected and was warmed to see Sophie Ryland. He remembered the irritation he had caused Marchmont when he took her on a flight over Mirabilly. They had a rapport which had survived his crass handling of the aircraft, their night in the outback *and* the appalling embarrassment and shame of meeting Ellen. Sophie would be about twenty-three now, he calculated.

"It's something, huh?" She indicated the grandiose hall as though it was as new to her as to him. "I'll show you to your room."

She led him up the curving marble staircase. They went along a hall to a room overlooking a wood and a river, the Nar according to Sophie. The room had a shabby elegance, chipped gilt chairs, a frayed tapestry on the wall, marquetry cabinets and heavy red drapes shot with gold threads. The bed was a canopied four-poster. He went into the bathroom. The marble tub stood in the middle of a tiled space.

"The bath is big enough for a bullock. Haven't they heard of showers in this part of the world?"

"We thought you'd appreciate one of the original rooms, Paul. There are more modern ones."

"It's fine. Some home."

"I wouldn't call it home. That's my apartment in Greenwich Village."

"This is the summer place, right?" He pulled his shirt off and began to remove his crumpled clothes from his bag.

"I'll see you downstairs," Sophie said.

He bathed in near-cold water, dressed in a crumpled jacket and took his time on the stairs peering at the smoky portraits, some dating back to Elizabethan times. The Marchmont ancestors were pale and pink and fair, as he was dark-haired and sallow like his mother. He worked his way down to the library and pushed in through the heavy swing doors. The room was high and light, stacked with tiers of books almost to the frescoed ceiling. A gallery with carved mahogany rails ran around the walls to give access to the higher levels.

He was beginning to look around when a golden

Labrador ran past him and started to make plaintive sounds to somebody hidden from view in one of the high-backed Regency chairs. The golden halo of Sophie's hair came into view. She too had changed quickly into a summer dress.

"Hi, again," she said, making a fuss of the dog.

The dog barked and Marchmont burst through the doors. "Well, well, Paul Travis no less!" He offered his hand. "Delighted to see you my boy!"

Marchmont was a youthfully jaunty fifty-six. His figure was solid and his smooth face would have fitted a number of the portraits on the stairs; it testified to a lot of ease and satisfaction. Paul sensed the same atmosphere about Marchmont as he had when he met him as a youth. The cornflower blue eyes made him feel, momentarily, like an iron filing in a magnetic field. Marchmont stood back and assessed Paul like an item of prime stock.

"And an entrepreneur..." he mused.

"I'm here to meet some of my mother's folks."

Marchmont relaxed on a leather couch and waved him to an opposite chair. Grayson appeared and served drinks. Sophie joined them.

"This is a historic first," Marchmont said, holding his gin and tonic aloft. "A man of Mirabilly sitting in this room! I'm glad you wrote, Paul, glad you were able to accept my invitation. And I think that there is a little business we could talk about later."

"Sure." He saw Sophie, out of Marchmont's view, press her lips together and raise her eyebrows.

"How did you become involved in this... *thing*... Paul?" Marchmont asked, as though the thing was something despicable.

Marchmont's manner was quiet and friendly; he was smiling, but clearly very curious.

"You mean the boundary issue? I became involved because I had visited the native land as a boy and I flew over it many times in my teens, when the station was checking or mustering stock."

"Then you must have seen that it was Mirabilly land. Worked for generations by the station."

"The local belief always was that it was Aborigine Trust land. I had an opportunity to join the mining syndicate which had an agreement with the trustees to mine."

"I know that. And I know you've been clearing a road, that's why I'm suing you and your friends for trespass."

Wanting to fight Marchmont was instinctive and it was difficult for Paul to explain why to himself. In the silence that followed Marchmont must have realised that he was suddenly exhuding an un-hostly chill.

"Anyway, we'll have an opportunity to talk later. Drink up, my boy."

The evening was warm and Sophie, neatly groomed in a long summer dress, was on the glass covered terrace when Paul arrived; here he would meet the family before supper. The sky was purpling. Chairs and a table with a white cloth had been placed overlooking the gardens. On the table, a magnum of Bollinger rested in a silver ice-bucket with champagne flutes and jugs of orange juice.

"John seems keen to talk business," Sophie said.

He didn't answer. He was surveying the scene and trying to imagine what it would be like to own this stately house and land, thoughts that his mother as a servant here might have had.

"Was it tough to come here?" Sophie persisted.

"Yeah, tough. I had to come, but part of me didn't want to come."

"What about you and John? I mean, about him being your father?"

"You ask the damnedest questions, Sophie. Forget it. It's not a subject that can be taken any further."

He didn't say that his mother had confirmed the rumour before she died. He couldn't tell Sophie. She was close to Marchmont. She would surely tell him and what would be the repercussions of that? Marchmont would think he was sucking up, crawling for recognition. And Marchmont would oppose him.

"Oh, shit!" Sophie said. Just at that moment, Grayson presented a tray of fizzing glasses to her and by a slight flicker of his eyelids seemed to signal his despair of the modern woman. "I just happen to think it should be resolved," Sophie added.

Before Paul could reply, Alex Rainham Marchmont, the son of Marchmont's deceased wife, sauntered on to the terrace. When Sophie introduced them, Alex gave a supercilious smile. "Ah, yes, the wild colonial boy. We've met."

Paul remembered the pallid kid he'd pumped full of champagne at the celebratory dinner at Mirabilly years ago. Once again, he saw that from an appearance point of view, Alex could easily have passed for Marchmont's natural son.

Marchmont appeared in a maroon velvet jacket with Linda Ryland on his arm. She was a ripely attractive woman in her late forties in a cream-coloured cocktail frock with emeralds at her throat. Nothing in her appearance squared with the tough times of former years which Sophie had once explained to him. She was elegantly at home in this luxury.

They talked on the terrace until it was cool and nearly dark and Marchmont suggested they go inside to dine. At that point, Emma, Alex's sister, arrived. She snatched a glass of champagne, made a fuss of one of the Labradors and then gave Paul a kiss on the cheek. He hadn't seen her since he was a teenager caught in her bedroom with his shorts at his knees; although it was another occasion of shame, Emma had remained in his mind as a symbol of exquisite but forbidden sex. She had blossomed into a voluptuous, rather over-weight woman.

In the dining room, under the chandeliers, the meal was served by uniformed girls on silver platters, while Grayson supervised with his eyebrows and dispensed the claret. The spaces between the diners around the table were wide and there tended to be only one conversation, but it never flagged or touched family matters. Paul didn't press his opinions too far, saving the Marchmont family from too much exposure to his squashed vowels. The meal indeed was a salad of accents, Paul's, the clipped rapidity of Emma and Alex's English public school tones; the more stately, throaty version of the same from Marchmont, Sophie's soft eastern seaboard drawl and the resonating, nasal New Yorkese of Linda Ryland.

At the conclusion of the dinner, Marchmont asked Paul to join him in the library. "We may get a chance to talk," he said, in a jocular way.

When Paul went into the library Marchmont was already in a wing-back chair by the fireplace. The drapes were open. The moon was up over the lawns. The trees on the rise were in sharp outline, with the summer-house folly like an Indian temple. Grayson put a cup of Turkish coffee beside Marchmont. He had a large cigar which sent up cords of smoke. Sophie was there. Paul refused the cigars and brandy, but not because he didn't use them occasionally.

"So, there's gold, copper and uranium on Mirabilly," Marchmont said with a cat-like smile.

"Not as far as I know. It's on the trust land next door," Paul smiled.

"No, on my land," Marchmont said dimissively.

"I know your claim," Paul said airily as though it would hardly bear inspection.

"And we'll win, and you and your friends'll lose a lot of money." Marchmont had a confident grin.

"I don't think so. The legal advice sounds conclusive to me," Paul replied woodenly.

"Ah, legal advice, Paul. There's nothing more uncertain. The law is a quagmire."

"I know what you mean. Do you want to settle the claim?" Paul asked, trying to be as unemotional as possible.

"What are you offering?" Marchmont looked at him haughtily.

"I can't make you an offer, but I can tell you what I would recommend to my partners: that you join the syndicate on the same terms as us."

It was a weakness if Paul disclosed his position so early, but again for reasons he couldn't articulate clearly, he didn't want to haggle with this man. He wanted to get it done. He anticipated Marchmont's rejection.

"Why make that suggestion, Paul, if you're so sure of yourself? It'll only dilute your payout, assuming there is one."

"We don't want the syndicate to be bogged down in court proceedings."

"I'll think about it. There would be a lot of small print to be worked out."

"Sure. And one piece of it would be that you return the stone in the Big House with the cave drawings on it."

Marchmont looked surprised. "What an extraordinary request! It's been at the house since Heron's days. We're talking about mining rights worth millions and you're concerned about a bit of painted stone."

"The Aborigine Trustees want it. It's an important precondition. And my mother thought it should go back. Didn't she ever speak to you about it?" He felt calm enough to mention her.

"I can't remember." Marchmont looked confused.

"I'm not sure we can get much further with this. I think I'll take a walk around the lawns before bed, if you'll excuse me." He left the room with a friendly wave.

Paul met Sophie after breakfast in the walled herb garden. They walked together. It was going to be another sultry day, but the lawns and manicured box hedges were fresh.

"There's a kind of dampness..." he said.

"It's the fens; it's usually raining and blowing. How long are you staying?"

"Until I've seen my relations, assuming I can find them."

"You'll have to find out what John thinks of your proposal."

"I think I know. He'll check up with Oz and decide he can win."

"Can he?"

"There's a very slight chance."

"I don't think I'm breaking any confidences in telling you that after you'd gone last night, he said he's certain the mine is on Mirabilly."

"And what else did he do? No, don't tell me. Let me tell you, Sophie. He rang Sydney. 'There's no way the son of one of my stockmen is going to con me!'" Paul mimicked.

"Okay, smart-guy. You got it about right. Why do you two have to behave like a couple of stags?"

"It would mean something to me if we could settle."

"Paul, the bit about the stone really riled him. 'Bloody nerve!' he said. I said I thought it was a fair enough suggestion and that annoyed him even more. It's a beautiful piece of art and I suppose history, isn't it?"

"How would I know, Sophie? I've never been inside the owner's wing of the Big House."

Paul had a ploughman's lunch with Sophie at the Green Man; it was cheese and pickle on a chunk of bread. "They call it a shearer's sandwich in Sydney," he said.

Sophie insisted that they have a pint of Mulgrew's Special Bitter, brewed in the wood, but she couldn't finish hers and left it for him. He liked it.

While they were eating, he took a small leather-bound volume of the New Testament out of his pocket. He opened the cover and showed the inscription to Sophie. 'To Ellen Colbert on her confirmation, October 1947.' It was signed 'Hugh Prendergast, Vicar, St George's-by-the-Ouse.' Ellen herself had written underneath, 'Ellen Louise Colbert, 16 Blakiston Row, Barton, King's Lynn.'

"This is where the search starts, Sophie."

"Do you need to do this, Paul? I can't imagine trying to search out my relatives in the backstreets of Detroit. I don't think I'd want to know them. It's like digging in a grave where you might find out all sorts of nasty secrets."

"My mother told me her story when she was dying. She had nothing to hide, but for years she was defiant about not disclosing her past. It's not that I don't trust what she told me. I just want to get the feel for the family's view."

"She was certainly a strange woman."

Paul remembered how rude Ellen had been to Sophie when he introduced them years ago and she had virtually ordered Sophie to get out of the house. Ellen had instinctively loathed Sophie by proxy as the daughter of Marchmont's mistress. But the only reservation Paul had about Sophie and what held him at bay, was her close connection with Marchmont; she worked in the publicity department of his company in New York and evidently admired him.

Sophie offered to borrow Alex's car and drive Paul while he did his detective work. He bought a map at the Barton newsagents. They drove on to town and stopped at the Duke's Head Hotel in Market Square to have a cup of coffee and plan their moves.

King's Lynn, a thriving port for coasters 150 years ago, had lost its sense of importance. Although they were seeing it on a fine day, the lash of rain and winds from the Wash had left the houses with a faded look. They navigated their way through narrow streets to the place where Ellen Colbert once lived.

Blakiston Row was a line of red brick terraced houses, each with a narrow room and a doorway at the front and another room above; they were near an unused wharf. One or two properties in the street appeared to be occupied, but most were deserted and boarded up, including number sixteen. The houses were built close to the street. All Paul had to do was push open the creaking gate, take a pace to the doorstep and look through a crack in the front window-boards. Inside was damp, dark and appeared to be full of trash. The house was a frowning ruin that never seemed to have provided a space where you could visualise that a family had lived.

Sophie parked Alex's incongruous shiny red Porsche and they walked down the block to the next street. The houses were in the same decayed condition, but they found two old men talking on the pavement. The men remembered the family name, Colbert, and said that one of the girls had married a stonemason and lived 'out Meadowcourt way'.

They found St George's Church, not by the river, but by a scrap dealer's yard guarded by Alsatian dogs. They enquired at the nearby rectory. The parson, who answered the door, looked crumpled and dozy. After Paul had explained his mission, the parson brightened and said immediately, "Ivy Colbert married Cyril Harris, a stonemason, in this church, after his first wife died and I officiated. Poor old Cyril didn't survive too long, but he left Ivy comfortably off. She'll be in the phonebook." He brought the phonebook to the door and looked up the address for them.

They drove to the more spacious detached house of Mrs Harris in Meadow Drive, where the streets were wide and had long lawns in front. Ivy Harris had moved up the social scale from Blakiston Row. Paul was against telephoning her in advance because he felt it might be hard to identify himself as a genuine caller. "Let's play it at the front door," he said to Sophie.

A heavy, sixty-ish woman, her features squeezed in a doughy face held the door open slightly and looked suspicious as Paul explained. He produced a colour photograph of Ellen, taken in the front garden of the house on the Hill, with a wattle tree and flowers in the background. The woman took it gingerly between finger and thumb. She devoured the small scene with her small eyes and opened the door. "I had a sister, Ellen."

She beckoned them inside. In her fleshy looks there was still a suggestion of Ellen. She invited them to sit in a lounge stuffed with furniture and ornaments, while she made tea.

"So you're Ellen's boy," she said, as she handed around a plate of scones. "And his wife," she added as an afterthought.

Paul didn't correct the 'wife'. He talked about Mirabilly without mentioning his mother's descent from the Big House, to the Hill and then the Village, but it must have sounded like the far side of the moon to a woman for whom Norwich city was the centre of the civilised world.

"Well there's not much good to tell here, Nephew. Ellen got in tow with one of the local nabobs, name of Marchmont years ago. She sailed off with him in his yacht and never came back."

"She didn't keep in touch?" Sophie asked.

"Too ashamed. She left her husband, a cripple in a chair, paralysed, left him flat, left me to look after him!"

Ivy Harris sat on the sofa with her feet together, her hands clenched in her lap and took no tea or scones herself. Sophie had opened the floodgate.

"You see, Ellen thought this Marchmont was going to marry her. Can you imagine it? Him a high society figure and her a slushy in his mansion? You'd have to be daft to think it could happen anywhere except in story-books, wouldn't you?"

Ivy Harris was taut, her figure a shapeless sack, her cheeks puffed and her eyes glittering with fierce excitement.

"Ellen first became a maid, then a lady too grand to speak to us, living on presents from this man. She always thought she was better than us. And then this Marchmont goes and dumps her on a farm at the other end of the world! She couldn't show her face here after that, could she? There was a terrible fuss. Her husband Peter killed himself with sleeping pills. Poor man, so young and handsome he was when he first went into that chair. You can understand why Ellen couldn't hold her head up here. Nobody would give her the time of day."

Paul shrivelled up inside as she spoke. She was in an ecstasy of bitterness. She saw him pale.

"It's just the truth, Nephew. What you came here to learn."

A silence.

"You haven't had your tea, Nephew. It'll be cold now. I'll..."

"We have to go," Sophie said.

"Where are you staying?"

"At the Grange," Sophie said.

"Goodness me, is that a hotel now?"

"No, it's still owned by the Marchmont family."

Ivy's face shadowed. "Really?" she said, puzzled.

Paul stood up to leave without being able to say anything. Sophie gave their thanks.

As Ivy was showing them out, she said mildly, "Come round for tea next time you're here, Nephew, with your wife."

Paul searched her face. Her eyes had receded into deep pin-pricks. She was serious.

"You're not so lively tonight," Marchmont remarked to Paul that night after dinner, as he shepherded him into the library for coffee.

"I met my mother's sister, Ivy Harris, this afternoon."

"Indeed?" Marchmont said, intent on the cigar-cutter and his Davidorff.

"Yes, she told me how my mother came to leave King's Lynn and go to Australia."

"Sit down, my boy and have a port." He stretched out comfortably on the couch. "There's often a lot of embroidery in the telling, you know."

"It wasn't embroidery that you went to Australia with my mother."

Marchmont seemed completely at ease. "No, that much is true. We were very close before she met your father."

"And my mother was a maid here?" Paul looked up at

the plaster cherubs on the lofty ceiling and became aware that Grayson was still fussing with the drinks tray in the corner. The conversation was about to stumble forward when Linda Ryland swept into the room.

"Darling," she said to Marchmont, "none of that awful old tawny port for me. Grand Marnier, please, with ice."

Paul excused himself and went up to his room without finishing his coffee, impatient with the idle conversation, but after about an hour Marchmont telephoned him and asked him to go to his office on the first floor. Marchmont and Sophie were there. The trio stood between the desks and office machinery.

"I wanted to tell you the answer to your suggestion about settling the case," Marchmont said.

"It was, as you say, only a suggestion," Paul said.

"Never mind what it was. The answer is no."

"You're making a mistake."

"Why settle for part, when I'm entitled to the whole?"

"We didn't start this venture without anticipating what might happen."

"How could you know I'd sue?"

"Because Mirabilly has always treated the land as its own. We anticipated you'd support that. We examined the title deeds and surveyed the land long before we put a cent in."

"Why would we treat the land as our own if it wasn't?"

"Because the Gudijingi River, which was given as the boundary in the original lease, changed its course over the years and began to flow through the native land and your predecessors moved their operations with it, on to the native land."

Marchmont gave him a hostile glare for a moment and then softened. "We'll see."

Paul thanked him for his hospitality and said he'd be

leaving early in the morning. He felt calm because he had expected Marchmont's reaction. Sophie went with him when he left the room.

"I want to get back to the clean air and the sun," he said to her.

He wanted to get out of the damp smell of the old house, with layers of Marchmont history absorbed deep in its walls, even some part of the history of his mother.

"I'm sorry you had such a bad time with Mrs Harris," Sophie said.

"It was never going to be fun, only something I had to do."

"And you never did talk to John about whether you're his son."

"I never intended to, Sophie. Now, all there is on this subject, is a page of notes taken by a drunken lawyer twenty something years ago."

"I know it's kinda late now, Paul. You don't *need* a father, but isn't it important for both of you that you *know*? A DNA test would prove it."

"Sophie, for Marchmont to accept that he was my father would mean admitting a whole lot of things he'd rather forget. It's not going to happen. It's all too late."

"Perhaps you're right… John would have a terrible sense of deprivation. I know what he would have made of a son. Alex is adopted and frankly he's useless; Emma's nice but more interested in being fashionable. John treats me as a kind of quasi-son."

"I'll probably get away before breakfast," Paul said, when they were outside his room and he kissed her on each cheek very formally. And then he kissed her properly.

"Call me when you're in New York," she said. "And even when you're not. I like you, Paul."

186

"Let me get this visit behind me."

His feelings for Sophie Ryland had outlived a number of his girlfriends in the Territory, but at that moment he was too caught up in the echoes of Marchmont and his mother to deal with her.

At 6am in the morning Paul was coming down the main stairway of the Grange with his bag over his shoulder. Grayson was waiting at the foot of the stairs, round-shouldered and fully attired in his white shirt with a black bow tie and a frock coat.

"I've ordered your taxi, sir. It should be here at any moment."

"Thanks, Grayson. You didn't need to be here. I could have managed." Paul thought he looked anxious.

"Some breakfast, sir, surely? The cab will wait."

"No, I haven't enough time, thanks. I'll get off."

Grayson drew himself up it seemed with effort. "May I ask a question, sir?"

"Certainly."

His thin lips quivered as he prepared to address Paul. "It's about... Ellen Colbert."

"My mother. She's dead, Grayson. Cancer. She told me about you. She liked it here. She was very fond of you."

Grayson bowed his head slightly. It seemed more than he expected to hear. "She... said that?"

"She did. She said that when she was here, if she had been free to marry, you were the sort of man she would have wanted. And tell me, how did she get on here?"

"We all cared for Ellen. She brought joy to all those around her."

Paul clattered down the steps to the cab, leaving the old man with wet eyes.

18

Sophie Ryland felt excited as she reclined in her seat after the aircraft had attained cruising height. She had a dizzy-high feeling from a first glass of champagne.

The Marchmont team were flying from JF Kennedy Airport, New York, to Sydney. Sophie was in the main cabin of the business jet with Sean Donnelly her assistant and the engineers, geologists and finance people who were going to work on the case. John Marchmont and Curtis Lefain who was co-chairman of the board with Marchmont, an elder statesman of the company, were in the forward cabin.

Sophie was to handle the Australian end of public relations, working with Martin Thorpe in New York. She had chosen Sean Donnelly to assist with press releases and contacts with the news media. It was a valuable assignment for her and one in which she had already had some experience from her previous post in a PR company. She actually looked upon herself as Martin Thorpe's helper. He had said she had a flair and could do the Australian end. He was a veteran. The challenge had helped her to put behind her the sudden death of her mother during a minor operation.

Marchmont placed a lot of weight on good PR and Thorpe had pointed out to her that an important part of the case was going to be fought in the newspapers, on TV and in lobbying state and federal politicians. Marchmont wasn't the kind of person who would give her the job merely because he liked her, at least not this kind of job. He too apparently believed that she was skilled. She wasn't quite so confident, but never showed it. She had scraped through her liberal arts degree at New York State and regarded herself as an indifferent student, but she had taken to PR work.

They made the flight in twenty-five hours via Hawaii without a stopover and collapsed for a day at the Regent Hotel. Sophie woke up the next morning to open the drapes of her room; she was greeted by a view of a deep blue harbour with ferry wakes chalked on it and the opera house on its promontory, like a prehistoric creature with an armoured shell basking by the water.

She had her breakfast off a tray from room-service, cold fresh orange juice, fresh brewed Brazilian coffee and toast with honey. She looked through the *Sydney Morning Herald*, glancing out the window occasionally at the busy harbour, wishing she was free to take a ferry ride. In the finance pages of the newspaper there was an article about the dispute over the Mirabilly mine with the implication that the business reputations of Marchmont *or* Paul Travis, as the leader of the mining syndicate, were at stake. The heading was 'Somebody Made a Big Mistake'. Then the telephone started to ring. First, it was Sean Donnelly with a pile of faxes and emails from New York. Then Curtis Lefain. Then Marchmont. This sequence ended for her in a page of scribbled notes and a long list of duties and promises.

Sophie took the time for a shower and a quick look at herself in the mirror, in a pale blue linen summer suit and oatmeal court shoes. She picked up her heavy briefcase and let herself out of her room in good time. The party were to start a meeting in the hotel with their lawyers at 9am.

In the boardroom MCM had hired at the Regent, Sophie met Max Haldane the heavy, drawly Sydney lawyer to whom she had often spoken on the telephone. Haldane was acting for them on the boundary claim and he was reputedly a skilled operator and a man of wide influence in Sydney. The introductions to his large team were hasty; they were now running a few minutes late. Marchmont's advisers jostled for the best seats (close to him) around the wide oak table, as Marchmont took his, squarely across from Haldane. Sophie sat on one of the chairs along the wall with her notebook and pencil.

After jovial greetings and frivolous mention of Sydney's perfect weather, Marchmont launched his opening question without humour. "What are my chances, Max?"

Haldane slipped his jacket off to reveal a faultlessly laundered and starched white shirt, which provided a backdrop for his flaming silk tie, florid complexion and helmet of swept-back, steel-coloured hair. He wasn't to be hurried, flanked by two of his partners and numerous legal assistants. Sophie thought that for just a fraction of a second, he gave his client the kind of supercilious look which suggested that laymen always asked these simplistic and unanswerable questions; but he quickly covered this with a thoughtful frown.

"It's a difficult case, John," he said, his eyelids fluttering.

Marchmont's opaque blue eyes watched the performance expressionlessly, the lawyer's plump paws moving limply in the air to express the inexpressible, his mouth forming words but not uttering them. "Very difficult," he said at last, decisively.

"I know already it's a bloody difficult case! You don't have to tell me that, Max. But it wasn't so difficult last summer. Routine, you said. I told you Travis & Co would have problems about getting a road to the site. You said you knew somebody who could make sure they did have trouble. A formality, you said. You got your friend Barry

Clavell on to it. You asked me to get Clavell a job when he retired from government and I did. But Travis got his damned road."

"Barry delivered, John, as far as possible. Access isn't Travis's problem, or ours. A lot of things have happened since this first came up. We've done a lot of work..."

"And charged a fortune for it. And now I hear it's a difficult case! Do you realise that if I lose this action I have to write off maybe a hundred million US dollars? I may be able to flog off the mining equipment we've ordered, but this is a fleabite compared to loss of the Mirabilly mine. What's it worth? Nobody knows. Conservatively ten billion dollars over a decade, more likely twice that."

"I'm well aware of that," Haldane said, making it sound as though the magnitude of the loss wasn't of first importance.

Curtis Lefain, the southern gentleman, winced at the bluntness. "Gentlemen, we're all on the same side. Let's say we all have a lot to lose."

Lefain didn't add that if the case was lost Argo, Paul Travis's company, would take MCM over, but everybody around the table knew it. Marchmont was fighting for his reputation as the *Herald* had suggested.

"I understand how serious it is, John," Haldane said. "It's serious for Travis too. They've staked all their chips on winning the boundary claim. Let me tell you the story as I now understand it."

Haldane leaned his beefy body back in his chair. He smoothed his already sleek hair, loosened his tie and lit a small Dutch cigar with an acrid smell. Marchmont waited, slightly red-cheeked, impatient with his ponderous adviser.

Haldane started with a name Sophie had heard the first time she visited Mirabilly, Captain Heron. Heron, who founded the station, had lived on the Hill in the 1850s and was buried, with his wife and some of his sons, in the cemetery in the red cedar grove on the east side of the Hill. Sophie could remember walking through the ruins of Heron's house, built of stone to last a thousand years but now roofless and windowless, a frame for creepers and vines and a talking point for guests viewing the cemetery and the orchard.

"When Heron obtained his grant from the New South Wales government, the eastern boundary of Mirabilly was hard up against a no-man's land which became a native reserve. The boundary between the two was the line of the Gudijingi Creek.

"The Gudijingi was and is described as a creek, but at times it's more like a river. It runs through deep gorges, over falls, heading north, down across the savannah and grasslands to lose itself in the floodplains and swamps near the Gulf of Carpentaria."

"This is a geography lesson?" Marchmont interrupted.

"No John, the river was an obvious feature to use as a boundary and no doubt Heron and the surveyors of those days preferred it to notional lines across hundreds of miles of desert and scrub.

"But there was a peculiarity about the Gudijingi. Many years before 1850 the creek had forked for about thirty miles and then joined up again. So there's a long strip, four or five miles wide, call it an island, between the two watercourses. On that island is the Mirabilly mine."

Haldane placed his cigar carefully in the ashtray and raised both hands as he approached his climax. "The question is, which branch of the Gudijingi did Captain Heron and the officials of the state of New South Wales set as the boundary? If the eastern, where the creek flows now, the mine is part of Mirabilly Station. And the Mirabilly managers have always treated the land as theirs. If the western branch was intended, Mirabilly Station ends there, on the western line and the mine is on native land."

Marchmont appeared to be half-bored with a story he had heard in a variety of tellings over recent months. He was silent when Haldane had finished. Sophie knew it was hard for Marchmont to reconcile that his own business future and some of his personal wealth was in issue, as a result of what a few, possibly ill-trained and perhaps drunken surveyors, did in the outback a century and a half ago.

"Interesting speculations, Max," he said, "but surely as occupiers we have a title?"

"Not to mine native land, if it is native land."

Haldane heaved himself up and looked significantly at his partners. "John, old mate, don't get down about it yet. We're working on it, and of course we've had a re-survey."

"What does it show?" Marchmont snapped.

"On balance it does not reconcile with what we treat and regard as the boundary. It's against us."

"Christ, man! You mean Travis is right?"

Haldane held up his large hand cautiously. "As a preliminary view, yes. The old charts, measured strictly, support the Mirabilly boundary being on the west, but there are a lot of inaccuracies in the surveying…"

Marchmont brushed away Haldane's further words with a gesture. "What I want to know, is how Travis and his friends knew this. I mean, we're talking about land that has always been part of Mirabilly. We're proposing to invest a fortune in a venture *on our own land*. And we find somebody else has already started to mine! We're one of the most expert mining companies in the world. You're telling me that a stockman's kid, who's still got dust in his ears, can

193

come out of the desert and take it all away. How did he know what nobody else knew? I'm paying for the smartest advisers in the world and the son of a jackaroo tops the lot of you!"

There was silence around the table; it was a criticism which seeped beyond the lawyers to the finance and engineering advisers.

"John, I understand how you see the Argo people, but…" Haldane began.

"John, it won't get us anywhere to blame people," Curtis Lefain said gently, inclining his head of white curls. "This is a question of property law."

Then Haldane spoke with the dispassion of a solicitor who has many other substantial clients and who is neither hurt or even greatly concerned if one of them is annoyed by his performance.

"Yeah," he drawled. "I've been thinking about that. How did Travis know? He sure as hell didn't know what was in the old deeds, unless he's some kind of antiquary and that doesn't sound like him. I reckon he learned from the Aborigine Trustees. They've always regarded this land as theirs…"

"They say that about the whole continent," Marchmont said derisively.

"Not in the same way," Haldane persisted. "They say this is sacred land. Their tjuringas, sacred stones, are buried there. As a kid on Mirabilly, Travis would have heard this from the Aborigines on the place. They probably told him about the two branches of the Gudijingi. It's the sort of story that's handed down through the years. Travis could have heard enough from locals to think about checking up on the boundary line. It wasn't a problem to the managers at Mirabilly. They weren't being told to get off native land.

They wouldn't have been interested if you told them. They just went on grazing the land up to the eastern river boundary."

Sophie remembered going with Paul Travis to the cave near the east ridge and their odd conversation about spirits, although it had been more than ten years before. It was a private memory; nothing that would aid this discussion, nothing she felt obliged to reveal.

Marchmont accepted Haldane's explanation grudgingly. "When Travis came to the Grange over a year ago with his so-called proposition, he must have known about this. He gave me some cock-eyed stuff about checking the boundaries. He must have known I'd tell him to get lost. I mean, the bloody nerve!"

Sophie remembered that Paul Travis had actually explained that the river boundary had changed, but there was no point in reminding Marchmont in this company.

Haldane made a colder appraisal. "He walked you right into it, John. Our enquiries show he's had an agreement with the Aborigine Trust for four years, subject to settlement of boundary rights. Rather than come at *you* directly with a claim of trespass, he's pushed a road through and brought his machinery in, leaving you no option but to sue *him* for trespass and now…"

"Don't you tell me what he's going to do!" Marchmont said, standing up and glaring. "Unless you want to go and work for him!"

Haldane's cheeks purpled; there was a spark in his bloodshot eyes. Marchmont recovered himself quickly and laughed as though the remark had been a joke. Curtis Lefain sighed. He didn't like doing business like this.

Haldane smoothed the moment over. "We've still got a lot of fight in us yet!"

19

The Mirabilly boundary dispute was due to be heard in a week's time by the Aborigine Land Commissioner, a judge of the Northern Territory Supreme Court, in Darwin. John Marchmont had decided that Curtis Lefain and Sophie, with a few other key executives, would stay at Mirabilly in the Big House and join the rest of the group later at the Intercontinental in Darwin.

However, Marchmont insisted on Sophie joining him on a flight in the Falcon jet to Townsville. He had been preoccupied with the case and not his usual urbane self since their first meeting with Max Haldane. He and Sophie had hardly spoken except on business. On the flight to Townsville he explained himself as they settled back in the spacious seats in the forward cabin.

"I want to see the partner of this dead lawyer, Lucas, who acted for Ted Travis," he said. "I want to try to get to the bottom of the rubbish you told me about Paul Travis being my son. The partner has promised to go through the firm's deeds but he won't deal with me on the telephone."

Sophie was surprised. Up to now, Marchmont had appeared to have the subject in a locked recess in his mind. "Good. I think you should make the enquiry," she said. She already knew that he was confident that he was right. Paternity would have mattered to him if he had thought it was a real question, but he didn't and never had. As far as he was concerned it was all malicious gossip and vindictiveness.

As the Falcon cruised smoothly at 20,000 feet, Marchmont turned his head toward her. Intimacies about their lives were perhaps easier in that solitary cabin.

"Do you realise that Ellen Colbert married after about two months of my departure from Mirabilly? A couple of months! I'd gone back to Britain to sort out the family business and she acted without a word. She never wrote a letter or even picked up a telephone. She got married to one of the stockmen. I'd been expecting her to come to London. I even left her with airline tickets. I tell you Sophie, I cared for Ellen and I was shocked at the time. I could hardly believe it."

"Maybe two months is a long time if you're alone on Mirabilly. And couldn't you have written to her or called her?"

Marchmont's glance had a quiver of unease. It was rare for Sophie to hear him speak of his emotions in anything but a facetious way. At this moment he had lost the patina of brightness which was like a mirror shell around him, reflecting every approach, admitting no penetration to what was underneath. He appeared now to be looking inward, far back across the years.

"I'll tell you," he said quietly. "I loved your mother, but Ellen was my first love and I suppose you would say the love of my life. I've never stopped thinking of her, never stopped wanting her and never understood what happened between us. I went to London and got tied up with business. The next thing I learned is that she was married. Two months! It hurt. I had to assume she didn't care for me as much as I cared for her."

"Perhaps she loved you but thought you'd deserted her."

"Two months? No. And don't you think it's a bit thick to suggest that her kid could be mine in these circumstances?"

"She never suggested it, did she?"

"No, for the obvious reason that it wasn't true."

"Why? The child could be yours biologically. If she was just pregnant when you left she could have married another man and pretended the child was his. The story, I suppose the gossip, is that Ted Travis knew. That was said to be the deal he had with Ellen. Marriage to her in return for keeping quiet and bringing the child up as theirs. But he was worried about it and opened his heart to his lawyer."

"I know that is the story, but can't you see why that couldn't have happened?"

"No, I can't," Sophie said uncertainly, wondering whether she had overlooked something stunningly obvious.

"Because if I'd been the father she'd have told me immediately without a doubt. Isn't it true? She had everything to gain. I was rich. At worst she'd have had support for herself and the child. At best, marriage. Yes, in all probability I'd have married her. Ellen wasn't educated but by God she was smart. She'd have worked out what I've just said in a trice."

She noticed his hesitation on marriage. To Sophie, Marchmont's view was solid and polished, lodged in his mind like a river stone, but like a river stone it was cold. She wasn't so sure a woman would necessarily be that calculating.

"John, you just said you'd have married Ellen in all probability. I guess she might have understood that as doubt on your part. You have to understand how a woman sees things. Money may be important but it's never everything. Status isn't everything. And maybe she wasn't going to behave like *any* girl who gets pregnant. Maybe she was too proud."

"Balls!" Marchmont hissed and looked out distractedly

at the brightness over the green carpet below. "Ellen never had ten cents of her own in her life."

"Uh-huh." Sophie gave up. "So what are we doing here?"

"Ah-ha! I want to find out for my own satisfaction why Paul Travis wants to ruin me."

"When you were outwitting Paul at the Grange, you told me it was just business. That's what you said. Perhaps it's just business for him. He sees an opportunity to make money and he takes it."

"I've been set up," Marchmont said pompously.

"Oh, come on, John. If you'd been Paul Travis, a hungry young guy on the make and you'd worked out that you could take the Mirabilly mine and the company trying to work it, you'd have done it and said it was only business."

Marchmont was adamant. "What you don't understand Sophie is that the Marchmont interests aren't another five and dime company started by a stockman's kid from the back of beyond. It's an institution, an empire, it has a history, it's worth more than money."

"You're changing the subject. We're talking about Paul Travis's motivation. Why should he care a prune about the old colonial empire of the Marchmonts?"

Marchmont was angrily silent.

Sophie wanted to say that maybe Marchmont was history and a stockman's kid an inevitable successor, but she didn't. She rang for the steward and asked for a glass of iced lime juice.

When the Falcon landed at Townsville they took a cab from the airport and found the ANZ Bank building on Barlinnie Street. Sophie left Marchmont to go into the lawyer's offices on his own. She asked the cabbie to let her out in the main street. She bought a ticket to see the sharks in the aquarium and had an ice cream sundae. She liked the little she could see of the town; it was small-scale and colourful and safe. She tried to imagine what it would be like to be married to a man like Paul Travis and live here, quietly, on these unforgiving shores.

Sophie met Marchmont an hour later, in the town centre, as they had arranged. He was expressionless. Instead of stopping for refreshment, they decided to have a snack on the plane and were soon in a cab heading for the airport.

As soon as they settled in their seats on the aircraft Marchmont said with a triumphant gleam, "What you told me, Sophie, can't be substantiated. Lucas, the lawyer, as I said, is dead. Struck off by the Law Society before he died. The fellow I saw has taken over all Lucas's files and there's nothing in them of the kind you mentioned. No notes of interview. There are routine files about the winding up of Travis's father's estate, sale of property etc. Nothing else. I think we've got a put up job here. Another bit of mischief by Travis."

"A DNA test?"

Marchmont was quiet for a moment. "I don't know how you can suggest that, Sophie. I should crawl to the man who wants to strip me and say, 'I think I might be your father. What about a DNA test? I mean, would you mind, old chap?'"

Sophie didn't reply, but she believed what Paul Travis had told her.

Soon they were airborne, flying west toward the Gulf of Carpentaria. They climbed over the Great Dividing Range and gradually they began to see more clearly the mangrove swamps of the Gulf and to the south the arid lands of the artesian basin.

The aircraft flew over the Flinders and Leichhardt rivers which wind down from the Selwyn Range through the tropical rain forest, cypress and palms to the Gulf. After nearly four hours they began to lose height over the grey-brown soil of the Barkly Tablelands, the pasture country where Mirabilly bred its hardy cattle.

The Falcon drifted silently down on its approach past the Hill to the airstrip. Sophie could see the familiar Big House, shadowed under its high orange-tiled roof, its wide verandas, bright green lawns and the smaller houses around it huddled coolly under the gums. And then, lower down the slope, the Village and beyond the mass of sheds and stockyards all amid a tangle of dirt roads, baked and dusty.

When they landed they were greeted by the general manager, Jim Lomas, whose ageing face Sophie vaguely recognised as that of the pilot who flew into the bush to rescue her and Paul many years before. Lomas stowed them in a Ford minibus quickly and switched on the air-conditioning. The late afternoon was oven-like.

Lomas drove them to the Big House, shaded in a grove of gums and beeches. The drive leading to the house had been sealed since Sophie's last visit, so the cloud of dust which had followed them most of the way from the airstrip was left behind. Sprinklers were scattering fine spray over the lawns and there was a fountain and pond at the main entrance which Sophie could not remember.

All the quiet splendour of the 'Owner's Cabin' inside was preserved, the feeling of a continent strange and different. The rugs on the polished hardwood floors; the paintings by Sidney Nolan, Russell Drysdale and Arthur Boyd like internal eyes looking out to that strangeness. Still in place were the cabinets and occasional tables, inlaid with native timbers and the stone panel plundered from the cave where Paul had taken her. Sophie could feel the fragility of the veneer of civilization over the stark wilderness.

She was alone in the drawing room for a moment and she felt tense as she looked at the stone. It transformed the room with its vivid ochre pigments of red and yellow, white clay and charcoal, delicately touched with orange and blue colouring. She saw the picture with new eyes: the male figure in head-dress, with a hair belt and decorative pendants, carrying throwing sticks; and the female figure carrying digging sticks. Both the man and the woman were following a star. She remembered Paul telling her that the Aboriginals would paint the images on themselves and assume the journey of the figures. At the feet of the figures on the stone were drawings of a goose-wing fan, perch and barramundi. Paul had treated the presence of the stone in the Big House as wrong. Captain Heron's sons or the early Marchmonts, in breaking the stone panel from its place in the cave, had not seen it that way. To them, it was an engaging picture. Paul had said that the Aboriginals believed that the removal of the stone was a violation of the mythology of the dreamtime and sent bad vibrations down through the generations.

Sophie stood looking out the window as the light faded. She could see the gum trees with their golden shadows and the dry landscape beyond them. Only the red and yellow parrots in the trees moved with energy and colour. A wedge-tailed eagle far above and beyond the Hill was stationary in the sky.

Marchmont came bustling in, showered and changed and jovial.

"I thought I'd have a quiet look around to bring back memories," she said.

"Yes, it's a very touching place this, my dear," he replied, assembling gin, tonic, ice, lemon and glasses on a tray from the drinks cabinet. "I heard I'd inherited the Marchmont fortune at the dining room table. Opened the letter with my breakfast! I've had good times here. I came first out of curiosity. You know, the back end of the world. What could it possibly be like?"

"It's hard and unforgiving."

"You think that? I can understand. And yet I've come again and again. I've had little sentiment about selling chunks of the Marchmont inheritance when necessary. You have to move on. But I've never been tempted to sell Mirabilly. Never will. Let's join the others on the verandah for a sundowner."

As he was leaving he looked back and saw that Sophie had her eyes on the stone, the faint glow in the room lighting the heads of the two painted figures.

"Nice bit of work, isn't it? As good in its own way as a portrait by Picasso. A damn sight cheaper too. Comes from somewhere around here. It's the stone Travis referred to at the Grange, if you remember. And do you know one astonishing thing? I've had a letter from the Aborigine Trust asking me to return it – return it, mark you. Like the Elgin Marbles. It's been here more than a hundred years. Damned insolence!"

Sophie went to bed early that night after a business session with Marchmont and Lefain. They were worried by the way the case would affect the share price of MCM and discussed publicity to restore shareholder confidence. She had a lot of material to edit and pass to Martin Thorpe, arguing that they would win the case and explaining why Argo's offer to buy MCM wasn't worth accepting.

She was in bed, looking through the papers, when

Marchmont knocked, came in without asking and closed the door. He had a glass of cognac in his hand and she thought he was more than a little intoxicated.

"Sophie, my dear," he said, sitting down on the bed proprietorially. "When this is all over I'm going to ask you to marry me," he slurred.

"Drink up John and don't make silly jokes," Sophie said.

"I'm serious," he said, levelling his eyes on hers with difficulty.

"Oh, really? I don't think you have anybody to play with tonight."

"Why won't the woman believe me?" he said, rolling his eyeballs upward.

Her mom had driven herself to the edge of sanity to hear those words and perhaps Ellen Colbert before her, but they made little impression on Sophie. She didn't believe Marchmont. She thought that even if she had believed him, she didn't want to marry him. She liked him in a daughterly way, respected his abilities and although he had a sexual spark which was attractive, bed and marriage would be two steps too far.

"Maybe we ought to try it out, see what it would be like... you know..." Marchmont looked at her sideways with a satyr's grin.

"You're angry with Paul Travis and you want a sweetie to comfort you. Well it isn't me, John."

"Never?"

"I think of you as my father. I could never begin to give even the faintest consideration to such things so soon after Mom's death."

"Hey," Marchmont said, suddenly irritated and slopping his drink. "I can't make out whether you're an elder of the First Baptist Church in Peeknuckle or one tough lady."

He sat in an aura of cologne and cigar smoke. Sophie recognised that he was undeniably a valuable suitor. He was the golden goose. But that wasn't enough. Her selfish thoughts in relation to him were of a much smaller order, but, she felt, more capable of realisation: she hoped to conclude her role at MCM with experience that she could trade for a better job with another company if necessary. She had seen her mother's suffering; it was about the uncertainties of survival and she instinctively feared the kind of survival that is dependent on a man's goodwill, a man's whim.

"Sophie, I care a great deal for you…" he began, but he saw that her attention had returned to the papers on her lap. When she raised her head, there was a blurred look in her eyes which declared that the conversation was over. He rose and wavered toward the door.

He turned on the threshold. "I know you met Travis years ago and you and Emma both liked him, OK, but you're loyal to me, aren't you?"

"Absolutely, John. You can count on it," she said, surprised at his insecurity. She *was* loyal, but she nearly joked that it was just business and then thought that he was in no mood for jokes.

The Marchmont party moved their residence to the Intercontinental Hotel in Darwin, where they flew from Mirabilly the next morning and met Max Haldane and his assistants.

The hearing was only a few days away and it was up to Haldane to reveal what he could do. Sophie thought she could tell, even as they were getting their cups of coffee at the sideboard and settling behind the meeting table, that the news was bad. All Haldane's team were muted or looked grim.

The men lined up facing each other as they had at the Regent, Marchmont and his executives on one side of the table and the lawyers on the other. Max Haldane swallowed importantly but didn't hesitate.

"I'm sorry, John, but our concluded view is that we have no case, no reasonable argument to put forward. We can throw a bit of dust in the judge's eyes, but the charts are reasonably clear. You've been on Aborigine land for over a hundred years. We've checked and measured everything on the ground against the deeds and charts. We've checked the authenticity of the deeds. We've even had infra-red examination to see if they've been altered. It's true the Gudijingi now flows along the eastern route, but the deeds plot the western route, nearer to Mirabilly."

A silence fell in the room. All eyes were on Marchmont. He was calm and expressionless, a poker player confronted with four aces. "Since the pistol is pointed at my head, what do my advisers advise? That I allow the trigger to be pulled quickly?" He spoke lightly.

Now, with the bad news delivered, Haldane could allow a small smile at the corners of his mouth. "Sue for peace, John. Let me see what terms I can get from Travis. After all, he came to you a year ago with a proposal."

"It was an offer he knew I'd refuse. Any businessman would. You don't give away ten billion dollars to somebody who looks over your fence, sees something valuable in your backyard and says it's his. You'll get nowhere with Travis. He's out for the kill."

"John, we must try to settle," Curtis Lefain urged quietly.

"Try by all means!" Marchmont said, contemptuously.

"I think this is wise, very wise," Lefain said, pressing his gleaming moustache nervously.

Marchmont and Lefain left the meeting while Haldane

began to talk to his assistants and Marchmont's advisers about how they should approach Travis's lawyers at the Sheraton. There was a sense of relief and lightness in the room. Everybody had been expecting an explosion from Marchmont. The fact that he wanted to talk peace relaxed them all.

Sophie listened to the doom scenarios that were, the advisers all hoped, behind them. The debacle of having spent millions on a mine without rights would be seen by stockholders as gross negligence and mismanagement. They *had* to settle the case. Marchmont's career was in issue as well as a lot of money. But Sophie was left with an uncomfortable feeling about how John had taken the news. He seemed at ease. She knew John's moods and attitudes very well and this was not the reaction she had expected from him. The John she knew would explode, swear the air blue – and then settle.

In the talk around the boardroom table there was a flavour of covert admiration of Paul Travis's tactics and Sophie was suddenly sorry for Marchmont. He was like a blind man groping toward a precipice. She thought his usually sound business judgment had been impaired by his obsessional feelings about Paul Travis and his own emotional connection with Mirabilly. And Paul didn't really need to do this, no matter how hurt he was about the past. What had seemed to her a practical disagreement about a boundary, which, after some posturing on each side would be resolved in a businesslike way, had emerged as something else: a personal contest between the two men.

20

When Sophie went to her room after the meeting, she found a message from Emma Rainham. Emma now used her natural father's name, rather than her stepfather's. She too was staying at the Intercontinental Hotel. Sophie rang Emma's suite and Emma, sounding miserable, asked Sophie to come up.

It was a penthouse suite, the view of the molten metal sea shut out by closed blinds. The air-conditioning was icy. Sophie hardly recognised the bulky, brown, oiled female who came toward her in the shadow of the reception room. Emma's belly and the flesh of her hips hung over her bikini. Her thighs quivered as she walked and her big-nippled bare breasts swung on her chest like udders ready for milking. She saw Sophie's surprise.

"Pretty awful, huh?" Her eyes had a hopeless look.

"What's the matter, Emma? I didn't know you were in the country," Sophie said as the two embraced.

Emma, the stepdaughter, and Sophie, the daughter of Marchmont's subsequent mistress, had always understood the similarity of their positions as part of the furniture of Marchmont's life.

"I've only been in Darwin a few days," Emma said. "I'm going back to New York. I came out here to see the fun, but I guess I'm so much on the sidelines that I won't see much anyway. Paul is too busy working out how to finish off John. I didn't get to see Paul much. He knows he has my vote on the MCM takeover. He doesn't have to sleep with me to get it."

Sophie had learned how Emma had become a problem for Marchmont. She was the biggest single holder of MCM shares inherited from her father and bought from her brother, Alex. She was the key to Paul Travis's acquisition of MCM. With her shares and those he had bought in the market, Paul probably had a majority and could win on a vote. Sophie didn't know why Emma was so antagonistic towards her stepfather.

Emma was self-conscious as she saw Sophie's gaze measuring her contours. "Sure, I could lose a little weight," she said flopping on a couch and moaning. "I'm going on a diet next week. This week, I'm going to do as I please."

Emma beckoned the Aboriginal maid who moved a portable cooler on a trolley toward her. Emma looked inside and selected a chocolate walnut ice-cream sundae, spooned whipped cream on top, adding maple syrup and two fan wafers.

"Have one," she said to Sophie, "or have a boring sandwich if you want. Rita will fetch it."

Sophie declined and had a cup of iced tea from the trolley while they talked casually. Emma ate with a long spoon. There was enough ice-cream for two or three helpings and when she finally put the spoon aside, there was some left. Emma plunged the fingers of both hands into the dish, scooping out the remainder. She stood up holding the sticky mess in the palms of her hands looking at it and then smeared it over her breasts and belly like massage oil.

Sophie watched without comment as Emma waddled through the glass doors to the shower faucet by the pool on the terrace. She turned on the water and shortly floundered back to the room with a towel around her. She slumped back on the couch.

"Bring me a coke, will you?" she snapped at the maid. She shook her head in bewilderment. "Let me ask you, Soph: do you think you'll end up marrying John?"

"No definitely not. Your dear brother has asked me," she laughed.

"Oh, that!" Emma said with a shriek. "We Rainhams are losers. Look at my father. My mother. And Alex; I never thought of him as a serious contender for you."

"He's not, but I have to admit he's kind, good-looking and rich."

"He's weak and useless and he would drive you mad, much as I'd like to welcome you to the Rainham family." Emma swung her head to stare at Sophie with her sceptical green eyes. "Do you find John magnetic, let me ask you, sexy, hypnotic, what?"

"A little of all those things I suppose. He's a complicated man."

"He'll be a feeble old fart while you're still a vigorous woman," Emma said lighting a cigarette. "And he is a one hundred percent proof asshole."

Sophie couldn't work out her own feelings for John precisely, let alone explain them to Emma. What was important to her about John was the present when he was a vibrant influence, not some imagined future.

"There's something I should tell you," Emma went on, taking a deep toke on the cigarette. "It has to do with your purpose here…"

Sophie shuddered inwardly at what she might hear. The Marchmont family had as many hidden twists and turns as a coil of twine.

Emma concentrated now on drawing the coke up through a straw. "Bit of a hangover," she explained. "John's had his pecker in so many pies, it gets confusing. Paul's mother. My mother. Your mother. And, of course, all the rest of his stable of bitches and maybe you at some time in future…"

Sophie shook her head negatively and knowing that, unstable as she was, Emma wasn't a fantasist or trouble-maker, she braced herself. Should she listen to this? Was it necessary? She was left with the thought that on balance it was better to know everything.

"You better understand my motivation, Soph. You're John's emissary. You represent him and he trusts you. You should understand why I'd rather *give* my shares away than help him… When Dad had a heart attack and ended up in the mortuary, I was twelve and over from Roedean at half term. We had a suite at the Sherry Netherlands in New York. On the evening of the morning Dad died, my mother was partying with Marchmont in the bedroom she had shared with my father. The shameless cunt was having the orgasm of a lifetime while Dad was cooling down in a mortuary drawer a mile away. John was Dad's partner and best friend. You don't forget scenes like that."

Sophie began to understand a little more about the unruly and disrespectful stepdaughter.

"Dad died on an aircraft, a private charter flight from the US to England. John was on the flight with him. Only two passengers. When the plane landed, there was an issue with whether it should have landed somewhere where my father could have received medical help. The pilots said they didn't know a thing about the heart attack until their arrival in London. They remained in their cabin although there was an intercom. Dad was of course dead on arrival. The coroner asked the pathologist at the inquest about the likelihood that my father died quietly. He said it was possible, but most likely there would have been a period of intense pain, during which my father's condition would have been apparent and first aid would have been possible. Dad carried a pill.

"John admitted at the inquest that he knew about my father's condition and about the pill, but neither saw or heard anything to alert him. He said he slept for part of the flight. I think he knew. Sitting in the seat alongside my father while he was dying. I feel John was implicated in the death. But that could just be a little paranoia of mine. I went to the inquest.

"John really is an arch bastard and a character to be wary of. He plotted to get Dad's interests in the company on the cheap, but the deal hadn't gone through when Dad died. That didn't worry John, because he thought my mother would inherit everything anyway. That's what they were celebrating that night. Well, Dad knew what was going on and had already changed his will, leaving everything in a trust for me and Alex. Dad never went near Werner Fliegler – their old lawyer – but got some smart Wall Street guy to change his will. Werner would have wised John up. When Alex came of age, my trustees bought his interests as you know, making me the key shareholder."

"How do you know all this?" Sophie asked.

"I know what I saw at the Sherry. Mom talked a lot when she was stewed. The lawyer who drew up the trust talked to me. It's true, Soph."

It helped Sophie to see Emma as she sketched in this other part of herself. It explained the tension between her and John. It provided a possible reason for Emma's waywardness: expelled from two schools, taking drugs, associating with a man who ran a bar in New York who was a convicted child molester... Emma had quite a background.

212

"I guess John is wasting his time in thinking he can win you over," Sophie said.

"Yeah," Emma said, stubbing out her second cigarette. "And it didn't help when he treated my mother badly, although God knows she deserved what she got. She was besotted. I think he only married her to keep close to the shares. You know, adopting us. He drove her to the bottle and then, you know, the car smash. You can tell John it wouldn't matter if he came here and licked my shit off the terrace. He'll never get his hands on those shares. So Paul's takeover is safe, even if he doesn't give a damn for me."

Emma's blasé manner concealed bitter hurts. Sophie sensed too that Emma was saving face by going home.

"Is there anything I can do?" Sophie asked softly.

"Yeah, kick that big Aussie in the butt and marry him. I'm being generous in defeat. Alex is a joke even if he is my brother. Don't waste your time on him. As for John, you don't deserve such a fate."

"I'm working for the opposition team. I couldn't do anything about Paul even if I wanted to."

"Bang both their silly heads together."

Later, Sophie went with Emma in a cab to Darwin International Airport and they sat together waiting for boarding time silently, watching Aboriginal youngsters fooling with pinball machines in the lounge and occasionally begging for change.

When Emma had checked in and Sophie was about to say goodbye at the security barrier. Emma kissed her and said, "Paul is sore about you. He thinks you're Marchmont's property. It gives him the needle!"

"Well, maybe I am his property, at this stage. I take the golden shilling," Sophie said uncertainly.

21

When Sophie returned to the Intercontinental from the airport she received a message at the desk that a meeting had been called to discuss Haldane's peace mission. She met Sean Donelly in the lift and he didn't know the details, but the word was that Haldane had done well. As they assembled in the conference room later there was certain optimism in the air.

One surprise for Sophie was that Werner Fliegler, John's New York lawyer and friend, was there; modest, quiet, smiling, chatting to Max Haldane and his advisers about legal matters which had nothing to do with the case.

They took their seats at the conference table, Fliegler beside Marchmont. He had just flown in. He was an elegant, birdlike man with thin, plastered-down black hair, a beaky nose and a sallow complexion. He was uniformed rather than dressed in a tailored six-button double-breasted suit.

Max Haldane reduced himself quickly to shirt-sleeves, a loose Gucci tie and a cigar. He prepared to unfold his account of the discussions with Edward Carvello, Travis's solicitor.

"We were well received," Haldane began, "Ed Carvello's an old friend of mine, and apparently Travis feels the war has gone on long enough and welcomes an agreement."

"I'll believe that when I hear the offer," Marchmont said quietly.

Haldane twisted his heavy lips confidently and launched into a long introduction showing how hard he and his people had argued and he threw about a lot of legal phrases like 'best evidence' and 'balance of probabilities'.

Sophie felt herself dozing off.

Marchmont eventually cut Haldane off. "Let's get to the offer."

The lawyer was annoyed but he was used to demanding clients. "This is what we worked out, John: split the mine three ways. You, Travis's syndicate and the Aborigine Trust. You return the sacred stone you have at Mirabilly. It's a trivial point but the Aboriginal side make a lot of it. The roads and workings of the mine are to be kept apart from the sacred ground. Again, this is not too difficult. Finally, you agree to Travis's company taking over yours, with you to stay on the board as chairman for a year, always with the option of accepting re-election. Argo appear to have sufficient votes to take MCM by vote, so it represents a gain to keep you on the board. I think this can be presented to look good for you and MCM stockholders."

Haldane smiled and looked round for approval. His own group were plainly enthusiastic and nodding. Marchmont's team looked at each other and began to nod too. Curtis Lefain was unhesitating in his praise: "Nice work, Max. I'm sure we couldn't have done better."

Curtis looked round at the rest of the Marchmont team seeking confirmation. There was a general murmur of approval around the table as they whispered and listed the pros and cons on their fingers or in their notebooks. The consensus seemed to be that Travis could have driven a harder bargain. Yes, it was a good offer.

After a few moments the talk stilled as they realised that John Marchmont himself was silent and poker-faced. Werner Fliegler's black dome shone and his button eyes were bright, but he too had said nothing.

"That's it, is it?" Marchmont asked loudly, silencing the talk. "There's no more?"

Max Haldane looked surprised. "That's a lot, John and a very good offer in the circumstances. Of course there's small print to be worked out…"

"And if I don't accept?"

"Frankly, Travis will have you for breakfast. You'll lose MCM, your reputation and a hell of a lot of money," Haldane said with blunt, almost malicious confidence, drawing in a lungful of smoke from his cigar and half-closing his eyes.

Marchmont raised his eyebrows and turned slowly to Fliegler. Fliegler returned a small, modest smile but said nothing. The room fell silent.

They all knew then that something was wrong. The seconds ticked by awkwardly, perhaps half a minute elapsed.

"Max," Marchmont began, his voice rich and gentle. "I employed you to fight this action and you come back with a proposal that I get a third of what is mine. And another proposal that the control of my whole company, with all its interests will pass to a meat-fisted bushwhacker, interests that have been in my family for generations. What kind of mutual settlement is that?"

"Better than a disaster. Certainly some billions of dollars better over a period of years," Haldane said, affronted. "Your other assets will be in no way diminished."

Marchmont's tone changed. "Who are you working for?" he snarled. And then he shouted: "Fight! I said fight! Don't you understand plain Australian? I haven't even begun to fight yet!"

Haldane rocked back in his chair. He tightened his tie and brushed ash off his shirt, leaving grey streaks on the white cotton. "John, my old friend, I well understand how you feel but you have to be realistic. Travis is going to wipe you out."

Marchmont let the words settle and swept cold eyes over the Australian legal team. "You're fired, all of you, as of this moment!"

Haldane's face pulsed with sheer astonishment and then a stiff smile. "It may give you a good deal of satisfaction to say that, John. I know how strongly you feel about Mirabilly. And I can take it. But I beg you in your own interests to think again. You're a few days from trial. You can't possibly go ahead without representation. Nobody could pick up a brief like this immediately. It's too complicated."

"You're fired, Max. Take your partners and hangers-on and get out. I'm instructing a small local firm, Michael Davros. Hand everything to them tonight. Mr Davros is in the next room. I'll arrange an introduction because I don't expect you are on conversational terms with him. He'll give you a cheque for your costs to date when you've had an opportunity to formulate your bill. Goodnight, Max."

"Good grief, John…" Curtis Lefain began, alarmed but apparently stilled by Marchmont's determination. "Can't we talk about this…?" his voice trailed off into the noise of people muttering and packing up their files and departing. The hurt in the air was palpable. Nobody was listening.

Haldane reared up at the table, his usual detachment gone. He must have known with the mention of Davros that there was an established plan to sack him. Otherwise Davros wouldn't be in the next room. Sophie could see that there never was going to be a deal. Haldane had been working his ass off for nothing, except money. His face was blotched red and yellow. He jerked his head at his team to say 'clear out!' It was all over.

As they filed out of the door, Werner Fliegler, who had not spoken a word, was saying goodbye, shaking hands and whispering, "I'm sorry it had to end like this," dissociating himself from the rude and difficult client they shared.

To Sophie, Marchmont seemed to have seized the opportunity to reject Travis's offer without weighing its intrinsic value. He was inviting rather than avoiding disaster. She couldn't try to reason with him. He normally valued her views but on this he would be unapproachable.

22

The next day when John Marchmont's executives and advisers took their seats in the conference room the air itself seemed bruised. Nobody smiled. Few spoke.

It now appeared that Werner Fliegler was in charge. He took the chair at the head of the table with Marchmont on his right and Michael Davros, whom none of them had met before, on his left.

Fliegler smiled charmingly when they were settled and bid everybody good morning. He was dressed more casually today in a tan garberdine suit, a fawn silk shirt and a plain green silk tie. "This is Mr Michael Davros who will be representing us in court." He gestured toward the thick-necked, bullet-headed man in his mid-thirties, who looked to Sophie more like a paratrooper in a civilian clothes. Davros was short, crop-haired with large eyes and a nondescript grey suit, which bulged at the strain of containing his muscular physique. He nodded, half-rose from his chair and then fell back.

Fliegler kept the floor. "I'm afraid our amigos from Sydney have not quite got the right idea. Nor has Mr Travis. Mr Travis has a tiger by the tail. Oh, yes, he's been quite clever up to now, but it's time for the tiger to turn and bite."

Fliegler smiled in a disarming way, talking as though he was saying the obvious, his shiny head bobbing round to fix a glance on various members of the team as he did so. "You see, litigation is not just a process of measuring the evidence of one side against another, it is a tactical weapon and we have to use it as such. Mr Travis has what seems like a good case I must admit, but by the time we have contested every word of it and every line, in every court available to us in this fine country, appeal after appeal, years will have rolled by. Years, my friends! Where will Mr Travis be then? His offer to buy MCM will have lapsed. His partners in Argo, who want to exploit a mine not to fight in court, will have deserted him. The Aborigine Trust will realise that they have a turkey for a partner. Victory will not be so sweet three or five years from now, if victory it is, because litigation is also a dangerous game! Our main man, Mr Davros, will be in charge of this part of our strategy."

Sophie could feel that the members of the team who had been grimly wondering what could possibly happen next, were beginning to perk up and see a new viewpoint. This approach sounded practical and feasible. Marchmont sat back with a slight smile while Fliegler went on in complete command.

"The second string of our strategy will be to beef up our campaign with stockholders. Martin Thorpe in New York and Sophie Ryland here will blitz them with material showing up the Argo jackasses – or should I say dingoes? Of course we are vulnerable if Travis can amass a majority of the stock, but John is satisfied that he can rely on the vote of his stepdaughter, Emma, who has a very large holding. Or get a majority without her. And even if not, the acquisition process is very complicated. It can and will become a long and wearisome process when we have thrown a few legal spanners into the works. I will deal with this part of the case."

Fliegler paused, seeking approval in the faces of his audience and finding it. His attention darted to each of them; each felt specially important. Even Sophie felt Fliegler spoke as though he was speaking personally to her.

Satisfied, he went on. "The third part of our strategy will be to lobby local and national politicians, pointing out that Argo are holding up a development which will be highly beneficial for the country. John will head this initiative personally."

The maestro paused again to make sure his message was not only received but accepted.

"And the fourth and final aspect of our strategy will be to ask my friend Nathan Kowalski from New York, who runs one of the most effective private investigation outfits in the US, to have a look at the credentials of Paul Travis."

Sophie shivered. There was an evil tint in Fliegler's grin as he searched the table again for approval.

"Nobody makes as much money as quickly as Paul Travis without cutting a few corners. We need to know his peccadilloes, his sins and his crimes and so do our stockholders and the politicians of this country. Don't forget, mining uranium is a hot potato politically. It can only be done by Mr Clean. I've given a first instalment of Nathan's work to Martin Thorpe for dissemination in the right places."

Fliegler turned to Marchmont with a modest inclination of the head. "That, John, is your strategy," he said flourishing his arm.

"Sounds great to me, Werner," Marchmont said, lighting a cigar. "This is fighting talk!"

"It'll cost you a few million dollars, but a lot less than accepting Travis's offer. It will protect your reputation and I'll bet anybody here ten bucks that we get a better offer from Travis eighteen months from now."

Nobody took the bet.

In her naivety, Sophie had been certain that Marchmont

was beaten and was behaving like a selfish child. She believed most of the team thought so too. But suddenly this softly confident little New York lawyer had conjured up a campaign that was credible, a war of attrition. It had nothing to do with the merits of the case, but struck at its heart; it was focussed on stalling and damaging Paul Travis personally.

It was apparent to her now that there was nothing new about these plans. Werner Fliegler had been beavering away for some time. Marchmont must have suspected from his early meetings in Sydney that Haldane was not going to meet his requirements. Sophie's instinct now was that it was not Marchmont but Travis who was in danger.

The Marchmont team ended that evening with a champagne dinner. The court case which they had launched against the Aborigine Trust and Argo that had rumbled to a halt was now beginning to gather speed. They would probably lose the argument but there would be an appeal. And another. And another. What mattered was the war, the long, bitter campaign. The executives and advisers who had been quietly prophesying Marchmont's ruin were now convinced that he would survive. Sophie thought that some of them believed they had conceived the plan themselves it was so natural and obvious. They were already criticising Haldane and his ludicrously inadequate proposal. All except Curtis Lefain.

Lefain was troubled by the general acceptance of the strategy. Jostled by Marchmont to show approval after they had finished the meal, he said "I don't like working this way, John. Now if you'll excuse me."

When he had left the room, John laughed. "Poor old Curtis, he's got no balls!" The others in the room joined his laughter, except Sophie, but her opinion didn't rank in that company and nobody even noticed her reaction.

23

Sophie flew to Mirabilly with John Marchmont, Werner Fliegler and Curtis Lefain the next morning for the weekend. The case was to begin on Monday and except for Sophie they were in good spirits. She tried to be the unemotional public relations executive and carry out Marchmont's wishes. The atmosphere in the team was now buoyant. One event in a long campaign was not difficult to face and no reputations were immediately in issue.

On the plane, Werner Fliegler, who was sitting beside Sophie, told her he had been asked by John to look into the case a long time ago. "Max Haldane is a very nice man," he said, "but he's too well fed. He's two generations of Geelong Grammar, a patrician. Now Davros is clever and hungry. *We* don't care that he wouldn't know the difference between *Madame Butterfly* and *Madame Bovary*. His father had a fish market stall at Bondi. Davros will fight to the last ditch without gentlemanly concessions. We've kenneled our borzoi and got us a rotweiller! It's a game, my dear."

Fliegler also passed her a copy of the notes from Nathan Kowalski on the investigation into Paul Travis's private life. She scanned them quickly in revulsion. She had never thought a court case could become so personal. Travis was said to have run his early aircraft business without properly certified pilots or planes. He was supposed to have ditched his partner Karantis when he sold out to Ansett, clearing the way for them to take over the company. In his mining company it was alleged that he had abused Aborigine interests to further his own. A trawl of his sexual life had hooked two fish. A girl in Brisbane claimed he was the father of her baby and he was said to have had an affair with the wife of a leading federal politician.

"This isn't much," Fliegler said, "but by the time you and Martin have written it up, it'll look fairly nasty. And of course there'll be more. And better. Trust Nathan for that."

"Not much?" Sophie said, sickened. "It's filthy." Fliegler had his mouth open and she could see his long, yellow teeth. "This is not right," she said, staring straight ahead, avoiding the man's gaze.

Fliegler read her astutely. "You don't like wounding Mr Travis?"

"I have scruples about doing business this way, Travis or no Travis," she snapped, thinking she would do everything she could to stop the material going out.

"It's what you're paid for, my dear," Fliegler said in a fatherly way.

"I'm not paid to do dirt," she said, pulling on the earphones and switching to a pop music channel on the plane's sound system.

When they arrived at the Big House, the operator in the radio room passed a message to John Marchmont that Paul Travis would be arriving shortly in Mirabilly. Paul usually visited Mirabilly from time to time to see friends and visit his mother's grave. Like most of the hundreds of visitors each month he flew in and out without notice, but the operator, in common with most of the station's staff, knew about the case and guessed the information might be significant.

Marchmont was enraged. "This man is being

provocative. He's doing his best to crawl right up my nose!" he said to Sophie.

She was glad to hear of the visit because she wanted the opportunity to see Travis. She wanted to talk to him about the case. She didn't feel she would be acting disloyally. She simply wanted to tell him that he was in danger. She knew an approach by her would probably be misconstrued by both Marchmont and by Travis himself but she was determined to make it.

"Why shouldn't he visit his mother's grave? It isn't going to hurt you," she said.

"It doesn't seem unreasonable, John," Curtis Lefain said.

"It's indelicate – at the present time," Marchmont replied.

"Oh, come on, John, this is a town not a homestead," Sophie said.

"I suppose you want to renew your acquaintanceship with him?" Marchmont said angrily.

"I'd like to see Paul, yes."

Marchmont shook his head uncomprehendingly. "I trust you," he said, and stalked out of the room.

"He's a man of touching faith," Werner Fliegler said to her with a sugary smile.

Sophie ignored him and went to the radio shack. She got the time of Paul's arrival from the operator.

The next day at noon, dressed in jeans and a t-shirt, Sophie went down to the old Heron house, which was near the cemetery, to wait. Half an hour later, Paul arrived with an armful of white carnations and went into the graveyard. There were about thirty people buried there, going back to the 1890s; the inscriptions on the crumbling stones stirred thoughts that were vignettes of Mirabilly life over more than a century.

When Paul emerged from the cemetery and paused by the gate in the shade of a red cedar, Sophie came out of the ruins of the old house and approached him on the narrow, dusty path. She felt nervous. He looked serious and very unlike a man of business, with his hands deep in his pockets, unkempt hair and loose shirtsleeves.

He had no change of expression when he saw her. "I guessed you'd be around somewhere. Come to see the shootout at the OK Corral?"

"I wanted to see you, Paul."

"What's the message from Marchmont?"

"I have no message. He hates me speaking to you."

"You're under orders are you? I might have known it. Then why bother to speak? I'll see you in court."

"I'm bothering because… I care for you. I'm begging you to stop this case, Paul. It's madness. It's going to screw up both your lives."

"You're forgetting. I've tried. Twice. Once at the Grange. And only the other day with your Mr Haldane. You forget. I'm the one being sued. I'm going to have a clean win. But even if I don't I'll take MCM. There's nothing surer. Then all this will be mine," he said, gesturing toward the Hill. There was no triumph in his voice only a cold certainty. "And Marchmont won't have his empire to play with. He can take what's left of his money and retire to Acapulco or Bermuda. He won't be in any demand as the chief executive of any half-way decent company any more."

Sophie stepped forward and put her hand on his arm but he thrust her away. "Paul, you don't know what you're up against. This isn't the shootout. This is the beginning of a fight designed to drag you down. Marchmont will appeal and appeal. He'll try to smear you. I think he knows he's beaten in law, but he's going to fight and wear you down."

She felt no qualms about giving away the core of Marchmont's strategy, which Paul might possibly have anticipated, but not the intensity with which Marchmont would direct it. Paul showed a glimmer of understanding. He turned away from her and walked up the path a few steps, then stopped and looked back.

"Nice try. You've been trained well. You don't scare me. My reputation can stand anything that Marchmont can throw at it. You go back and tell him I'm taking the Mirabilly mine, Mirabilly Station and his company and he can go to hell!"

Paul walked on up the path and Sophie called after him but he didn't respond.

24

On the morning that the case was due to open at the New Territories Supreme Court in Darwin it was a hot, damp spring day. The colours of the city were bright; people in the street wore shades or narrowed their eyes. To Sophie it seemed odd in this weather to have to go into a shadowy panelled room which was very cold and argue over pieces of paper.

That morning Michael Davros assumed charge and Werner Fliegler retired to his role as the ingratiating observer – and stage-master. Davros was assured, his saturnine grin dominating and easing the others. He seemed taller as he conferred with their surveyors and engineers and seated them as he would have them in the courtroom. John Marchmont was at his side in an off-white suit.

Sophie was unobtrusively at the back of the courtroom. She planned to listen to the opening and then go back to the hotel to deal with the public relations material. She anticipated a dispute with Martin Thorpe and John about the personal dirt against Paul. She thought her loyalty would come into question and perhaps even her job, in view of Marchmont's temper. She didn't want to face this. For the moment, she was safe in the courtroom watching the gladiators shape up.

The Aborigine Trust and Argo, Paul Travis's company, were to be represented by a Queen's Counsel, Gerald Sleeman from Sydney. He was sleek-haired, paunchy and dressed in a black jacket and striped trousers. He was assisted by a young woman junior counsel. Davros, a solicitor, was carrying the entire weight of the MCM case alone. It was unusual for a corporation like MCM, which could have afforded to import glittering counsel from Sydney or Melbourne, to rely on a local man whose reputation for flair had apparently been acquired in the criminal courts.

All Sophie could see of Paul was the wavy dark brown hair at the back of his head. They all stood for the Commissioner Mr Justice Fowler to take his seat on the bench. His registrar was settled into the desk below and in front of him. As they sat down, Sophie had a feeling of emptiness in her stomach; those few seconds before a roller-coaster begins its ride. After the case was called and counsel had announced themselves, the judge smiled agreeably.

"I've read all the papers and studied the maps," he said. "I think I can see the issue. This is a major boundary dispute and I've never heard such a case yet without viewing the site. It's going to make the evidence of both parties more meaningful. I believe you've anticipated the possibility of a view and made some tentative arrangements. I'm afraid it's going to be very hot and unpleasant out there," the judge removed his spectacles apologetically, "but I don't see a way of avoiding it."

The judge invited Davros to open his case if he wished to, but after discussion between counsel it was agreed that the case should be adjourned now for a view of the site. It would have been impossible to complete the flight, 600 miles each way, in one day including the time taken for inspection. At Marchmont's invitation, the judge, registrar, the parties and their witnesses would all fly to Mirabilly for the night. The following morning they would depart in

229

lighter aircraft for two landing strips close to the mine, where helicopters would be waiting.

The judge, registrar and lawyers were accommodated at the Big House and Travis and his party at a vacant house on the Hill. There was an embarrassment when the judge said he couldn't dine with either Marchmont or Travis. That night he and the lawyers dined alone, the Travis team stayed in their house which Marchmont had provisioned and equipped with a cook and a bar. Marchmont and his executives dined together in another room in the Big House.

The next morning the entire party flew in three Cessna planes to the airstrips near the mine. Sophie asked John if she could go and he agreed; anything to postpone her work on the Travis smear material. She had the last seat.

The planes circled the boundary area for an overview. The fork in the Gudijingi Creek was clearly visible with the two legs imprisoning the mine and then rejoining. The 'island' was studded with boreholes and abandoned earth-moving equipment. All the syndicate's work had been halted when Marchmont filed his claim of trespass.

The planes landed at the southern airstrip and the party walked through a tinder-dry woodland of grass, mallee and brigalow scrub with scattered acacias and thin beeches and gums, toward the fork. The judge's group were ahead and seemed to take a long time. Those who were waiting sheltered in the mottled light of the gums. It was blisteringly dry and bottles of water were passed round.

Sophie looked down into the deep cleft where the creek ran. Although it looked black from the air, the water was a muddy red. As the eroded banks testified, in the past, huge volumes of water had swept through.

"Are there any crocodiles down there?" she asked Billy Tjakamarra the Aborigine Trust manager.

"Not here," he said. "A few miles downstream. The water runs underground, through caves and there are crocs there. They retreat downriver or advance upriver depending on the season."

She shivered. There was a sense of menace about the northern shores beyond Mirabilly with their crocodiles, snakes and spiders and the poisonous jellyfish and sharks in the warm seas of the Gulf.

It was two hours before their view was complete and they climbed aboard the planes for a flight of a few minutes to the northern airstrip. Sophie remembered this place from the night she spent there over ten years ago. The same old sheds and stockyards cooking in the blinding light.

When they landed, staff from Mirabilly had opened up the sheds and put a thin canvas up to shade the entrance to one of them; it was too hot to go inside. Cool boxes full of beer and coke had been brought in the planes. There were also bread rolls stuffed with freshly roasted beef and tomato. The three groups had to meet to eat in this shade and there was some restrained chatting and joking. Sophie found it uncomfortable to be so close to Paul but unable to speak to him. If his eyes rested on her he appeared not to see her. He was serious and aloof.

A plague of flies and midges drove them on with their task. The intention was to see where the Gudijingi rejoined the dry bed and flowed in one stream.

One of the surveyors led the judge and lawyers, sweating in their white shirts and shaded by broad brimmed hats, toward the escarpment; they would inspect the dry creek and then walk about 300 yards to where the Gudijingi rejoined the flowing stream and formed one watercourse.

Marchmont had never been on the ground in this place and he was interested in the access arrangements through the native reserve. He asked his surveyor to point out the route. The surveyor said it would be necessary to go down the escarpment and cross the dry creek to get a view. "When the judge has finished his deliberations, we'll go and have a look," he replied.

They waited in the mouth of the cave which Sophie had visited years before with Paul. She would like to have seen the paintings again, but it seemed like a diversion from a serious task to ask. The three groups walked to where the channels joined. Here the vegetation thinned and there was little shelter. The judge and his party unfolded the umbrellas they had been given at the landing strip and took their time.

The contestants waited under the thin trees running with sweat. Sophie began to feel strange in the heat and hoped she wasn't going to faint. She thought for a moment as she looked out across the country that her vision was playing tricks. The horizon blurred and quivered. She saw the then distant fires she had seen from the plane as they flew across Mirabilly.

Sophie and the surveyor gave in to Marchmont's impatience to see the proposed accessway and followed him through the dry grass and scrub, up the hill. They were soon out of sight of the other parties. On the way, they passed clearings where test bores had been made. A rusty Caterpillar bulldozer was idle in the sun with two giant dump trucks beside it.

"You could fry eggs on them," she said.

"That's all they'll be good for," Marchmont replied. "Unless I buy them at a cut price from that bloody son of a jackaroo."

They walked for ten minutes and from a rise, the

surveyor was able to point to a path winding through the reserve. "You can see where the dozer has broken through the undergrowth. There's a distinct track. That's about the line of the road. The only sensible way to go."

"On to native land beyond Mirabilly," Marchmont observed.

Marchmont examined the area though his field glasses. This was a road that would avoid the escarpment but lengthen the journey for the ore.

On the way back, Sophie heard the whine of an aircraft and had a quick glimpse of the white fuselage and green trim of the judge's plane as it headed back to Mirabilly.

"He's finished at last! He's not going to bother having a look from a chopper," Marchmont said. "The sod will be sitting in the Big House drinking my whisky and soda while we're still humping around out here."

They walked back through tall grass for another fifteen minutes and then the surveyor began to slow down and look around. He said at last, "Look, I'm a bit confused. I know the maps and charts, but I'm not so familiar with the ground."

They stood still looking at each other under a gum tree. Marchmont was annoyed. The surveyor was feeling a fool. And Sophie was immediately apprehensive. But they could fly back to comfort in a plane that was only minutes away. They could have a cold shower. Being so close to home reduced her concern and that of her companions.

Sophie felt the indifference of the land which didn't care to give any sign-posts to the traveller. Indeed, there were no travellers. They were rare intruders. The country was designed to mystify, full of features, yet featureless. 200 hundred yards on was strangely like 200 yards back. Her fluttering thoughts were shattered by the sound of another aircraft.

"That must be Travis's group. Ours will have to wait," Marchmont said.

The three of them agreed the general direction and headed through the grass with the surveyor leading. He was a bearded six-footer with a shirt open on a sun browned chest. If he hadn't already lost the direction Sophie would have had a lot of confidence in him. He looked as though he was at ease in the outback.

When they had walked about a quarter of a mile Sophie noticed that the pall of smoke she had seen earlier was now a lot closer. They stopped. What was ahead was a heat-haze with spurts of flame.

"We seem to have walked further than when we came," Sophie said.

"Good God, we'll have to hurry or be cut off!" the surveyor said.

Sophie could detect the panic in the surveyor's voice. She looked at Marchmont. His, at first, mild annoyance had mounted. He was a man who expected simple matters like what path to take to be worked out for him. He employed staff to do this. When the surveyor continued leading them down the slope Sophie followed.

Marchmont remained standing. "Stop. That's not my recollection of the way. It's more on the high side."

The surveyor stopped and shook his head silently in disagreement, but his credibility was too low to make a case.

"You've lost us once," Marchmont said angrily, "I suggest you go your way and we'll go ours."

"We need to keep together," the surveyor said. "It's just elementary bushcraft."

"All burn together?" Marchmont strode off up the hill and Sophie, doubting the surveyor herself, followed her boss up the hill.

25

In a few seconds, Sophie lost sight of the surveyor and they might as well have been miles apart, for all the possibility of finding him again. Or he could be just beyond the bushes a few yards away. They were in an area where the dry grass and underbrush was waist-high in places and in others, thinned to scrub and sand. Overhead were thin trees, beeches and gums which would live through a burning. Sophie had heard about the burning in summer; how the fires could cover thousands of acres, a haircut that would leave the trees and land, as the flames passed, ready to start fresh new growth before the wet season. What was incredible to her, was that country which seemed to invite walking and navigating with ease, actually hid their way as they progressed.

They came to what Marchmont had said was the top of the rise and would give them a view, but it was a false rise capped by another. Their climbing was not over. They stopped. Sophie's hair was hanging in damp strings across her face. Marchmont was puffing and for the first time his redness spelt exhaustion and concern rather than anger.

"That bloody man's got the water bottle!" he spat.

Sophie heard the exhaust crackle of another plane, probably their own, heading back to Mirabilly.

"They won't leave us here," Marchmont said. "All we have to do is make the sheds on the airstrip before dark and we're OK."

Sophie followed Marchmont it seemed for miles, but always there was another rise, another cleft, or what seemed to be a track but as in a maze, they never gained a vantage point. The sun burned the back of her neck despite her hat and she could see that John was unsteady on his feet.

"We'll have to rest for a bit," Marchmont said. Sophie looked around warily. The burning seemed to be closer. The air was full of smoke. They settled into the shade of a rock for a rest. Marchmont insisted that he had been noting landmarks as they moved and that they were going in a more or less straight line, but Sophie doubted it. The alarming possibility was that they had been circling the same place. Apart from the screech of an occasional cockatoo and lizards in the grass, they saw no living creature. They heard the chatter of helicopters. Sophie reckoned they had been lost now for about three or four hours, but it felt more like days. Tiredness rose in her and flooded out the fear and she fell asleep.

Sophie awoke suddenly out of a confused and senseless dream – it was dark and her body was chilled. Marchmont snored beside her. The sky was full of stars. Although she could not see it, she knew that there was a big moon behind the rock. The bush screamed with cicadas; creatures moved there unseen. The air was still laden with smoke. Flickering in the distance she could see fires. She huddled against Marchmont, dozed and they were both awake at the first finger of dawn.

"We should march away from the rising sun toward the west, the dry creek and the Mirabilly escarpment," Marchmont said.

They set off, hungry, ash-stained, thirsty and weak but the urge to get on was strong in both of them.

"There's no need to worry," Marchmont said, "they'll have dozens of people looking for us this morning. By God I'll stir up some of those idiots about this. They could have got us out of here yesterday, if they tried!"

At first the sun was gentle, stretching golden rods across the bush, slowly dissipating the deep purples of shadow. But when the sun had levered itself higher, the rays began to prick Sophie fiercely, red hot knives which burned the already scorched skin on her neck and shoulders. Sophie slogged on as the sun blistered through her thin shirt from behind, streaming through her cotton sunhat, down every strand of her hair into her scalp. She could hear the helicopters and she surged with hope.

They had no way of knowing where the fires were because they had no perspective across the bush. When they came to a place where they might have been able to a see a few miles, the view was obscured by smoke. A layer of thin smoke, orange in the light, now pervaded the land before them. But what had been distant burning changed rapidly as they moved. At some points, they faced a wall of flame and had to swerve from their westerly course. The conflagration in the grass was so fierce at times that it was almost invisible and Sophie had to look up to see the tips of flame. The quivering curtain breathed and roared like a dragon.

Marchmont stopped and turned to her and she could see for the first time that he was as afraid as she was: "We'll have to run for it! Go back, back!" he shouted.

They fled back the way that they had come, stumbling, falling at times, too weak to run sure-footedly, the smoke now following them, the crackle of burning grass in their ears. Sophie ran and ran until her legs ached, the smoke grating her lungs, choking her and she fell and felt the stones grind into her breasts and thighs.

Marchmont, behind her, groaned, "Keep going Sophie!" He grasped her arm and she struggled to her feet and they ran on together.

As she lurched forward, Sophie saw two figures rise up in front of her, two thin black giants who seemed to be seven or eight feet tall. The two men held out their arms to catch her and dragged her and Marchmont into the shelter of a crevice and gave them water. It was the most beautiful drink she had ever had in her life. She didn't know how long they stayed there while her body tried to recover. She could hear Marchmont talking to one of the Aboriginals, Mike or Johnny, as they said they were called; questioning him slowly, calmly, patronisingly, about what they were going to do. She could hear the words but was too dazed to follow the meaning.

Marchmont said to her, "They're saying that to get back we have to skirt the burning and that makes sense. But instead of going directly west we have to cross in front of the fires and then turn west."

"We have to do what they say," Sophie said.

"We've got surveyors and pilots and Christ knows what in the way of people who ought to have been able to find us in five minutes."

"The helicopters couldn't see us and we couldn't see them," Sophie said.

"All we've got to do is cross half a mile of open ground that way." Marchmont pointed toward the open ground and the escarpment which they could now see at times, as it appeared through the smoke.

"Mike says we have to go round," Sophie said.

"He does. How far?"

Mike raised two fingers then three.

"Miles?" asked Marchmont scornfully.

Mike assented.

"What does he know?" Marchmont exploded. "I can *see* where we have to go."

Sophie looked at the Mike for reassurance. He shook his head negatively.

"What in hell does he mean?" Marchmont shouted.

"Crocodiles," Mike said.

"So we're going to risk our lives trying to beat the fires, instead of skirting around a pool of crocs?" Marchmont said, his cheeks shaking.

"We can beat fire. Let's go now," Mike said.

"Fuck you!" Marchmont said, "I'm going across that stretch and up the escarpment to my plane! Come on, Sophie."

"No!" Mike held up his arms to bar Marchmont. "Tjuringas."

"Ah, now we've got it. A spiritual objection. I've never heard such arrant bloody nonsense in my life!"

"He's saying that their sacred stones are buried there, John."

"I know exactly what he's saying. That, against our lives? Come on, Sophie," Marchmont said, taking her arm and pulling her with him.

Something inside Sophie told her that Marchmont was wrong. It was better to try Mike's way even though it was risky. She pulled away and Marchmont looked at her in surprise and then with derision. For her, it was a simple gut matter of the best way to save her life. For Marchmont it was perhaps more.

"These men *know*…" Sophie said.

"You'll get back all right," he said sarcastically. "But I'll be there hours before you. I'll make sure a hot bath is waiting for you."

Marchmont strode off in the direction of the

escarpment. The two trackers shook their heads and turned their backs. Mike took Sophie's arm. They headed across the front of the fire. "We can do it," he said.

Marchmont was out of sight almost immediately and with Mike in the lead and Johnny bringing up the rear, they pushed along a low cliff edge. Occasionally they could hear fierce crackling as the fire consumed dry wood. Mike made a fast pace and Sophie had trouble keeping up. Her feet were sore and swollen; the trainers she was wearing were so soft on the hard ground that every stone bruised her bones.

She kept looking back to try to get a view of Marchmont but she couldn't see him. It was the weird effect she had already noticed. The place looked at first so benign and even open, but people disappeared from view very quickly. The trees and grass and scrub absorbed them into a world with no landmarks.

Mike stopped and offered her water and she asked him what there was to fear in crossing directly to the escarpment. "Crocodiles," he said again.

She couldn't weigh the importance of the Aborigines' belief that the crocodiles there embodied the spirit of their ancestors and guarded the sacred site; for her it was the mere presence of crocodiles, so inert and yet so lightning fast.

Mike began to drag Sophie after the first mile. "Not far now," he said. "Creek there." He pointed through the smoke. She could see that their path followed a sheer drop chiselled out by past watercourses. It was dangerous to go near the crumbling edge. The slope ran down to the dry course of the Gudijingi in about half a mile. Once they were there, they were safe. The danger was that the bush in front of them was being consumed in a line which was moving ever nearer to the cliff edge along its whole length.

"We're trapped!" Sophie shouted to Mike when they had gone 200 yards. With a fifty foot drop on one side, they were confronted by a red army on the other which could drive them over the precipice. Looking back, she saw that the flames had advanced behind them. There was no going back. Mike grabbed her, the silent black man whose skin shone as though it was steely hot. He pulled out her shirt and tore a strip off the tail. He doused it with water and tied it across her lower face. Then he knotted the strings on her hat under her chin, tucking her hair inside. He rolled her shirtsleeves down and tucked her jeans into her socks. For himself, he took a dirty rag from his pocket, wet it, and tied it over his mouth. "We now run pretty fast," he said. "No stopping."

He set off into the flames with Sophie loping behind and Johnny behind her, three fire-walkers, Mike holding up his arms to fend off the branches of trees and saplings that they could hardly see. Sophie followed his stained white shirt, stumbling, branches tearing at her clothes and lashing her face, feeling the heat touch her clothes, run its fingers over her body. Her chest was exploding and she couldn't feel her feet properly; they had become numb and the numbness obscured the pain of the stones. Her eyes streamed and she was near blind. But she tried not to lose that jigging white shirt before her. And then she smashed into a tree trunk, feeling an intensity of pain in her forehead and chest, and then…

26

When Sophie awakened, she was lying on hard ground under a makeshift awning, insect bites swelling around her eyes, scarcely able to breathe. Flies buzzed at the net over her face. Men whom she didn't know were standing around. Two were preparing a stretcher. She felt painful all over. Her shoes had been removed. Her feet and hands were roughly bandaged. She felt a sudden horror that she had been burned and sat up trying to touch her face.

"You're OK Miss Ryland, take it easy," one of the men said. "You're scorched and bruised but you're quite fit."

She sank back with relief and then thought of John and the tall black man who saved her. "Where is John Marchmont? Is he safe? And Mike and Johnny?"

"Mike carried you in. We don't know about Mr Marchmont. He's out there somewhere."

Mike came over to her. She thanked him in a few agonised words. He hardly appeared to be the worse for his ordeal. "Paul Travis and his boys, they will come back. Mistah Marchmont, I don't know." He shook his head depressively.

Sophie was carried on a stretcher back down the dry creek, up the escarpment to the sheds by the airfield. Here she insisted on getting up and trying to walk around but it hurt. Her bones ached and the soles of her feet were bruised. She had an iced lemon drink made by one of the pilots and sat in the shade of the huts, where the temperature was nearly a hundred degrees. She refused the offer to be flown back to Mirabilly and instead waited with the pilots and the first aid team. Mostly, they sat in worried silence. She could hear the distant roar of the fires and the spluttering of a helicopter, far away.

She fell asleep sitting in a plastic chair and when she awoke she heard fresh voices. Three or four men were approaching. One was the almost unrecognisable Paul Travis. His hat had been replaced by a soiled burnous, his shirt torn and blackened. His arms and face were blotched with charcoal. His expression as he approached her was hard, tight-lipped.

"He's dead," he said quietly when he was beside her.

"Do you know what happened, Paul?"

"I was never close to him but I saw him moving from a distance."

"Are you going to tell me?"

"He seemed determined to move directly toward the escarpment, which meant crossing close to a pool and through saturated ground. He may have slipped or simply been bogged down. He was taken by crocs. The boys in the chopper hoisted up… what was left."

"Horrible! Could you have gone there?"

"Not if I wanted to live."

"Mike warned him."

"Anyhow, you're OK, Sophie."

She sank down in her chair with Paul towering over her. A few hours ago Marchmont had been breathing venom and determination, lashing others with his words and now – no more. She sobbed and then saw, behind Paul, two men carrying a bulging black plastic bag that was not really a human shape. The bag was hefted into the luggage space of one of the planes and everybody started their silent, weary preparations to fly to Mirabilly.

At Mirabilly Sophie found that after a shower all she had was a few aches and cuts, burns on her hands and arms, another burn on her cheek, bruised feet and breasts and singed hair. She changed into slacks and a t-shirt and went into the drawing room. The judge's party had left.

Curtis Lefain had quietly taken charge of the MCM team, who were preparing to leave. He had asked Paul to come to the Big House. When Paul came in, he too was showing no more than a few cuts and bruises. He was pallid under his tan. He had an unfocussed look of shock in his eyes. Werner Fliegler stood back, for the first time startled and confused. Curtis Lefain embraced Paul and thanked him warmly for his efforts. "Now, Mr Travis, this is not a time for business. It is a time for mourning, but we are thrown together here in an unusual way…"

"Curtis, surely you're not going to try to talk business now?" Sophie said sharply.

"It's OK," Paul said, "talk about anything you want to."

"Hear me out, Sophie," Curtis Lefain said gently. "You won't be offended. I know John was a friend of yours as well as an employer. As he was for most of us in this room. What I have to say will do his memory no violence. You, Mr Travis and your people, along with Mirabilly staff, have just risked your lives to save John and Sophie and you have our grateful thanks. I will say no more about the case between us today, but I have hopes that we can meet in Darwin in the next few days and resolve matters."

Sophie, sickened by what she thought would segue into business talk, walked on to the verandah and in a few minutes Paul followed. They stood looking across the lawns, the heavy scent of honeysuckle in the air, a cockatoo screeching in the blue gums.

"You'll get what you wanted – at a price," she said.

"It's a painful price. I wished no harm to Marchmont."

"Haven't you got enough?" she asked, frowning and going back into the house.

A week later in Darwin, Sophie was at a meeting between Curtis Lefain, Paul and their advisers.

Lefain said, "When I received details of your offer to settle the boundary claim my personal view was that it was generous and I urged John to accept. He did not, but now as chairman of the board it's my duty to deal with this litigation and I am proposing that we accept your offer if it's still open. Mr Travis, can we end this battle?"

"Yes," Paul said, immediately.

There seemed to be a collective sigh of relief. In any other circumstances, there would have been a popping of champagne corks. The advisers moved quietly away while Werner Fliegler buttonholed Paul in Sophie's hearing. Fliegler, the architect of the planned psychological blitzkrieg of yesterday, was the most fervent admirer of the peace of today. He said to Paul that he had always shared Curtis Lefain's view.

27

When the meeting at the Intercontinental Hotel finished, Paul asked Sophie to have a drink with him in the bar. He steered her to a remote couch. He waved the waiter away.

"Up at the Big House when we talked, Sophie, you asked if I had enough."

"Well you do, as of about an hour ago."

"You know what I'm talking about. I think you're very upset…"

She didn't reply. After a pause, she swallowed awkwardly and reached her hand across to his.

"What are you thinking?" he asked, troubled.

"That night on the Gudijingi Creek when you couldn't start the aircraft. I was sixteen."

"We've missed a lot of time together, Sophie."

"There's time ahead."

His mood changed abruptly. He smiled and dropped his hunched shoulders. "There's something I have to tell you…"

The words flattened Sophie's rising spirit. She imagined what he meant was, 'Wait a minute, there's something I have to confess and maybe you won't want to go on with me.' The dirt which Werner Fliegler was beginning to unearth had reminded her that few single, healthy men of thirty would have an entirely uncomplicated background.

"If you think you need to," she said, reluctantly.

"Ellen told me on her deathbed that I *am* Marchmont's son." He shot the words out.

They hit Sophie like a bullet. Her mind lurched, partly in relief at not hearing the tawdry story she had expected, but more at what this vastly different confession meant. Paul had kept this to himself in the years since Ellen's death, despite their talks. The course of her life, where it touched John and Paul, reeled through her thoughts. She raised her hand to her brow for a moment, trying to sort out the confusion in her mind.

"It's all past history now, Sophie," Paul said softly. "But I wanted you to know."

"Why didn't you tell me when *you* knew – or when you came to the Grange?"

"Because you wouldn't have given up trying to convince Marchmont. Could you have succeeded? I doubt it. He would have viewed me as some kind of fortune hunter."

"I'm crying inside at the folly, Paul, the terrible folly of the three of you. John's arrogance in what he *thought* he knew and what he missed. Your mother's vindictive sense of inferiority and the life she missed and only had to reach out for with her little finger. And your wounded pride in not being able to take a step, even a late step, toward the man you *knew* was your father. So much folly!"

Her words must have seemed like stones grinding on each other inside Paul's head. His mood had changed. His cheeks were hollow. His lips quivered uncertainly. "I never... saw it like that."

"I guess you thought of yourself as modest and undemanding, standing back."

"I did, yes," he said in a choked voice.

"Self-sacrificing..." She shook her head negatively, emphatically, but with sadness.

It obviously hurt that Sophie, the only person now who knew the secret definitively, was able to identify instantly what she regarded as his fault. "My mother was, as she saw it, rejected," he said in a low voice.

"You know, Paul, John's belief that a pregnant Ellen would have unhesitatingly claimed that John was your father if that was so, wasn't an unreasonable view for a man to have."

He began some sort of a defence of himself: "We're not talking about the generality of 'a man' here, with macho male attitudes. Marchmont completely misread Ellen. He just didn't understand. She believed *she* had been rejected. The pregnancy was something that came along afterwards. She simply wasn't the kind of woman to cry and say, 'Never mind if you don't love me. I'm having your baby so you better marry me or give me a decent allowance'. Marchmont ought to have understood what she was like. Actually, she believed that he wouldn't have married her anyway whether there was a child or not. All that would have happened, Ellen thought, was he would take the child away from her, by sending it away to expensive schools in Sydney or more likely England. Getting money for herself never came into it."

"Well, wasn't that selfish on her part? What a different life you'd have had."

"How would you feel about losing your son? And it would be loss. I'd be thousands of miles away from her in Australia or abroad. Yes, it was a selfish position but as a woman, can't you see how much against the grain it would be?"

"I can see that, Paul, but mothers make sacrifices for their children."

Sophie thought that they would probably always see this from different points of view.

A group of about thirty mourners, Mirabilly hands, Paul Travis and Sophie Ryland, were gathered in the shade of the gum trees beside the old cemetery on the Hill. It was fiercely hot and still and the air seemed to quiver. Beyond them were the worn and slumping gravestones and one new empty burial plot, strewn around with flowers; beside it, a polished coffin.

An Anglican minister from Darwin, bare-headed, swayed in the full glare facing them. He spoke of John Marchmont, whom he had never met, with distant awe.

It was a surprise to Paul and the Marchmont family that John had expressed a wish in his will to be buried at Mirabilly, alongside Ellen Colbert. No, it was more than a surprise to Paul; it was a shock. He told Sophie it made him think again about what he knew of his mother's story. Perhaps her feelings of inferiority were too hasty. Was it all a misunderstanding? This was a conundrum of human behaviour which he supposed he would turn over in his mind all his life at times when he thought of his mother.

As they stood near the grave, with ripples of heat rising off the parched grass, he remembered Ted Travis's funeral and how shocked and angry he had been with Ted at the graveside, a man whom he had since remembered with forgiving love. Perhaps his present negative feelings for John Marchmont would change.

Paul had been more open with Sophie after Marchmont's death. He admitted that he had foreseen the conflict over the Gudijingi mine, an investment he would probably never have made otherwise. He had even invited the conflict, knowing that if he had not been behind it, Marchmont might well have reached a cool and sensible compromise with the Aborigine Trustees. He could never have foreseen that the conflict would bring about Marchmont's death, but that fact cast a deep shadow.

Now, he had told Sophie, he had at least a sense of closure, shadowed as it was.

The headstones were similar plain white marble, Ellen's now graying with the years, engraved only with names and dates, but Paul said to Sophie that he thought he could see the words 'King of Mirabilly' on one, and 'Queen of Mirabilly' on the other.

A year later, Sophie and Paul Travis were married in Townsville. It was a quiet wedding on a sunny day at the registry office, a fitting conclusion to what they could both look back on as a long and fraught courtship. Paul wondered whether he could ever have concluded the courtship with marriage if Marchmont had lived.

At the ceremony there were just five young friends of Paul's, two girlfriends of Sophie's from New York and Emma Rainham. Afterwards, they sailed on Paul's yacht for about an hour and came back to dinner at the Yacht Club.

Marchmont's company settled the lawsuit, as they agreed. The stone at the Big House was returned to its place in the cave and Sophie saw its disturbing beauty, in its natural place, for the first time.

It was an irony that Marchmont left a large part of his estate to Sophie, whom he seemed to treat as the son he never had. In this oblique way, Paul became close to the inheritance he never had. But it was the missing middle of a life, which Marchmont could have given him, that he often pondered about; experiences that would have made him a different man. What *might* have been had to be dismissed as fantasy, but he fantasized: a degree from a British university, perhaps even Oxbridge, or one of the Ivy League colleges in the USA in law or history, a career as a civil servant or a politician or an academic...

Sophie and Paul decided to live in Sydney and visit Mirabilly when they could. Paul said he felt a sense of being home when he was there, sleeping in the same bedroom as his mother, the room where in all probability he had been conceived, but he never visited that place near the company store where the Juduba flows.